doomsday

The PHOENIX FILES

Chris Morphew

doomsday

Kane Miller
A DIVISION OF EDC PUBLISHING

First American Edition 2013
Kane Miller, A Division of EDC Publishing

Text copyright © 2013 Chris Morphew
Illustration and design copyright © 2013 Hardie Grant Egmont

Design by Sandra Nobes
Typesetting by Ektavo

First published in Australia in 2013 by Hardie Grant Egmont

For information contact:
Kane Miller, A Division of EDC Publishing
P.O. Box 470663
Tulsa, OK 74147-0663

www.kanemiller.com
www.edcpub.com
www.usbornebooksandmore.com

Library of Congress Control Number: 2011935704

Printed and bound in the United States of America
1 2 3 4 5 6 7 8 9 10
ISBN: 978-1-61067-102-6

To Mum and Dad,
For more reasons than I could possibly list here.
Thank you.

Chapter 1

LUKE

We ran.

Flashlights swept through the bush behind us, closer every second. Soren wailed in pain as Jordan and I dragged him through the mud.

"Quiet!" hissed Jordan, steering us back towards the entrance to the Vattel Complex, but Soren kept right on shrieking. He writhed under my grip, swollen, bruised, slick with the blood from his interrogation.

A flashlight beam sliced past us and I caught a flash of Jordan's face, stretched tight with anger. She shot a dark look at Soren, like she was half-tempted to throw him to the guards and be done with it.

"No!" Soren gasped, losing his footing. "Please – I did not mean to –!"

He broke off into another wail as Jordan jostled him again. "You didn't *mean* to?"

We'd thought Soren was dead. We'd *seen* him get gunned down, back in town. But apparently he hadn't been gunned down enough to keep him from selling the rest of us out to Shackleton.

I looked back, stomach churning. At least five guards were crashing through the undergrowth behind us, and there was no mistaking the towering silhouette of the guy up front. Calvin. Back on duty after weeks out of action, just in time to ring in the end of the world.

The sky above our heads crackled with electricity. Moments before Soren's arrival, Shackleton had unleashed the final part of his plan to keep Phoenix locked off from the outside world: a domed network of electrified cables, stretching out over the town like an enormous spider web. I couldn't see it anymore – after one brilliant flash as it powered up, the shield grid had faded into the darkness – but I could still hear it. I could still *feel* it pressing down on us.

Smoke billowed up from the south, blotting out the stars as the fire in town continued to blaze. Reeve and the others were still back there, fighting for control of the Shackleton Building. But they couldn't be doing much better than us if Shackleton had security guys to spare for a search party.

2

We reached the entrance to the complex and some-one inside opened the trapdoor to let us in.

"Stop! *Stop!*" Soren demanded, digging his heels into the dirt, like he'd only just realized where we were taking him. "We have to get *away* from here!"

I ignored him, hitting the stairs as soon as the gap was wide enough, my feet sliding on the moldy concrete. I wasn't about to just abandon Mum and the others.

"Run!" he railed on. "*Leave* them! There is no time!"

"You want to stay out here?" Jordan snapped, releasing her grip on him. "Fine. *Stay.*"

Soren swayed, almost collapsing, and latched on to Jordan again.

There was a shout from the bush, way too close, and I swore as another flashlight beam caught me in the face. I turned and hammered down the stairs, brac-ing for an explosion of gunfire, but it never came, and a few steps later I heard the entrance rolling shut above our heads.

"We need to get the others into the panic room," said Jordan. "Barricade the corridor. Hold Calvin off."

My head swam. "Jordan, how are we meant to –?"

"You've killed us!" Soren wailed. "You've killed us! There is no way out!"

Jordan didn't want to hear it. She tore down the

stairs, three at a time, hauling Soren behind her.

I staggered down after them, feet heavier with every step. It wouldn't take Calvin five minutes to get through that trapdoor. And in the meantime, I knew the Co-operative weren't the only ones who wanted me dead.

He was down here somewhere. Peter. Out of his room and hours away from putting a knife in my chest.

Earlier tonight, Crazy Bill had dragged Jordan and me down into the depths of this place, to the half-buried lab he'd finally finished excavating out of the concrete. He'd cornered us, watching with wild excitement as Jordan's body began fading out of existence, into one of her "visions" of another time.

Almost like he'd known it was coming.

As always, I'd grabbed on to Jordan, fighting to stabilize her, to drag her out of the vision and back into the present before she disappeared completely. But this time, things had spun even further out of control than usual.

For a moment before she returned, Jordan had somehow gotten caught between the two timelines; one foot in the present and the other in wherever she'd been fading away to. She'd become a kind of gateway between our time and the other one. And in that moment, Bill had run at her – run *through* her – and disappeared. Into the other time.

A minute later, he'd returned. And suddenly, Crazy Bill wasn't so crazy anymore. Somehow, his trip through Jordan, through *time*, had cleared his head enough for him to tell us the truth about who he really was.

Bill was Peter. A twenty-years-older Peter who'd spent the last two decades trapped in the past. Because this wasn't the first time he'd used Jordan as a time machine.

Sometime in the next seventeen hours – in Bill's past, and our future – Jordan was going to fade out again. And when she did, she'd become a gateway between our time and another: a day twenty years ago. One we'd seen replayed over and over again on Kara and Soren's old surveillance video.

The day of my murder.

I was going to go back in time, armed with a message that just might help us save the world. And Peter – our Peter – was going to follow me back. He was going to kill me. And then he was going to dive back through the gateway, back to the present.

But he was going to be too slow. The gateway was going to collapse, spitting him out, stranding him in the past with no way back to the present except to wait out the next two decades until it all happened again. And the next time Peter showed his face in Phoenix, it would be as a mentally unstable homeless

5

man who seemed to know a bit too much about what the Shackleton Co-operative was up to. Which was all very tragic and whatever, but given the part of the story where he stabbed me to death, I wasn't shedding any tears for him.

And I *was* going to die. I got that now. If there'd been any hope left that I could escape all this alive, it had disappeared the moment that trapdoor had closed over our heads.

Bill was right: there was no undoing the past. This wasn't just *going* to happen. It had *already* happened. More than that, it *had* to happen. The only reason we had any clue how to stop Tabitha eating humanity alive from the inside out was this: I'd gone back to the past the first time around and delivered our message to Kara.

Take Tobias to the release station.

That was it. Everything we had. A one-sentence save-the-world plan based on –

Based on *what?*

I stumbled down the last few stairs. Sick. Emptied out. It would have been the easiest thing in the world to just let it all go. Curl up into a ball right here on the stairs and wait for the end to come. But some stubborn corner of my mind kept me stumbling forward. If I had to die, I was going to make it count for something.

6

It was chaos in the corridor. Mum raced to meet us at the bottom of the stairs, an appalled look on her face at the sight of Soren's mangled body. Cathryn stood behind her, sobbing violently, still bleeding from the gashes Peter had scratched into her face on the way out of his cell. Jordan's mum was leaning against the doorway to the surveillance room – on her feet, which was something – with a screaming Georgia clinging to one leg and a minutes-old baby cradled in her arms.

Tobias.

The annihilation of the human race was scheduled for five o'clock this afternoon, and the weight of the world was resting on someone who couldn't even support the weight of his own head.

Mum opened her mouth to speak, but Jordan immediately shouted her down. "RUN!"

"What's happening?" Georgia wailed, burying her face in her mum's leg.

"They're coming! They're already at the entrance! All of you, get down into the panic room!" Jordan dragged Soren over to Cathryn, dumping him in her arms. "Take him."

Cathryn shook her head. "I don't –"

"Take him!"

"Where's Peter?" I asked, grabbing hold of Mum.

"I don't know. We heard noise in the kitchen, but –"

"GO!" Jordan screamed. "GO, GO, GO! *NOW!*"

They got moving, Soren limping against Cathryn, Mrs. Burke dragging Georgia along with one hand, clutching Tobias in the other. I waited for Mum to fall in behind them, then moved to follow.

I'd only taken two steps before I realized Jordan wasn't with us. She'd run off into the surveillance room. I doubled back, stomach sinking even lower.

"No!" said Mum, shooting out a hand to grab me. "Luke, you're not –"

"Right behind you," I said. I reached into the back of my jeans and pulled out the pistol I'd picked up on our trip to the Shackleton Building earlier that night. "Here."

Her eyes went wide. "Luke, no, I wouldn't even know what to –!"

She twisted around at a sudden moan and a splattering sound behind her. Cathryn let out a nauseated shriek. Soren had just thrown up all over the ground.

"*Please,*" I said, pressing the gun into Mum's hand. "They need you."

She sucked in a shuddering breath and took the pistol, holding it away from her like she was afraid it might spontaneously combust. "All – all right. But ..."

She pulled me into a hug, then ran off to get the others moving again.

I raced to the surveillance room. Static spat from the circle of laptops that had once fed us footage from the cameras in town, back before Mike blew up the security center. I glanced around the room, half-expecting Peter to come bursting out from under one of the desks.

Jordan was across the room, staring at our one remaining eye on the outside: the camera feed from the entrance above our heads. Then she dashed past me, taking hold of a desk near the door.

"He's up there," she said, voice hard, eyes red with tears. "Calvin. They're all around the entrance. But I can't —"

Smash!

Jordan lifted up the desk, upending it, knocking a pair of laptops to the floor. "— I can't see what they're doing. Too dark." She ran the desk out into the corridor.

I followed her out. "Jordan, what are we —?"

There was another echoing crash as she threw the desk to the ground, ramming it between the walls of the corridor.

"Come on," she grunted, almost knocking me over as she ran to grab another desk.

A barricade. Or at least, an attempted barricade. Pointless. No way was this going to stop them, or even hold them up for more than a minute or two.

But there was a glint in Jordan's eye that told me this was not a good time to argue. Her family was in danger. We were way past reason now.

I ducked back into the surveillance room, upending another desk, hands barely keeping their grip on it. Maybe Peter wasn't going to finish me off after all. Maybe it wouldn't even get that far.

A few more desks, and we'd made a heap that stretched to the ceiling. But it would take just one solid push to send the whole thing crashing to the ground.

Jordan stayed at the barricade, trying to wedge the desks more tightly together, while I sprinted back to the surveillance room for some chairs to shove into the gaps. I returned just in time to see Jordan lose her grip on the desk at the top of the pile, sending it clattering to the ground on the other side. She screamed in frustration, pounding her fist against the wall.

I tried again. "Jordan –"

"Pass me that chair," she snapped, wrenching it out of my hands. She jammed it between two of the desks, and the whole pile shifted, almost collapsing.

"Jordan, listen, I don't think this is –"

She wheeled around, face twisted in desperation. "They're not getting in here, Luke!"

"Yes they *are!*" I said. "You know they are! You've *seen* it! You want to help your family, we need to get down to the panic room and keep Calvin out of *there!*"

She twisted away from me, sprinting down the

corridor. I ran to catch up, relieved that she was actually listening to me. But then –

"Beds," she said frantically, veering through another doorway. "They'll be harder to move."

"Jordan, *stop*, they won't even –"

I froze at the door, catching sight of the mess spilling out from the kitchen at the end of the bedroom. It had been completely ransacked. Drawers yanked open, cupboard doors ripped from their hinges, ground littered with the smashed remains of mugs and bowls and –

And cutlery.

Knives.

This was Peter's work. He'd found his murder weapon.

I shivered, creeping into the kitchen to investigate, and almost jumped out of my skin at a loud scraping behind me. Jordan, shoving a bed at the door. There was a clatter of rusty metal as it slammed into the doorway and got stuck. She dragged the end around, throwing her weight against it. The bed shifted a few centimeters and got lodged again. She cried out, rattling the bed with both hands, panic threatening to swallow her completely.

I came up behind her, resting my hands on her shoulders. "Look –"

"Would you help me with this?"

"*Look*," I said again, pointing at the mess in the kitchen.

Jordan's eyes dropped to the floor, taking it all in for the first time. I felt her shoulders slump, and some of the manic energy seemed to drain out of her.

"Please," I said. "Please, can we just get out of here?"

Jordan turned around, cheeks still glistening with tears, an agonized look on her face.

"C'mon," I said, moving to drag the bed back out of our way.

My hands had barely hit the bed frame when an explosion rang out above our heads, echoing down the stairs. Then a distant shout and the sound of thundering footsteps.

They were here.

Chapter 2

JORDAN

"Crap!" Luke heaved at the bed, but it was stuck fast. He gave up, vaulting over, nearly slipping as his foot skidded in the puddle of vomit on the ground.

I leapt out behind him, finally dragging my head back into the game, hurling silent abuse at myself for letting the panic take over like that.

What was I thinking? What was I *thinking*, wasting time on that joke of a barricade when I could have been getting Mum and Georgia to safety?

And Tobias.

Tobias.

My baby brother, who hadn't even been alive long enough to see a sunrise, but who was somehow meant to be the answer to all of this.

If we could even get him out of here alive.

We pounded down the corridor. I could hear voices approaching from the other side of the barricade. They were already –

Crash!

The barricade collapsed, my misguided attempt at protecting my family exploding in a pitiful avalanche of furniture. I ducked, screaming, as someone opened fire on us.

BLAM! BLAM!

A fluorescent tube fell from the ceiling, shattering on the floor at our feet.

"Freeze!" Calvin boomed.

But I'd already stopped running. Calvin didn't miss that shot. Not from ten meters away in an empty corridor. It had been a warning. That was the only reason we were still alive.

"Turn around," he ordered.

I turned, heart hammering, but keeping my head up, forcing myself to look at him.

Calvin waded through the mess of upended furniture, flanked by four guards, all armed with Shackleton's standard-issue assault rifles. Whatever had been keeping him out of action these past few weeks, he'd clearly gotten over it.

Luke slid a hand into mine. He was shaking like

14

crazy, and I felt a throb of guilt for keeping him up here when he could have been finding a place to hide.

One of the guards let out a snicker.

Something flashed behind Calvin's eyes. Just one tiny, fleeting moment, and then gone again. He kicked aside the last chair in his path and paused a few meters short of us, sneering at our filthy nest of a hide-out, probably wondering how on earth we'd kept it a secret all this time.

He raised a red-gloved hand, aiming his pistol again. "Where is it?"

Neither of us spoke.

I clenched my teeth, blinking the tears out of my eyes, stomach roiling. It couldn't end like this. It couldn't. What was the point of finally figuring out Tobias if we were going to die before it even had a chance to matter?

Calvin's men stood poised behind him, waiting for an order. I'd run into all of them before at one time or another. Seasoned officers who Calvin could trust to stay loyal and get the job done.

At the back of the pack stood a guard I'd seen down here once before, in a vision of this place, destroyed and abandoned. A vision of today.

"The baby," Calvin growled. "Where is it?"

I swallowed, remembering the picture Georgia had drawn earlier tonight – Calvin standing out in the bush,

Tobias in one hand, a gun in the other – and the ominous words that had come with it: *That's what the baby wanted a picture of.*

The silence stretched out.

I squeezed Luke's hand, my mind whirring frantically and coming up with nothing. But if Calvin thought I was going to spend my dying breath selling out my family –

"Answer him!" snapped one of the guards, losing patience. It was Officer Cook, hands still caked with Soren's blood.

Calvin held up a hand, signaling Cook to lower his weapon. "Last chance, Jordan. We will find that child one way or another. The only decision you are making here is whether or not you'll live long enough to see it happen."

"You sick freak!" I said, dropping Luke's hand and striding forward, rage boiling over. "How can even *you* be okay with –?"

Calvin rushed up, meeting me halfway. He shot out an arm, grabbing me by the throat and shoving me into the wall. "*Listen,*" he snarled in my ear. "Believe me when I tell you, this is not a fight you can –"

WHAM!

Calvin was flung into the ceiling – two meters, straight up – crunching with shocking force into one of the light fixtures. I ducked out of the way just in time to avoid getting crushed as he plummeted to the ground again.

Before he'd even landed, the corridor filled with panicked shouts as all four of Calvin's men were thrown off their feet, tumbling backwards through the air like they were caught in a hurricane. They crashed to the floor at the end of the corridor in a heap of desks and chairs and limbs.

Another startled cry and Luke rocketed past me, sliding across the floor. He reached out a hand, somehow managing to catch hold of the bed still lodged partway out of the bedroom door. He dragged himself to a stop and a wild, inhuman scream rang out behind me.

Peter. Red-faced and rabid, fist clenched with white knuckles around the handle of a knife. *The* knife.

For a second, it was like the whole universe had stopped in its tracks.

Then the guards began to stir.

Luke scrambled to his feet.

Calvin felt around for his pistol.

"LEAVE!" roared Peter, charging. "LEAVE HER!"

Luke dragged me sideways into the surveillance room just as one of the guards opened fire with his rifle. Peter screamed again, and a sick thought flashed through my mind: *He can't kill Luke if they kill him first.*

We raced across the surveillance room, stumbling through the pile of smashed laptops to the door on the other side. But we were only stalling. This was all just a circuit. The surveillance room led through to Kara's laboratory, which opened into the corridor again through a second door. Nowhere to run but back into the fray.

We burst through to the lab and I slammed the door behind us. Luke ran to grab one of Kara's old operating tables and shoved it up against the doorway.

He took a breath. "Now what?"

Rifle fire split the air in the next room. One of the officers started shouting, but it was swallowed up in a scream and a smash and dull thud.

"We need to keep going," I said, lunging across the lab. "Find the others."

Luke cringed. "Yeah, but …"

"We can't stay here," I said. "And we'll come out right up at the other end of the corridor from where we started. We might be able to sneak –"

SMASH!

A massive crack appeared in the door we'd just blocked off as something – or someone – heavy was hurled into it. The table Luke had shoved back there rattled away across the floor.

"GET OUT!" cried Peter, voice breaking. "YOU DON'T GO NEAR HER!"

"Quick," I said, already at the second door, peering into the corridor.

I could only see one guy out there. Only one still on his feet, anyway. Officer Blake or something, the one from my vision. He was staring into the surveillance room, weapon halfway raised, like he knew what he was supposed to be doing but didn't want to risk catching Peter's attention.

I heard Peter scream, and Blake reeled away in fright. I looked across the lab just in time to see the first door splinter apart and the limp form of a security guard come sailing through the air towards us. The body thudded to the ground and rolled to a stop against the wall.

Luke shoved me into the corridor.

Officer Blake twitched around, spotting us. He raised his rifle and fired. Too late. Moldy plaster exploded from the wall behind us, but we were already through the door at the end of the corridor and out into the dark, debris-strewn passageway that wound through the bowels of the Vattel Complex.

After only a couple of seconds, I heard pounding footsteps, and a pair of flashlights tore up the corridor behind us. But here, at least, we had the home-field advantage. We sprinted along on autopilot, ducking and weaving instinctively to avoid the countless bits of jagged, rusting shrapnel spiking out from the walls and ceiling – the familiar hazards of a place that had been blown up and concreted over and dug back out of the rubble again. I heard one of the guards cry out, swearing bitterly as he collided with something sharp.

Ahead of us, I spotted the place where the passageway widened out, leading off to the room where we'd been holding Peter. Still no sign of Mum or Georgia. Good.

I pushed forward, and almost tripped over a small, dark shape in the middle of our path. I leapt over it, glancing back at Luke. "Watch out –"

"Argh!" Luke stumbled, kicking the thing over. It toppled onto its side and I realized it was some kind of gas canister. There was a bit of string tied to it, leading off down the passageway.

We kept moving and the string changed course, running in under the door to Peter's room. Suspicion flared inside of me and I shoved the door open, ignoring Luke's moan of protest.

Inside, Soren was crouched behind Peter's broken bed, holding an old lighter to the end of the string.

"*Come on!*" he barked at us, bloodied fingers twitching on the lighter. "*Come on! Come on! Come on!*"

There was a spitting, crackling sound, and a spark ignited at the end of the string. It shot along the fuse, way faster than I'd expected, across the floor and out into the passageway.

"Close the door!" Soren shouted. "Close it!"

I heaved the door shut and dived behind the bed, dragging Luke –

BOOM!

The whole world flashed bright-orange and I rushed to shield my head as the bed was blown back into us. A cloud of dust and smoke rushed into the room, swirling into my nose and mouth, and I curled up on the concrete, coughing violently.

Everything was black, the lights above our heads destroyed by the explosion. Finally I could breathe again, and I sat up.

Luke's hand came down on my arm, groping in the darkness. "You okay?"

"Yeah." I dragged myself to my feet. "Soren?"

A flashlight flicked on beside me and I saw Soren's battered face suspended in a haze of gray dust. He stood, grunting, and stepped over the bed. I helped Luke up and we followed him back into the passageway.

Soren swung the flashlight back the way we'd come. But instead of lighting up the empty corridor, the beam shot straight into a sprawling heap of concrete boulders. An entire wall of rubble that hadn't been there two minutes ago.

He let out another grunt. "*There* is your barricade."

Chapter 3

LUKE

THURSDAY, AUGUST 13, 12:21 A.M.
16 HOURS, 39 MINUTES

"I hope they kill each other," Soren growled, wincing in pain as I half-supported, half-dragged him up the passageway. "Peter and Calvin. Solve both our problems."

"Hurry up," I said, shoving him along. Jordan was pulling ahead of us, shining Soren's flashlight around at the walls. The passageway was starting to smooth out again by now, the debris clearing as we moved further away from the center of the explosion that had ripped through the place two decades ago.

A shadow slid across the wall and I flinched.

Just the flashlight.

Surely there was no way Peter could have made it through before the cave-in. But that didn't stop me seeing him around every corner. Didn't stop my mind skittering between hair-trigger panic at the thought of him leaping out at me and a cold, creeping dread at what would happen when he finally did.

Jordan stopped at a row of lockers along the right-hand wall. She pulled open the door of the last locker in line, and a scream exploded from inside. Two hands shot out, clutching a pistol.

Jordan leapt back. "Whoa! No! It's okay! It's us!"

The hands hovered in the air, still pointed straight at Jordan's chest, then finally dropped down again. My mum stepped shakily out of the locker. "Sorry. Sorry, I was …"

"It's fine," said Jordan. "Quick, get back inside."

Mum ducked back in and we followed after her. Straight through the locker and out the back, into the room hidden on the other side.

Jordan and I had set this up weeks ago. The lockers had originally been inside the room, but we'd dragged them out into the hall and punched the back out of this one. We had food in here for a day or two, and a couple of blankets to shield us against the worst of the cold. Not exactly Narnia, but it would keep us alive until the end of the world, at least.

"Where are they?" Mum asked, returning to her guard duty. There was something so horrible about the sight of her holding a gun that I wished I'd never given it to her.

"Back up near Peter's room," I said. "Soren rigged up an explosion and caved in the passageway."

"So we're trapped," said Cathryn, stepping out of the shadows.

"You were already trapped," said Soren, limping in behind us.

Jordan spun her flashlight around the little room and practically dived on top of her mum, who was over in the corner feeding the baby. Georgia was curled up next to her, sniffling. I looked away, not exactly clear on the breastfeeding privacy rules.

"So what do we do now?" Mum asked.

"Um," I said, still a little thrown by this bizarre new world where Mum turned to *me* for instructions. "Let's just sit tight for a while. Keep hidden. I mean, with everything going on in town, they might eventually decide to just give up on us."

Mum pursed her lips, seeing straight through me. But what else was I meant to tell her? She didn't know about Peter. Not the part about him stabbing me to death, anyway. And there wasn't much point dumping that on her now.

"How is he?" whispered Jordan, drawing my attention back to the family reunion on the floor. She

24

brushed a gentle finger over Tobias's head.

Mrs. Burke shrugged. "He seems fine so far. Normal. I mean, he's feeding like a super-baby, but so did you and Georgia."

Jordan shot me a sideways glance. End of the world or not, it's never okay for your mum to start discussing your "feeding" habits in public.

Her eyes drifted back to Tobias, and mine followed, the same question running through both our heads: how in the world was this tiny kid supposed to stop a killer virus from exterminating seven billion people? Somehow, that seemed even more impossible than the rest of Phoenix's cavalcade of insanity.

And what if it really *was* impossible? What if Tobias wasn't the savior we all thought he was?

The only reason any of us believed Tobias was special was that *I'd* said he was, twenty years ago. But what did I know? What if this was all just some stupid endless loop of me fooling myself into believing something that had never been true in the first place?

Stop, I thought fiercely. *Stop it. You're not getting out of it that way.*

This wasn't about my doubts and I knew it.

This was about fear.

I knew what the right thing was. I knew I couldn't just ignore humanity's best chance for survival. And with a day left until the end, I knew I was dead whether I confronted Peter or not.

Which was all good and rational, but there's a pretty massive difference between *knowing* what's right and actually having the guts to do it.

All these weeks, I'd been wishing for a clear way forward. A tangible answer that I could pick up and run with. Now I had it. Or as close as I'd ever get, anyway.

And all I wanted to do was run the other way.

I sat on the ground, back against the cold wall. Stalling.

We'd been down here for what felt like days now, but was probably more like half an hour. Somewhere in that time, Jordan had remembered the phone in her pocket, the one I'd pulled from Ketterley's body earlier tonight. We'd crowded around as she tried to call Reeve, but we were way too deep underground to get reception, even on Shackleton's secret super-villains' network.

Jordan had pocketed the phone again and no one had spoken since. Cathryn was sobbing in one corner, Soren sitting silently in another, picking at a scab. Mrs. Burke was doing her best to keep Georgia from freaking out, but even a normal six-year-old wouldn't have missed the despair in the room, let alone a kid who could see inside other people's minds.

Mum hadn't left her place at the door for a moment. Not even when the rest of us were fixated on the phone.

And through it all, Tobias just lay there, sleeping. No sign in the world that he was anything other than an ordinary newborn.

But he had to be. He was all we had left.

Which meant I had a job to do.

I stared down at Tobias, so impossibly tiny and frail. Just a *baby*.

You'd better be worth it.

Jordan was circling the room, pacing like a caged animal. I reached for her leg as she passed. She dropped down next to me, knees bent up against her chest.

"Hey," I whispered. I put an arm around her and the dull ache in my stomach intensified. Not that we'd ever had great odds of surviving this place and living happily ever after, but it's one thing to see something coming a mile away, and another thing to be there when it arrives.

Jordan leaned into me. "This is stupid," she breathed. "We need to *do* something."

"Yeah," I said.

But for a minute, I couldn't get the words out. I just sat there, feeling her next to me, knowing it was probably the last time we were ever going to be together like this.

"We have to go back," I said finally, keeping my voice low enough that only she could hear. "*I* have to go back. I need to deliver that message to Kara."

Jordan straightened up.

"Don't," I said. "Please. Don't argue about it. It's hard enough –"

"So, what, I'm supposed to just stand back and watch you die?" she hissed.

"We need to know, Jordan! If Tobias is the answer to all of this, then we need to make sure we know about it. And if he's not – Well, I'm dead anyway, aren't I? As soon as Tabitha gets out, I'm gone. And in the meantime," I said, with way more courage than I felt, getting up before either of us had the chance to talk me out of it, "I can't just sit here. And I'm pretty sure you can't either."

Jordan got up after me, and Mrs. Burke jolted. "What's going on? Did you hear something?"

"No, it's okay," I said. "We're just going to duck outside for a sec. See how far along they are, clearing through the rubble."

"I don't think that's a good idea," said Mrs. Burke tersely.

Jordan glared at me, and there was an uncomfortable silence as she decided whether or not to play along.

"We'll be careful," she said finally, bending down to hug her mum. "Whatever happens, stay quiet and don't give yourselves away."

Jordan scooped Soren's flashlight up off the ground.

Georgia buried her face in her mum's side.

"Back soon," I lied, heading for the door.

And suddenly, I guess my survival instinct kicked in or something because every step became a massive effort, an order I had to force my body to carry out against its will.

After weeks of turning this moment over and over in my head, I was finally stepping out to meet it. It wasn't just an idea anymore – some weird, unexplainable thing we'd seen on an old video tape. It was actually going to *happen*.

Mum turned as I reached her, face barely visible in the darkness. She held out the pistol. "Take this."

I shook my head. "We'll be fine. You need to protect the others."

Mum hesitated, then lowered the gun. She put her arms around me and I almost lost it.

I'd walked into the jaws of death before, but not like this. Not with the outcome already decided and played out and caught on camera before I'd even started. Not *knowing* that I wasn't coming back.

I kept hold of Mum, a crushing hollowness flooding through my chest, like I was being pushed apart from the inside. I let the moment drag out as long as I could, knowing that this was it, that letting go meant *letting go*.

Mum made a noise in my ear. The sound was so

unfamiliar, so out-of-character for her, that it took me a second to realize she was crying.

"I'm sorry," she said, voice cracking. "I'm sorry I brought you here. I'm sorry I dragged you into all this. If I'd just looked up from my work for a half a second and stopped to think what you might be –"

"Mum, stop," I said, taking a breath to keep back my own tears. "*No one* knew what this place was! That was the whole point. And, listen, whatever happens to me – whatever happens to any of us –"

"Luke …"

"No, *listen*," I said, determined to get it out while I still could. "You need to know I don't blame you, okay? Whatever happens to me, I need you to know that none of this is your fault."

Mum held me out at arm's length. "Luke, why are you –?"

"Because it's the end of the world, Mum." I took another steadying breath, thankful she wouldn't be able to make out my face in the darkness.

She pulled me to her again. "Be safe out there, okay?"

"Yeah," I said, wrenching myself away from her.

She moved back into position at the door, and we slipped past her, out into the gloom of the passageway.

Chapter 4

LUKE

The nausea hit me as soon as I stepped outside. I pushed up the corridor, stumbling, everything fuzzy with tears, breaking into a run before I even knew what I was doing.

"Wait!" called Jordan, as soon as we were out of earshot of the panic room.

I kept running, like my dread was a monster bearing down on me, and all it would take was a moment's hesitation, one false move, and it would overtake me completely and –

"Luke!" Jordan caught hold of my wrist. "Luke, *stop.*"

I wiped my eyes clear with the back of my hand and realized that she was crying too.

"*Talk* to me," she said. "What are we doing here?"

"You know what we're doing," I said, walking again, but keeping hold of her hand. "You're going to send me back twenty years, and I'm going to tell us all about Tobias."

Jordan made an exasperated noise, but it got caught in her throat and came out more like a sob. "I can't just *send you back*, Luke. That's not how it works."

"No, I know, but –"

"And even if I could, that still wouldn't get us past Calvin. What's the point of knowing about Tobias if we can't even get back up to the surface?"

"I don't know, okay? I don't *know* anything, but – Seriously Jordan, what choice have we got? What else can we do but go back to the room from the video and see what happens? Maybe it doesn't have to go the way it did last time. If we go now, maybe you can send me back and I can deliver the message before Peter even knows we're there."

"You don't believe that," Jordan croaked. "You're the one who keeps saying that there *is* no 'last time' and 'this time.' That it's all just some big, unstoppable loop."

"And you're the one who says it's all happening for a reason," I said, more aggressively than I'd meant to. "You've been telling me since forever that there's some unseen purpose to all this. Do you actually believe that, or is it only true when it suits you?"

Jordan didn't answer, and on top of everything else, I felt a swell of guilt. "Sorry," I said. "That wasn't –"

But before I could even get the words out, Jordan pulled me to a stop again, stepping in front of me, eyes red and shining with tears. Her hand slipped up through my hair and she brought my head closer and kissed me.

I let out a sob, torn up and exhausted, sighing into her mouth, the impulse to run vanishing in an instant. My hands laced around behind her back, pulling her to me, and I could so easily have just stayed there like that until they broke through and came for us.

But eventually, Jordan split apart from me. Her hands slipped down my arms and she stared at the ground between us. For a long time, she was silent. I stood, holding on to her, knowing we should push on but not able to bring myself to do it.

"It's not fair," she whispered.

Which, even though it was the kind of complaint a four-year-old would make, was actually a pretty perfect way to sum it up.

We kept moving, neither of us speaking until we reached a little side-tunnel that had been clumsily cut out of the concrete; the pathway out to the last room I was ever going to see.

Jordan went straight past the mouth of the tunnel

and kept walking.

"What are you doing?" I asked as she let go of my hand.

"Checking on Calvin," she said. "Wait here."

I ignored her, trailing behind as she slipped up the passageway. Before long, we heard noise up ahead, muffled sounds of concrete on concrete. Jordan flicked off the flashlight and we continued on by touch.

After another minute or two, we rounded a corner and I flinched as a tiny shaft of light pierced through the blackness up ahead of us, twitching erratically and then flickering out again. Another flashlight, shining in through a tiny gap in the wall of rubble. They were quickly getting through.

I tightened my grip on Jordan as the noise continued. The shifting of debris, and frantic, breathless grunting.

There was an explosive *smash*, like a boulder getting hurled into a wall, and one of the guards shouted, "Hey! Watch –"

A roar rose up from the other side of the cave-in, silencing the guard.

"Leave him!" said Calvin, sounding unusually strained. "Let him work."

The noise dropped away, a momentary standoff on the other side of the wall, and then the grunting and smashing started up again.

"He's clearing the rubble," said Jordan, sounding sick. "He's coming after us."

Another flashlight beam shot through the rubble, bigger this time. We had a few minutes, maybe less. Jordan pulled on my hand and we doubled back, running, putting as much space between us and Peter as we could.

I think we both knew it wouldn't be enough.

We weren't going to change it.

I was already dead. I had been for twenty years. All that was left was to take back the message about Tobias and hope that my death made some kind of difference after I was gone.

In what felt like seconds, we got back to the low tunnel out to my murder room. Jordan made a half-hearted attempt to keep us moving past it, but I pulled away from her and crouched at the tunnel's mouth.

Jordan made a kind of gasping noise, like she'd started to say something and then given up. I closed my eyes, head spinning, fighting down the urge to vomit, knowing that once I started down that tunnel, I wasn't coming out again.

Move, I told myself, with as much resolve as I still had left. *Go. Either* you *die or everyone else does.*

I forced myself inside, not knowing if that was even true, not knowing anything anymore, my mind capable of nothing except pushing me through the tunnel, and hardly even capable of that. My whole body shook like it was coming apart, teeth chattering uncontrollably, arms barely holding me up off the ground.

Light flashed up the tunnel as Jordan crawled in behind me, flashlight clutched in one hand. I squeezed my eyes shut again, trying and failing to steady myself, half-expecting her to grab my leg and try to drag me back out of there. But she just moved silently up the tunnel behind me.

I almost rolled over the edge as the tunnel came to a sudden end. Thanks to Soren's dubious excavation work, there was a meter drop down to the ground on this side. I stretched out my arms and crawled to the concrete below.

Jordan dropped in behind me and flicked off the flashlight, but not before I caught a glimpse of the dull-brown stain smeared out across the floor. My two-decade-old blood, due to be spilled from my body any minute now.

I shivered in the dark, reaching out to Jordan, pulling her into a hug. Her breath was ragged in my ear, and I felt the moisture seep through the fabric of my shirt as she started crying again.

I steadied myself against her, soaking up the warmth of her body and the feeling of her arms around me, waiting for the telltale lurch that would signal the arrival of her next vision. Time stretched out.

And nothing.

No vision. No anything.

"You have to go," I said shakily after a minute. "When this is done. When I'm – You have to get out of here and go kick Shackleton's arse. Get your family out. And my mum. Make sure she's –"

Jordan loosened her grip, finding my face in the dark. She kissed me, missing my mouth. "Stop it! This isn't finished! Don't you dare just lie down and stop fighting!"

"I'm *not*. But Jordan, you know this is –"

We sprung apart as an enormous clattering and crashing of concrete echoed along the passageway outside, followed by a triumphant shout from one of Calvin's men.

The celebration was cut short almost immediately as a louder, wilder shout rang out over the top of it. There was a split-second roar of gunfire, quickly replaced by a scream from whichever of the guards had been stupid enough to get in Peter's way.

Silence fell for just a few moments before it was broken again by the sound of footsteps hammering up the corridor outside.

Chapter 5

JORDAN

"JORDAN! JORDAN!"

Peter's voice raged up the passageway, sucking the air out of my lungs.

"Wait here," I said, reluctantly letting go of Luke. "No – *wait*," I insisted, as he moved to follow. "Stay here. Let me check it out."

I shoved the flashlight – still off – into my back pocket and clambered into the tunnel again, blinking the tears out of my eyes, scrambling towards the sound of Peter's voice.

I'd told him.

Two days ago, I'd gone to see Peter in his cell and

I'd told him all about what we'd seen in the video.

What if I was the one who'd put all this in his head in the first place?

"JORDAN!"

A flashlight clicked on up ahead and I froze at the mouth of the tunnel, thinking he'd seen me. But no, not yet. He was still further up the passageway. I shuffled back a bit, pressing myself low against the base of the tunnel, and waited, grateful that I'd at least had the sense not to tell him *where* Luke was going to be when he murdered him.

The flashlight beam grew brighter, bouncing along in time with Peter's footsteps, and suddenly he was right in front of me. From this angle I could only see up to his chest, which I hoped meant he wouldn't be able to spot me without bending down. He slowed, catching his breath, flashlight in one hand, knife in the other, both arms covered in blood and bruises. He turned in a circle, crying out again. "JORDAN!"

Peter's flashlight beam flickered right over the top of me, and I was suddenly struck by the stupidity of what I was doing. If Peter found me, it was going to lead him straight back to Luke.

But the flashlight kept moving, shining back the way he'd come. Peter muttered something to himself, then turned around again, still bellowing my name.

The sound of his voice faded away. I inched forward again, craning my neck out of the tunnel to see along the passageway. Then someone somewhere stifled a gasp of pain, and I jerked my head back before realizing they were a little way off – a guard back up the corridor who'd just collided with something in the dark.

They were still coming. Hanging back, flashlights off, keeping their distance from Peter. But Calvin had come here for Tobias, and he wasn't going to leave without him, which meant –

A sudden jolt of energy shot through my body, and I leapt out of the tunnel, a wild, reckless idea bursting to life inside my head. I was back on my feet and sprinting after Peter almost before I knew what I was doing.

I flicked my flashlight on, no time for caution, ignoring the corner of my brain that kept insisting this wasn't going to work, that I'd never been able to change the past before and this time would be no different.

Almost immediately, I saw the beam from Peter's flashlight dancing up ahead. He wheeled around as I approached, face contorted with fury. But then he saw who I was and his expression melted into one of freakish, single-minded joy.

"Jordan!"

He threw his arms around me, mashing his lips against mine, like he was trying to swallow my whole

40

face. I squirmed, acid rising in my throat, but he just dragged me closer, and I felt the cold handle of his knife pressing into my back.

"Pete –!" I pulled back, coughing. "Peter, not now! They're coming!"

Peter's eyes narrowed. "Where's Luke?"

"Not here," I said, determinedly keeping my voice even. "Peter, please – I need your help."

Suddenly, I had his full attention. "What is it?" he asked, still not letting go of me. "What do you need?"

"They're coming," I said again. "Calvin and his men. They want –"

"I'm not scared of them."

"No, I know, that's –" I glanced over my shoulder, thinking I'd heard something. "That's why I need you to protect my family."

Peter may have been a murderous lunatic, but he was also the only one down here who could protect my family from Shackleton's security. And he'd do it, too. If he thought it would help prove his undying love for me, he'd do pretty much anything. And if I could keep him busy enough with that ...

Then maybe Luke didn't have to die. Maybe we could get the word out about Tobias and get Luke out of here before Peter even knew what was happening.

Peter took a step back from me. He stared down at

the knife in his hand.

I gritted my teeth, fighting the urge to scream at him. "Peter –"

"Yeah," he said, nodding emphatically. He put his hands on me again. "Yeah, of course. Of course I will."

I broke away from him and took off down the passageway. "This way."

The panic room wasn't far off. I sprinted along the last stretch of half-destroyed laboratories, into the more-intact section of the complex on the other side, with Peter right behind me, panting in my ear like a wild dog.

I told myself I was doing the right thing, that this was the best way to protect my family and keep Luke alive. But who knew what Peter would actually do when the time came?

A few meters short of the row of lockers that hid my family, I reached out my hand, bringing Peter to a stop.

"Okay, they're just down there," I said, already bringing up my mental map of the complex, trying to work out how I was going to get back to Luke without getting caught. "Whatever you do, don't let the guards – *Peter!* What –? No, *stop!* Let go of me!"

Peter's hands clamped down around my arms, terrifyingly strong. He hauled me down the corridor to the lockers, throwing a door open at random. I twisted under his grip, kicking at him, but it got me nowhere.

"What are you *doing?* Get –!"

"Quiet!" he snapped, shoving me in with one hand and finally letting go. I tried to jump out again, but I couldn't do it. I couldn't move myself forward. Peter was still holding me there, telekinetically pinning me to the back of the locker with his fallout-addled brain. He ripped the flashlight out of my hand, switched it off and slammed the locker shut again.

There was a *clank* of metal on the outside of the doors as Peter jammed something through the handles, locking me inside.

I stared out through a little grate in one of the doors. "Please," I whispered, as Peter dropped out of sight. "You need to let me out of here. I have to –"

"No," he panted. "I'm keeping you with me."

His flashlight clicked off, plunging the corridor into complete darkness.

I slumped down, losing my balance as Peter released his telekinetic hold on my body. I pushed against the doors, but they wouldn't budge, and I was too scared of attracting the attention of security to try anything that would make more noise.

"Shh!" Peter breathed through the grate. "Shut up. I'm looking after you."

For a second, I thought I heard Georgia's voice from the panic room. I strained my ears, trying to work out what was going on in there, but the sound had already disappeared. I put my face in my hands, barely keeping hold of myself. This was a disaster.

"How are you even going to see them coming?" I asked. "They could be right –"

"I said *shut up*," Peter snapped.

I heard his feet twist on the dirty ground as a tiny creak of metal sounded behind him. The door to the panic room cracking open.

"Jordan …?" whispered Luke's mum uncertainly.

Peter let out a growl. "Where's Luke?"

"Not here," said Ms. Hunter, even more nervous now. "He's with –"

"Shut the door!" I hissed.

"Jordan?"

"Do it!"

The door clanked shut, and I heard more shuffling of feet on concrete as Peter started after her.

"No, wait!" I said. "He's not –"

But the plea was silenced almost immediately by a furious spray of weapons fire. A rifle flashed from somewhere off to my left and Peter cried out, thudding to the ground.

My heart jolted into my throat. *Did he just –?*

"Lights!" Calvin demanded, and a pair of flashlights cut through the darkness of the corridor. I squinted away, blinded.

There was a fierce scraping of metal: the locker next to mine pulling away from its place against the wall. I opened my eyes just in time to see it go blurring past me, up the corridor in the direction of the guards. The air was filled with an ear-splitting clatter as the locker was hammered with bullets.

Peter gasped like he'd been holding his breath, and I heard the remains of the locker crumple to the ground. In the shifting light of the flashlights, I saw him stumble to his feet in front of my grate, exhausted but apparently unharmed. Then he disappeared again.

"Sir?" said one of the guards, spooked but still waiting for an order.

Before Calvin could respond, Peter let out a breathless shout and I heard the locker scrape up off the ground again. The guards cried out and the corridor fell back into shadow as their weapons clattered to the ground.

"Peter!" Calvin called. "Enough of this!"

"STAY BACK!" shrieked Peter, and the locker on my other side started scraping away from its place on the wall.

Calvin pushed on, raising his voice over the sound. "Do you want to end this? Do you want to protect your friends? Hand over the baby and we will spare the rest. I give you my word they will not be –"

"NO!" With an enormous crunch, the locker shot across the corridor and slammed into the opposite wall.

"Get back, get back!" said one of the guards as Peter, still out of sight, lifted the locker into the air again, angling it around to get a clear shot.

"Fire!" Calvin ordered. "Take him –"

"WAIT!" shrieked a new voice from the direction of the panic room, and I felt my heart crash down into my stomach.

Peter's locker dropped out of the air, filling the corridor with a deep, echoing clatter.

One of the guards found their weapon again, shining their flashlight in the direction of the voice, and a trembling figure stepped out in front of me, hands above her head. Cathryn.

No, no, no, no, I screamed inside my head, fists balled up in front of my mouth to keep myself from crying out. *No, no, no, what are you DOING?*

"You c-can't do this!" Cathryn said, taking a shaky step forward. "I'm Louisa Hawking's daughter!"

You IDIOT! I pressed my face up to the grate, panic washing over me, wave after wave. *You stupid, brainless coward! You think that's going to make any difference?*

Calvin laughed. "Your mother's wishes do not concern me, Cathryn."

"If you kill me, she'll –"

46

"She will do the same as the rest of us," said Calvin. "She will do what she is told."

Cathryn opened her mouth, but no sound came out. She looked back at the panic room, despair on her face. Her one bargaining chip had failed – of *course* it had – and now she had –

One of the guards let out a shout, and a dark blur spun across my grate. A rifle. Cathryn shrieked as it hurtled past.

I heard a grunt and a click as Peter caught the weapon, and then gunfire filled up the corridor again. The sound ricocheted inside my locker, pounding my head from all sides.

"EVERYBODY BACK!" yelled Peter, charging up behind Cathryn who was still on her feet, paralyzed with fear. "EVERYBODY –!"

One of the guards returned fire, drowning him out, and a scream rose up in the corridor. Cathryn collapsed, clanging noisily against one of the fallen lockers. Peter glanced down at her, focus slipping for just a second.

And suddenly Calvin was leaping into my field of vision, through the mess of battered, bullet-strewn metal, rifle swinging out over his shoulder like a baseball bat. He cracked the weapon down across Peter's head. Peter staggered, swaying on his feet, but didn't fall. Calvin pounded the weapon into his head again, and he finally dropped to the ground.

I slumped against the locker doors, my knees threatening to give way. The doors *thunked* into whatever Peter had jammed through the handles, but the sound was covered up by another wail from Cathryn.

Calvin glanced down at her for only a moment before turning back to his men, hand outstretched towards the panic room. "In there. Bring Tobias to me."

It took everything I had not to start pounding on the doors in an attempt to break out.

They rushed past me. Still four of them, even after the carnage back up near the entrance. Calvin must have roped in a couple of others after the corridor caved in.

"Do not harm the others," Calvin called after them. "Shackleton wants them alive."

One of the guards spoke up. It sounded like Officer Cook. "Sir? Barnett's orders were to —"

"Officer Barnett is no longer in command," Calvin said coldly.

An uncomfortable pause, then: "Yes, sir."

Screams flew from the panic room as the doors were flung open. Ms. Hunter started to yell, but there was a clatter of metal on concrete as her pistol was tossed aside. I heard Georgia wailing, Mum begging the guards to leave her children alone. Then one of the guards fired their weapon and my heart almost burst out of my chest.

The screaming stopped.

My insides went cold.

I slumped down inside the locker.

No, no, no, no …

"On your feet!" Cook boomed. "Now! All of you! Next person to speak gets a bullet."

Georgia sobbed again, and I felt the light flicker back on inside me. Just a warning shot. They were all still alive.

Footsteps shuffled into the corridor. A guard stepped into view in front of me, waving the others through. Mum came out after him, Georgia shuddering in her arms and the barrel of another guard's rifle poking into her back.

I pressed my face up against the grate, clenching my fists, telling myself over and over again that my best hope of helping them now was to stay hidden and wait until I actually had a shot at doing something constructive. It was excruciating, every second an eternity.

They paraded the others out, over the unconscious heap of Peter's body, with Cook at the back, cradling a silent Tobias.

Cathryn whimpered as Calvin dragged her to her feet. Cook came up to hand Tobias over. He looked Cathryn up and down, then rolled his eyes. She was completely uninjured.

Calvin shoved her roughly across to Cook, and then reached to snatch up Tobias. A smile broke across his face, eerily reminiscent of the one in Georgia's drawing.

"Everybody out," Calvin ordered, nodding at the entrance. "We've got work to do."

The guards filed past him, hauling my family away. I choked down a shudder, fingers clawing the walls of the locker, only barely managing to stay quiet.

"What about the others?" asked Cook in an undertone, hanging back to speak with Calvin in private. "Hunter and Burke?"

Calvin glanced back down at Tobias. I couldn't read his expression in the darkness, but the next words out of his mouth were clear enough. "We've got what we came for. If you find them, kill them."

Chapter 6

JORDAN

I held out for as long as I could, waiting for the guards to get some distance on me, hands wrapped around myself to keep from breaking down before they got out of earshot, head filled with so many blood-spattered images of Mum and Georgia and the baby that I barely even knew where I was anymore.

Finally, my resolve gave out and I started hammering on the doors of my locker, trying to shake loose whatever was holding the handles shut. The doors rattled but didn't budge. I felt the tears pricking my eyes again, panic threatening to boil over completely and send me into meltdown.

"Come on!" I pleaded, pounding the metal. "*Come on, come on, come on, COME ON!*"

I threw myself, screaming, at the doors. An explosive *bang* shot up and down the corridor and the locker rocked, almost toppling over. I backed off, panic shooting up my spine. The locker tipped into place again, and I crashed into the back wall, shaking.

I straightened up, trying to steady my breathing. *Think, you idiot! Get it together before you kill yourself.*

I stared through the grate at Peter, still unconscious among the bullet-riddled lockers, face lit up by the flashlight on his rifle. I swallowed hard, trying to work out if waking him up would put me in more trouble or less, and then a burst of clarity flashed just bright enough for me to see another way out. I couldn't tip myself forwards without crushing Peter's legs and trapping myself even worse in the process. But Peter had thrown aside the locker next to mine.

If I could knock this thing over sideways …

I spread my feet, digging them into the foot of the wall on each side of me, heart still threatening to punch its way out of my chest. With another furious shout, I threw my weight hard to the left. The locker rocked slightly, but clunked back down again.

I swung to the other side, building momentum,

then heaved left again. Another swing and a miss but I kept moving, back to the right, and then back to the left, and then right, left, right, left –

And then suddenly I was in free fall. I twisted around, trying to brace myself, barely even getting my hands down under me before –

CRASH!

My arms cushioned some of the blow, but not enough to stop my head thumping down into the ground. I groaned, head spinning, maybe even blacking out for a bit. As soon as I'd gotten my breath back, I rolled over and kicked at the door in front of me. There was a thump as whatever had been blocking the handles came loose, and the door fell open, crashing to the ground.

I jolted backwards. Peter was right there in front of me, face lit up like he was about to tell me a ghost story. Eyes closed, but still breathing.

I crawled out, doing my best not to touch him, skin crawling as my mind flashed back to the night he'd cornered me in his bedroom. My foot caught on the strap of his rifle and I almost face-planted into the ground. Peter stirred, mumbling something under his breath. I wrenched myself away, half-expecting to get thrown into a wall, but he settled into unconsciousness again.

My flashlight lay on the ground in front of him. I

picked it up and pushed myself back to my feet, still woozy from the fall.

What now? I thought, leaning against the wall.

The panic inside me had settled for a moment as I'd escaped the locker, but it was already surging to the surface again. I took a deep breath, forcing myself to focus.

Calvin would have them all out of the complex by now. Off to be interrogated by Shackleton. He'd keep them alive for a while at least.

Or would he? How did I know that? How did I know Shackleton didn't just want to slaughter them in person? And what about Tobias? Would he even make it to Shackleton, or would Calvin just wring his neck out in the bush somewhere? If Tobias died, so did everyone on the outside. So did –

Luke.

I had to find Luke.

I took off, but made it only a few steps up the corridor before skidding to a stop and running back to Peter. I crouched down again, tearing his rifle away from him. I ran my hands over the ground, searching for his knife, but it was like it had just disappeared.

No time! I screamed inside my head. *Just go!*

The panic took hold again and I abandoned the search, reaching down and rolling Peter over, into the locker I'd just escaped from. I slammed the locker shut and ran around behind it, pushing it over onto its front, sealing him inside.

Even dizzy with fear, I wasn't stupid enough to think that would hold him for long. But it might give us a few minutes, and maybe that would count for something.

I started running again, through the mold and the dirt and the decay, straight for the epicenter of the explosion that had started all of this. The explosion *I'd* caused, twenty years ago, on the night of Luke's murder.

My head was a dead weight, throbbing with the pain of my fall and still reeling from the revelation that everything we'd been through in the last hundred days had only been possible because of *me*.

I'd caused the fallout, which had caused my powers, which had caused the fallout.

What would happen if we changed it? What if Luke never went back in time? What if I didn't let him? If there was no trip back through time, then there was no explosion to bring down the complex, no fallout to attract Shackleton here in the first place, no *any* of it.

We could stop all of this before it even started.

So why hadn't I?

Surely I'd known all of this the last time around. But I'd still made the way for Luke to go back. I'd still let it all happen.

Why?

I kept moving until finally my flashlight lit up the entrance to the tunnel. Instantly, the impossible, circuitous time-travel questions flew from my mind and things became a whole lot simpler: I needed to get inside, get Luke out of here, and go after my family.

I crawled into the tunnel, head still pounding, but with a clear goal to latch on to now, at least. My flashlight shone into the room at the far end, slipping over the grimy walls.

"Luke!" I hissed. No answer.

I scurried forward, faster now, a fresh burst of dread shooting through my stomach. "Luke!"

I reached the end of the tunnel and dropped to the floor, spinning my flashlight in a frantic circle. He was gone.

I shone the light into every corner, as if I could have missed him the first time in this tiny, empty room, then dropped back against the wall, raising a hand to my injured head.

Calvin had found him. Luke must have left to come after me and gotten caught by security on their way back from –

I snapped upright at the sound of heavy breathing in the darkness, fingers playing over the flashlight as I debated whether or not to turn it back on again. The breathing grew louder. I couldn't take it anymore.

I switched on the flashlight and thrust it back in the direction of the tunnel. It was Luke.

My heart lifted for just a fraction of a second before plummeting back to earth as I realized what he'd done.

He'd been back out to the living area. He'd changed his clothes.

Luke crawled out of the tunnel, dressed in a mud-stained tracksuit with the hood pulled up over his head. His murder clothes. The same ones he'd been wearing in Kara's surveillance video.

He wasn't just *letting* things happen the way they had before. He was *making* them happen, making sure everything played out the way it was supposed to.

"No!" I said, backing off from him. "Luke, please – *please* – you're not doing this. You can't …"

Luke stepped towards me, eyes bloodshot and streaming. He opened his mouth to say something, but all that came out was a sob.

My arm was still frozen in place, lighting him up with the flashlight. Luke pushed it gently aside, closing the gap between us. He wrapped one hand around my waist and brought the other up to my cheek. His lips closed around mine, soft and slow, and the tears that had been needling my eyes since I crawled in here spilled over and ran down my face.

Luke's hand traced across my back, rubbing slow

circles between my shoulder blades. His thumb moved over my cheek, brushing away the tears, and I tightened my hold on him, overwhelmed with the deep, dark *wrongness* of it all – that this brave, beautiful boy should lose his life while a murderer lived to see another day and a sick old man built an empire on the back of –

What are you DOING?

I pulled away from him, overwhelmed with my own stupidity. Luke shows up in his murder room in his murder clothes on his murder day and I just stand there and *kiss* him? I dived at the tunnel entrance, ignoring his gasp of confusion, desperate to get out before history had a chance to repeat itself.

But I didn't get two steps before the nausea erupted in my stomach. I collapsed mid-stride, a breathless groan tearing its way out of my throat.

Luke was by my side in an instant.

"*No*," I pleaded, shoving him weakly away. "Run! Leave me! I won't let you –!"

The protest died in my mouth and I curled into a ball, wracked by another bout of uncontrollable gagging. The room hurtled in circles around me, the flashlight beam fracturing into a thousand tiny shards, and still Luke would not leave me. He cradled my head, both of us trembling out of control.

"Please …" I choked, not even sure I was saying it

out loud.

I could hear Luke speaking to me, trying to comfort me, but his voice was all warbled.

"I'm sorry ..." I murmured as he swam in and out of view above me. "I'm so, so sorry ..."

And then I was gone, falling to pieces in a hurricane of swirling blackness. I squeezed my eyes shut, blocking it out.

But slowly the pain died down, the universe straightened out, and harsh, white light blasted through my eyelids. I lay on my back, forgetting where I was for a moment. Forgetting everything. Then it all came flooding back and I opened my eyes and dragged myself up from the floor.

I was sitting in a stark, white laboratory. Completely empty. And spotless, unstained by Luke's blood. In front of me was a second room, sealed off from mine by a wall of glass. I'd been in a place like this before. Vattel and her people used these rooms to investigate the mysterious "events" at the center of their research. Events that, as it turned out, were me.

I wiped my eyes, dragging in shallow, shuddering breaths.

On the other side of the glass were desks covered in boxy computer equipment, which had been designed to pick up the trace or residue or whatever that I left behind whenever I popped in from the future. Previously, I'd seen Vattel Complex scientists working the computers, running scans to try to figure out what I was. Today though, the room was unoccupied.

I stood up, arms out to balance myself. This was it. The day from the video. The day of Luke's –

No. Not this time.

I turned, searching for Luke, waiting for him to appear like he did every time I faded out, the only one who could drag me back to the present.

A door clunked open behind me. I leapt back, some stupid part of my brain freaking out that it was Peter.

A head poked through the door, just below the handle. A little girl, Georgia's age or maybe a bit younger, with long brown hair and deep, penetrating eyes. A young Dr. Galton, back before Shackleton secretly adopted her. She peered furtively around the room, like she was looking for a place to hide. Her eyes swept straight through me without any hesitation. As far as she could see, the room was still completely empty.

Galton froze as a voice called along the corridor outside. "*Ashley!*"

She ducked back out of the room. The door swung wide and I saw her scamper away.

Any other time, I would probably have gone chasing after her, fascinated to find out what was going on out there. Not now. I didn't care about any of it. There was no room in my mind for anything but Luke.

"Ashley! What will your mother say when she finds out you've been sneaking off again?" The voice up the hall raced closer. Kara, two decades younger and gentler, but still unmistakable. She waddled past the open doorway and I caught a glimpse of a flowing white nightgown and an extraordinarily pregnant belly before –

Jordan! Luke mouthed, flashing into view, centimeters away from my face. I reeled back, startled, then reached out, grasping for his arms. My hands passed straight through him and I lurched, almost tripping over. He tried again, nose running, tears streaking his face with mud. But again, we failed to make contact.

Luke looked away for a second, like he'd heard something behind him, and I felt my chest turn to ice.

Peter.

"Run!" I screamed, trying pointlessly to shove him away. *"Go!* Get out of there!"

But where was he supposed to go? There was no other way out. If Peter was coming up the tunnel, then –

"– BACK!" Luke gasped, suddenly audible again, hands collapsing at my sides. His voice was all stretched and distorted, like a Skype call on a bad connection.

Out behind the wall of glass, the computers whirred to life – an automated process to track the "events" when there was no one here to do it in person.

Luke's gaze flickered back out behind him again and I could see the pale, sick dread rising in his eyes. "Please – please – you have to let me in –"

He flinched, almost losing his grip on me as I jerked backwards, convulsing. I clung on to him, nails digging in through his clothes. All around me, the room began to decompose, swirling away into a sludgy blur.

And then suddenly, it all sprang back into place, but now I could see the world of the present as well, one time superimposed over the top of the other. The room was pristine and destroyed, immaculate and filthy, gleaming white and dim and dark, all of it fusing together into a flickering, mind-bending mess.

Luke's hands trembled against me. I could still see the doorway behind his back, but now the ragged outline of the tunnel's mouth had reappeared alongside it. And there, barely visible in the glow of my abandoned flashlight, was the dark silhouette of someone moving.

"Hurry!" Luke cried, attention flitting back and forth between me and the tunnel. "Please! Whatever you – You have to let me in!"

The shadow in the tunnel scuttled closer. Light glimmered as the blade of Peter's knife caught the flashlight beam. I couldn't breathe. My chest felt like it was closing in on itself. The world began to break down again, my grip on the past slipping away, and all at once I understood what I had to do.

Luke was dead. If he was still in the present when Peter arrived, he'd be gutted right there where he stood. But if I could get him into the past, if I could give him somewhere to run …

Maybe this time it would be different.

Please! I begged, some deep, primal part of me crying out for help. *Please, don't let him die.*

The bile rose up in my throat and I felt the ground start to give way underneath me, but I held on, focusing whatever strength I had left on keeping up the connection between the two timelines.

A furious wind rose up, rushing into my ears and under my skin. I felt myself splinter apart, my vision blurring as my body lost cohesion. Over Luke's shoulder, I saw Peter shuffling closer, his dark form filling the tunnel now. Luke whirled around, letting go of me. He turned back, face drained of color, wrapping me up in a frantic, desperate kiss.

I love you, he mouthed over the tornado spinning through my head. I tried to respond, but I was too far gone, pulled open and stretched apart.

Peter twisted around and dropped to the floor.

Luke cast a terrified glance over his shoulder.

Peter raised the knife high over his head, screaming

something at Luke. Luke spun back to me, and I had to force myself to keep watching, keep the connection alive.

Don't let him die. Please.

Luke ran straight at me, and I jumped back – or would have if my body was still capable of moving like that. I looked down at my stomach, caught a fleeting glimpse of him blurring into me, and then he was gone. Somewhere in transit between the blood-stained ruin and the gleaming laboratory.

But he wasn't there yet. I couldn't let go. Not until –

Peter cried out in fury, loud enough for me to hear even over everything else. He rolled back his shoulders, knuckles white on the handle of his knife, glaring into me with bulging, inhuman eyes.

"*NO!*" I screamed, throwing my hands out as if that was going to do anything. The whole world shuddered and roared around me, like it knew what was coming next.

Peter looked into me, looked *through* me, a hideous grin spreading across his face.

He lowered his head and charged.

Chapter 7

PETER

He was getting away. Straight through her and gone, just like Crazy Bill before.

Coward. Filthy cheating coward!

I felt my fingers drumming on the knife. I knew what I had to do.

Straight through her and gone and kill the dirty thief and then finally – *finally* – Jordan would be mine again.

She swirled, glowing and brilliant and hardly even Jordan anymore but still beautiful, still mine. I smiled at that. The thief was trying to escape, but she was holding the way open for me to go in there and kill him.

Kill the coward and get back what's yours.

I ran, straight in, straight through, into her body that was not her body, light everywhere, spinning all around me. I grabbed hard on my knife, rocketing through the big, bright silence.

And then there was a room again, still bright, but walls and floor and solid. I landed wrong, almost falling but not.

And I saw him.

DIRTY UGLY THIEF!

Everything else was gone. Everything but the rage, rage, rage, filling me up and showing me what I had to do.

RUN!

He tried to shake his head, to open his mouth and scream, but he was too slow. Stupid and ugly and slow. I swung my arm, up in the air and down in his chest. The knife was blunt but I was strong and *now* the scream came out, all wet and pathetic.

BLOODY COWARD! BLOODY WEAK STUPID TRAITOR!

I took back my knife, sticky and oozing. Back into his chest again, hitting the bone underneath, and again, breaking something open, and the blood poured out faster and faster. He coughed and fell down, taking my knife with him, still *taking*, even now.

I looked back at Jordan, still there, a shimmering

perfect haze, ready to welcome me back to her. My chest swelled up with the thought of it. Time to go home.

The thief screamed again. I crouched down, getting my knife back, cursing him as he kept trying to breathe. Shallow, slippery gasps, like a fish. I stood, disgusted with him, and then froze, my eyes flickering to the ceiling.

There was a camera up there. It had been watching me the whole time.

I looked away. Not important. *Nothing* was important except that he was *gone* and the world was right again. It was done. Finally, it was done.

I ran back into her, into the glorious, consuming light. Anger gone now. No sight, no sound. Nothing but surging, soaring joy. So furiously bright, so all-consuming, tearing me up and hurtling me along and tossing me over and over myself, over and over and –

Something was wrong.

Where was she? Where was the filthy room with the stains on the floor? The first trip had been nothing. Seconds. This was too long.

The brightness dimmed. Sound rose up in my ears. Transcendent light covered over by gray, roaring mess.

No. This was wrong. This was *wrong*.

Turbulence rattled through me, pummeling muscle and bone. I was screaming. Burning. Not fire, but something, curling around me, licking up my body and into my mouth and nose, consuming everything.

Then *smack* into the solid ground, everything bright again. I was back. Back in the shining laboratory, in a pool of the traitor's blood. Still shaking.

The light was everywhere, cracking walls and shattering windows with a sound like an erupting volcano. Concrete and glass and dirt rained down from the ceiling. The whole world caving in on me.

And then it was gone.

Chapter 8

JORDAN

I saw it all.

I saw Peter charge out after Luke.

I saw his knife come down again and again.

I saw Luke cry out and fall to the ground, the life gurgling out of him.

I saw him drag himself across the room, streaking his own blood across the floor, out into the next room where he would spend his last breaths warning Kara about the end of the world.

I saw the whole thing play out exactly the way I'd seen it a thousand times over on Kara's surveillance tape.

And then the whole world blacked out and I didn't see anything.

I woke up, concrete hard against my back, and for one treacherous moment I was disoriented enough to blur the pain a little.

Then I opened my eyes and saw the dull-brown stains spread out underneath me, lit up by the glow of my abandoned flashlight, and reality set back in like a battering ram. I felt my chest cave in, my lungs collapsing, my whole body giving way under an avalanche of crushing, nauseating grief.

A groan burst out of me, long and low and guttural. My arms wrapped around my stomach, shivers rattling through me, tossing me against the dirty ground. His blood was everywhere. Smeared out around me, soaking into the concrete.

I had to get out.

I was on my feet before I even knew it, desperate to be *out* of there. My legs failed me and I hit the wall, hands crashing into the tunnel.

I started gagging. Not a vision. Just my body's pointless attempt to purge itself. I rode it out, head down between my arms, and then half-climbed, half-fell into the tunnel.

And then finally, the dam burst and the tears came flooding out. I crawled through the darkness, stopping and starting, overcome with ugly, unrestrained, shuddering sobs.

Some subconscious part of my mind registered a change in the way my cries echoed off the walls. I was back out in the corridor. I got up, only now realizing that I'd left my flashlight behind. I staggered aimlessly through the black until I collided with some spongy wood sticking out from the wall. I held on to it, keeping myself standing.

But why? Why even bother? Why not just curl up and die and be done with it?

Nothing had changed.

It was all over, and nothing had changed.

I'd held out for as long as I could, longer than I'd ever done before, watching him struggle and bleed and crawl out of the room, hoping against hope that something would step in and save him. But nothing. *Nothing.* Blow for blow, scream for scream, it had all happened exactly the way it was supposed to.

WHY?

Why let him get murdered? Why couldn't he have just delivered the message and come back? Why did he have to *die* for it?

For months, I'd been hurtling along on the strength of my stupid visions, convincing myself that they were somehow helping us along, guiding us through these hundred impossible days, that somehow we were *meant* to overcome the Co-operative and make it out alive. And now this.

I spun away from the wall, rage blazing up and bursting out. "YOU WERE SUPPOSED TO HELP! YOU WERE SUPPOSED TO SAVE HIM!"

After that, it wasn't even words. I screamed my throat raw, crying out into the endless darkness, until finally my lungs gave out and I stood, chest heaving, waiting for something, anything, that would justify what had happened here tonight.

But of course, there was no response.

Nothing but deep, deafening silence.

I started running. It was all instinct – some innate reflex kicking in below my conscious mind. I just needed to get away. I fumbled in the dark, somehow finding a path among the laboratories.

Light glowed faintly up ahead. The dying flicker of an old camping lantern. It was coming from Bill's excavation room. *Peter's* room. The place he'd spent two weeks obsessively digging up out of the rock. All in some deluded attempt to return to the Jordan he'd left behind twenty years ago. To return to me.

I pushed on, shakier with every step. Through the old laboratory with the floor covered in broken glass, through the remains of another decrepit corridor, into the room with the lantern that Bill had dragged us into, only hours before.

I stopped at the back wall, almost slamming into my own shadow, and sank to the ground again, dizzy and out of breath. Crying again. It seemed impossible that I *could* still cry. I felt so emptied-out already. But the tears kept coming, dredging themselves up from the depths of me and running together into deep, wracking sobs that left me gasping for breath.

He was gone.

Gone.

I realized now that I'd never actually believed it was going to happen. Not really. Even in my most desperate moments, I'd never let go of the stupid, stubborn hope that *somehow* this would all get turned around. And now it was finished and he was gone, and I realized I had no idea what to do next because every single one of the plans in my head had Luke in it.

I was paralyzed, the grief and the emptiness drowning out everything around me until there was nothing left in the whole world but to lie here in the dirt and weep.

"Luke …" I choked. "Luke …"

I winced, the sound of my voice driving daggers into my own injured head, but I kept crying out, as if I could call him back from the dead. "Luke …"

My eyes snapped open.

I gazed over at Bill's old camping lantern, my mind alight with a sudden realization. As I watched, the lantern seemed to shimmer slightly, waving out of shape, as though there was heat rising up from the ground in front of it. At first, it could have been just tears obscuring my vision, but the distortion quickly expanded and spread, growing brighter, more visible, like mist or steam or something.

Like *me*.

Another portal was opening up. The one from a few hours ago. The one I'd inadvertently created – inadvertently *become* – when Bill brought Luke and me out here to force his way into the future. This was the other end of it.

I sat up, staring into the brightening cloud. I'd seen all this before, from the other side. Which meant the other Jordan, the one from the past, could see *me*.

"JORDAN!" I yelled. "TAKE HIM! TAKE HIM AND GO! HE'S –"

My voice became a splutter and then gave out completely. What was the point? She couldn't hear me. Of course she couldn't. That had been *me* a few hours ago and I hadn't heard a thing. Nothing had changed, and nothing was going to. Despite his misguided attempts to avert events, Bill had been right all along.

It was inevitable. All of it.

I slumped back down again, blocking it all out, trying to ignore the roiling pool of liquid light burning on the other side of my eyelids.

It wasn't until a fierce *thud* struck the ground in front of me that I remembered I still had one more ordeal to survive before this was all finally over.

I sat up. Crazy Bill from a few hours ago had just flown out of the portal, filthy and stinking, barely covered up by the tattered remains of his medical gown. He'd landed awkwardly, sprawled on his back between me and the portal, the light in his helmet shining a spotlight onto the ceiling.

I slid away until my back hit the wall. Bill rolled over and stood. He sobbed loudly, lifting his hands to reach out to me, face taut with a kind of awestruck joy.

"I'm back," he said breathlessly, like he almost didn't believe it. "I'm back, Jordan. I'm here."

I pressed into the wall, cold fury spreading through my chest.

It was him. Peter.

He advanced on me, hands trembling, spreading apart to embrace me. "Jor–"

"MURDERER!" I yelled, lunging at him. "You *stupid – pathetic –*!"

He lurched away, shocked, like he couldn't fathom

why I wasn't pleased to see him. He gathered himself and stepped forward, trying again.

Then he stopped.

His eyes locked on to mine, slowly pulling themselves into focus as though he was just now figuring out how to use them. The smile slipped from his face. His mouth drifted open in dawning, horrified comprehension, like he'd suddenly realized where he was and what he was doing. Like he was waking up.

I slammed my fist into the side of his face, all pain and rage and adrenaline. "YOU KILLED HIM!"

He recoiled again, waving his arms, trying to speak.

"*NO!*" I cried, punching him in the stomach, in the ribs, in the mouth, fists pounding at whatever they could reach, beating and beating, sick, choking, blind with tears, screaming myself hoarse. He staggered under the blows but didn't cry out, didn't fight back. I kept going, hammering into him, head throbbing and spinning, arms aching from the effort, until finally my body said *no more,* and I collapsed at his feet, gasping for breath.

He stared down at me, an agonized moan slipping out between his rotting teeth, then wheeled around to look into the portal still swirling in the air. He steadied himself, head clutched in his hands, and took off at a lumbering run. Back through the shimmering cloud. Back into the past.

Almost as soon as he'd disappeared, the portal began to break down. The light grew brighter still, spreading out and filling the room, and the walls shook with the familiar sound of rushing wind. And I guess there was some part of me that still cared about preserving my life because I shrank into a corner, shielding my head as cracks snaked through the concrete and bits of the ceiling broke loose and fell away.

Everything turned white as the portal erupted in an explosion of light. And then it was gone.

The darkness returned, and I lay on my back, dust raining down on my face. My chest rose and fell, gradually regaining its natural rhythm, and I waited as my eyes remembered how to see again in the dim light of Bill's lantern. By the time they did, I seemed to have gotten some small part of my mind back as well.

I was still here. Still alive. The gaping, invisible hole in my chest hadn't gone anywhere, but I was starting to feel like maybe I could split my attention just enough to let some other thoughts creep in around the edges.

My family was still out there.

The *world* was still out there, however temporarily.

Luke had given up his life to warn the rest of us about Tobias. Was I really going to just lie here and waste that?

There would be time to grieve later. To do it for real.

But right now I had to get out there and *do* something, or else I was going to have a lot more to grieve over.

One more day, I told myself, slowly rising to my feet. *You can do that much. Keep it together for one more day, and then you can fall apart all you want.*

But even as I moved to leave the excavation room, I caught myself glancing over my shoulder, checking out of habit to make sure Luke was with me, and my insides gave another sharp twist.

Focus, I ordered myself. *Keep it together. Think. What's next?*

My first job was getting outside. I bent down to grab Bill's lantern, carrying it with me as I climbed back through the caved-in corridor and into the lab on the other side. The light was all but dead now. Still, it was better than nothing.

I jolted as my foot struck something heavy lying on the ground, and then swung the lantern down to see what it was.

Bill's pickaxe. The one he'd been using to hack this place apart. I shivered, remembering the night Dr. Galton had flung an almost identical pickaxe into my side, cutting me open on our way out of the medical center. Luke had carried me to safety. He'd saved my life. And now –

Enough.

I took a breath, hoisting the pickaxe up off the ground with my free hand. I wouldn't use the pointy ends. I didn't want to kill anybody. But one solid whack with the broad side would be enough to take care of any unsuspecting guards who were still –

I jumped again, backing up and hurriedly switching off the lantern.

Footfalls on gritty concrete. One of Calvin's men, still down here. Left behind to take care of Luke and me. Or maybe he'd just been too injured to leave with the others.

Silently, I lowered the lantern to the floor and wrapped both hands around the pickaxe. I edged across the lab until my shoulder nudged the wall, then felt along to the doorway out of here.

He was just around the corner. Hard to tell how close he was in the darkness. But close.

I brought the pickaxe out in front of me, feeling the weight of it in my hands. One chance. Either I got him on the first swing, or I got shot full of holes.

I held my breath, straining to hear him coming, and almost shouted as a flashlight beam shot out from back up the passageway, lighting up the wall opposite me. The circle of light grew steadily smaller as the guard crept closer.

I shifted my grip on the pickaxe, preparing to swing.

Three …

Two …

A rifle poked out from around the corner and I swung, throwing all my weight behind the weapon in my hands. It sailed out in a wide arc, almost pulling out of my hands, momentum carrying me out across the doorway. The guard yelped, leaping back, and a shudder ripped through my arms as the pickaxe swung past him and struck heavily into the wall. I squeezed down on the pickaxe, desperate to get out of the line of fire before –

"Whoa whoa whoa! Jordan!"

The voice cut through everything and I froze up. The pickaxe slipped from my hands, clanking noisily to the floor.

The man lowered his weapon, spinning it around to light up the space between us. And there, in the glow of a stolen rifle, dirty but completely uninjured, completely *alive …*

"Luke?"

2½ HOURS EARLIER...

Chapter 9

BILL

For the first time in twenty years, I had no idea what was supposed to happen next.

I limped along the dark road, eyes on the town center, my lungs rattling. Pain roared from feral gums, seeping cuts, and even worse going wrong on the inside. It was my same old screwed-up body, but somehow getting my head back together had turned up the dials on all of it.

I gasped for breath and it tasted like smoke.

Phoenix was burning.

Gunfire echoed in the streets, flames surged through the school and the mall, the whole town glowed orange in the light of the fire and the crackle of the shield grid strung out across the sky, and none of it even came close to the chaos raging inside my head.

I tried to block it all out. Focus. But I couldn't block out the sound of Jordan's voice. My head was full of it. The same word, over and over again, dark and poisonous and so unbearably freaking *true*.

MURDERER.

I was a murderer.

And now, finally, I could see it. I could *feel* it. Two full decades as a professional crazy person, and all that blood and death and guilt had finally come crashing down on top of me in one massive, soul-destroying heap.

And to top it off, it had all blown up just as I'd succeeded. Just as I'd *won*. Twenty years stuck in the past, twenty years waiting and scheming to get back to the girl I'd murdered for, and I'd finally *done it*. I'd gotten the portal to the future back open and made it home to my own time, just a few moments after I'd left it. And there was Jordan, all alone and crying on the ground, with no Luke to distract her from falling all over me.

All hail Peter, the romantic freaking mastermind.

And not only had my spectacular display of murder and craziness failed to impress Jordan, but somehow this second trip through time, this trip that was meant to be my big shiny victory, had ripped away the decades of insanity and brought me face to face with the sickening reality of who I really was.

MURDERER.

It was gone now. The haze of fallout clawing at my brain. Rewiring my thoughts. Twisting me around. In an instant, it had all been blown away. My sanity had been given back to me.

Crazy Bill was gone. I was Peter again.

Right. Like it's that simple.

Like I could just write the last two decades off as my "crazy years" and let myself off the hook. Like it wasn't me, right there, making every single one of those decisions. I might've been messed up by the fallout, but my mind was still there. It was still *my* mind.

What a twisted bloody nightmare to see yourself for who you really are.

I made it to the park at the end of the main street and crouched in the overgrown grass, knees cracking. Shouts rang through the shadows up ahead. Guards-turned-firefighters, swarming around what was left of the mall, spread too thin to do anything much. Whatever was going on inside the Shackleton Building, it had the Co-operative even more worried than what was happening out here.

I clenched my filthy hands around the key card I'd dug up from one of my old hiding places in the bush – the one I'd stolen all those weeks ago to sneak in and spy on Shackleton and Calvin.

Fear churned through me. Not the familiar, always-there crazy person panic. This was sane man's fear. Survival fear.

Deal with it, murderer. Move.

I stood, pain creaking up through my legs again, and lumbered out across the park, my dirty old hospital gown rippling out behind me. I yanked it up around my waist, and broke into the closest thing to a run I could manage.

And suddenly, there it was. Sliding into view from behind the mall, lit up by the fire but still in one piece. The building that'd been my prison for more than half of the last hundred days: Phoenix's medical center.

I forced myself forward, chest heaving, dodging the guards and the minefield of debris buried in the grass. My mind reeled with the long-lost terror of not knowing what was up ahead, the future suddenly wide open in front of me again.

It was bloody disorienting. For so long now, I'd been living my whole life according to the same pre-written plan, working obsessively to make sure history repeated itself exactly the way it was supposed to. And somewhere along the line, I'd convinced myself that all of it was inevitable. That my future was fixed because I'd already seen it happen.

And maybe that was right. Maybe I *couldn't* change

anything. Maybe it really was all locked in from the beginning and even now I was just playing into the same endless loop. But I was getting pretty bloody sick of second-guessing myself.

Screw time travel. All I knew was that right here, right now, I was making a choice.

I knew I could never unbreak it all. Even if this worked, I couldn't cancel out all the evil I'd done just by stacking some good on top of it now. But back in the medical center, somewhere in the blur of my imprisonment, I'd seen something. Something that might actually make a bit of difference. Not for me, but for her.

I crashed out from the grass at the edge of the park and staggered across the street to the medical center, firelight crackling over me. A firefighter shot past without even noticing I was there.

Up the side of the building to the main street. It was a war zone. Wreckage from the mall littered the street. This was more than just fire damage. Someone had tried to blow it up. A big hunk of concrete had punched through the razor wire around the front of the Shackleton Building, twisting it out of shape and demolishing the fountain on the other side. The security center had been destroyed days ago now, but no one had even bothered to rope it off.

Now and then, I saw movement in the darkness. Escaped prisoners, but not many of them. It seemed like most of the fighting was still going on inside the –

I lurched back, crouching in the shadow of a parked delivery truck as the Shackleton Building doors slid open. Two figures raced out into the light of the fire. I felt a little pull in my chest as I realized who they were: Mr. Larson, my old English teacher, getting dragged along by his wife.

Another guy ran out after them, dressed in black and armed with a rifle. He shouted at the Larsons to get back inside, and I felt another jolt of recognition, this time laced with icy hatred. Mr. Hanger, our monster of a history teacher. Trust him to sign up for Calvin's death brigade. He was never happy unless he was making someone else miserable, so this had to be pretty much the perfect –

I caught myself, disgust washing over me as a memory floated to the surface of my mind. My fists around Mr. Hanger's throat, smashing his face into the floor of the school gym while he begged me to stop.

If he was a monster, then what was I?

I shook my head, pushing it all away. No time for this.

Larson darted in front of his wife as Hanger charged over to meet them, still shouting but apparently unwilling to actually *use* the weapon in his hands.

I dragged my eyes away from them and kept moving, up the little wheelchair ramp behind me to the entrance.

My bare feet crunched on crumbled bits of safety glass. The front doors of the medical center had already been smashed open. I jumped across the threshold, thudding down on all fours on the other side.

I grunted, picking myself up. The lights were all off, had been for weeks, but an orange glow flickered in from the street, just enough to see by. I scratched at my beard, trying to remember. I hadn't been in through the front in years. Which way was I meant to –?

An arm shot out from behind me, wrapping around my throat and dragging me back into the shadows. A twisted bit of metal hovered in my peripheral vision: the broken leg of a food court chair. "Easy, mate. We don't want any –"

I shifted around, yanking free, my mind lashing out to shove him away, send him flying into a wall.

Nothing happened. The guy stayed right where he was. Someone screamed behind him.

I tried again, channeling all my adrenaline out into his chest.

Nothing.

I froze up, feeling suddenly defenseless, realizing for the first time that it had been a package deal. My trip through the portal hadn't just stripped me of my insanity.

It had taken my sci-fi mind powers away from me too.

"All right, mate. Just – just stay back." The man stepped shakily out of the shadows, clutching his chair leg like a caveman holding a spear. His voice registered in my head and I swayed under a sudden weight, realizing who he was a second before his face caught the light.

Dad.

Chapter 10

BILL

Dad's eyes narrowed at the sudden change in my expression. Mum came up behind him, freaked out but alive. Unhurt. Tears stung my eyes, and I stumbled to touch her, seeing both of them clearly for the first time in forever. She cringed away, terrified, and with an ache in my chest, I realized how I looked to them.

"HEY!" Dad stuck out his chair leg to ward me off. "Hey. That's close enough."

He might as well have run the thing straight through me. But what was I expecting? I wasn't their son. Not anymore.

"Listen," said Dad. "I'm sorry. I shouldn't have attacked you. We're only trying to –"

"How did you get out?" I asked, shocked at how

weirdly unfamiliar my own voice sounded in my ears. Dad didn't answer. "Look, I swear I'm not going to hurt you. I just …"

Dad cocked his head, like he was trying to work out how Crazy Bill was suddenly capable of coming out with a complete sentence.

"We were in the showers when the food court blew up," said Mum, and for the first time I took in her wet hair and the nurses' uniforms she and Dad had found to cover themselves. "They move us through in shifts during the night. We ran. Crawled through that hole in the fence."

Dad lowered his weapon and glanced into the shadows behind them. "I think we're all right, Alyssa."

A girl stepped out. Green eyes, caramel-colored skin, dirty Phoenix High uniform. Couldn't have been older than thirteen. She had a guard's utility belt hanging over her shoulder like a beauty pageant sash.

Alyssa looked up at me, nervous but standing her ground. She glanced sideways at my mum. "Are we bringing him with us?"

"Bringing me where?" I asked.

Dad frowned, figuring out how far to trust me. I looked away from him, pushing back another surge of tears. It was too much. Too familiar. How many times had I been on the receiving end of that look, back when the worst I'd been guilty of was skipping class?

"Vattel Complex," he said finally. "An old place under the town. It's where we were hiding out, back before —" He hesitated. "Hang on. Is that where —? Have you been down there with them?"

My gut turned in on itself. "Yeah. I have, but —"

"Are they okay?" Dad's hand hovered in midair, like he'd been about to touch me but then thought better of it. "Peter. My son. Is he …?"

"He's — alive," I said. "He's still down there."

Mum let out a little shudder of relief. She wrapped a hand around Dad's arm and swallowed hard. What was it going to do to her when she found out the truth?

I glanced around the reception area. I couldn't do this. I had maybe an hour left before Luke's murder.

"Hey, where are you going?" Dad called after me as I started towards a doorway across the room.

I ignored him, pushing through to the corridor on the other side.

"The tunnels?" he guessed, trailing after me, Mum and the girl right behind him. "Yeah, I thought of that too. But how are you going to get in without a —?" His eyes dropped to the card in my hand. "Oh."

I limped around a corner. Now what? I couldn't bring them with me. Not back to the complex. Not now. But I wasn't about to just abandon my parents.

Keep moving, murderer. Work it out later.

There was a *click* and a flash of light as the girl found a flashlight on her belt. She handed it to my dad.

I watched my shadow lumber along the walls in front of us, all huge and ragged, and that sickening sane man's fear flooded over me again. I was naked. Unarmed. Powerless except for my bare, blistered fists. A lifetime of hurling my problems across the room with my brain, and now –

"Shh!" Dad hissed, and the flashlight cut out behind me. Everyone fell silent. I strained my ears. Nothing but the muffled sound of the chaos outside. Dad flicked the flashlight back on again, shaking his head. "Never mind. Thought I heard something."

I hurried down the next corridor, even more on edge now. What was I meant to do if someone *did* come?

Dad's flashlight switched off again.

I skidded to a stop, just short of the next bend in the corridor, clamping my mouth shut, suddenly aware of how loud and rasping my breathing was.

A round of gunfire echoed in from somewhere on the street.

"C'mon," Alyssa whispered. "There's nothing –"

The whisper turned into a squeak as a door clunked open, just out of sight. There was a burst of light and a cold, venomous voice spilled out from inside.

"– honestly think him foolish enough to leave that option open to you? The countdown is *locked*, Louisa. Not even Shackleton can override it now."

I stepped back, crashing into my dad.

It was Dr. Galton. Shackleton's second-in-command, last seen as a hazy nightmare swimming past my prison cell. I stumbled to the nearest door and wrenched at the handle. It didn't budge. Mum yanked on Dad's arm, urging him to *run*.

Galton strode closer, footsteps splitting the air like gunshots. And in between, a buzzing sound. Another voice, coming through a phone. Whatever it was saying, Galton didn't like it.

"To protect himself!" she snarled. "To protect the *world* from invertebrate cowards who would have us turn tail at the first sign –"

Her flashlight shone around the corner, lighting us up. Ending the conversation.

Mum screamed. Dad dragged her back, waving his chair leg. Alyssa turned to run, but –

SMASH!

Before she'd even made it one step, she shot into the air and through the nearest window, tangling in the blinds. *How –?*

Galton. Steely concentration in her eyes. She was like me.

I charged, diving before she had time to react. Her phone and flashlight flew from her hands. Pain sparked through every joint I had as we dropped to the ground. She thrashed around but couldn't shake me. Her powers really were like mine: useless at point-blank range.

They worked fine on Dad, though. I heard frantic footsteps behind me as he rushed in, then a breathless shout as Galton threw him back up the corridor.

I got to my knees, still pinning Galton down, one hand mashed into her face. I felt the force of her mind against me, shoving me back, but I held on, bringing my other hand around to catch a fistful of her hair. Galton cried out, eyes squeezing shut. A massive over-reaction.

Too slow, I realized what she was up to. Her hand flashed around, all silky precision, aiming the pistol she'd just whipped out from her hip.

BLAM!

But the one upside to twenty years in the wild was that it kept your survival reflexes pretty sharp. I jerked sideways, deafened by the noise. Plaster raining down from the roof as the shot went wide. I grabbed Galton's wrist and smashed it hard against the floor, sending the weapon skittering away.

Galton snarled at me. She kicked and clawed, drawing blood. Her nails jabbed at one of my nastier wounds and a howl of pain burst from my throat. I dragged her head up off the floor, appalled all over again as I flashed back to the scene with Hanger in the gym.

Do it.

I smashed her back down again.

She cried out, whole body shuddering, and I flinched. A half-second of pity. Galton took it, rolling under me, knocking me to the ground. I rolled to catch her. Grabbed at her hair again. Missed. I threw out my other hand and caught Galton by the arm, just in time to feel her tense up and shriek as a spray can hissed into her eyes. Galton crumpled, face red and streaming.

I twisted around. The kid. Alyssa. Back out in the corridor, armed with the pepper spray from her guard's belt. She pumped another blast into Galton's face and I squinted away, catching the edge of it.

"Grab her!" Alyssa shrieked.

I heaved in a breath, half-blind but keeping hold of Galton's arm. I got back to my knees, hauling her towards me, then flipped her over and pinned her down again, my hands shifting uneasily back to her head. One solid thump and it lolled to the side.

The corridor went quiet again. I backed off from Galton, pushing down the sick feeling in my stomach, and turned to Alyssa, who was checking herself over for injuries. "Thanks."

She nodded weakly, pulling a set of handcuffs from her belt. I took them from her, locking Galton's arms behind her back, then flinched at a light and low buzzing behind me. Galton's phone, vibrating across the floor. I crawled over and read the name blinking up from the screen. *Louisa Hawking*. Cat's mum, calling Galton back.

I snatched up the phone and ended the call. Memories flooded back from a lifetime ago. Memories of countless afternoons at Cat's place, when I had no idea that Louisa was anything more than a kind-of-highly-strung mum. Memories of Cat, of a relationship requiring zero murders that might have actually gone somewhere if I hadn't been so bloody –

A rush of footsteps pounded the thoughts away. Mum and Dad, barreling towards me. More flashlights coming behind them.

I snatched up the key card and ran. Around the corner, down a little flight of stairs and there, finally, was the big steel door that led down into Shackleton's tunnel network.

"Stop! Stop right there!"

A furious, too-familiar voice. Mr. Hanger. *Officer* Hanger. Either Cat's mum had realized what was up and called for help, or this was just the latest in a long history of him magically showing up to bust me. Either way, I was pretty sure he wouldn't actually *fire* that gun until –

Gunshots shattered the air above my head. Alyssa screamed.

"Bloody Hanger!" I shouted, diving for the metal door with the key card in hand. The door clunked open and I hurried inside, tripping on my gown and almost getting trampled as the others rushed in behind me.

Hanger fired again. The bullets battered into the door as Dad heaved it shut after us, while Mum raced across the tiny, empty room to activate the trapdoor in the floor.

"He's – supposed to be – a teacher!" Alyssa panted. She jumped aside as the section of gray tiles she was standing on sank down into the floor, revealing a glimmering silver staircase. "Whoa. What *is* that?"

I ignored her, plodding down the stairs as soon as there was space, out into the light of a wide, narrow corridor. The Co-operative's secret medical research facility, aka Victoria Galton's House of Imprisonment and Torture. My mind flashed with groggy half-memories of drips and needles and "tests."

Dad looked at me out of the corner of his eye, pretty uneasy himself. He was the engineer who'd designed the containment machine that kept me trapped down here. "Sorry," he said warily. "For – for my part in all this. I had no idea who I was really working for. Truly. I had no clue about any of it. All I knew was that you were – They told me you were a dangerous monster."

"Yeah," I said, heading for a door to my right. "They weren't wrong."

A shout echoed behind the double doors at the end of the corridor.

"There's someone in there!" shrieked Alyssa, searching her belt for a weapon. The doors shook like someone was pounding them with their fists.

"The prisoners," said Mum. "The ones who didn't make it out last time."

"We need to get those doors open." Dad looked back at me, expectant.

"I – I can't," I said. "Something –"

Mum broke off from the rest of us, striding towards the doors. Dad ran after her, realizing what she had in her hands. Galton's pistol. She must have grabbed it on our way down.

I left them to it. Went through a door to my right, into a dark room filled with petri dishes and medical fridges. In the middle was a bed, empty and neatly made. More unwelcome memories. During my stay here, the bed had belonged to whichever of us the Co-operative were running their latest mad-scientist experiment on, which most of the time seemed to be a pasty-skinned kid named Jeremy.

I ripped open the nearest fridge, scanning through the labels on the vials inside. Four shelves, arranged by name and then by number: *Anderson, Burke, Burke, Kennedy.* Not what I was looking for. I slammed the door shut, then raced along the line of fridges and opened one near the end.

Bingo. Jeremy had a whole fridge to himself. I crouched at the bottom shelf and ran my finger along to the last vial in line: *J_Thomas_Tissue_Modification_Treatment_4-3-0*

This was it. Or at least, as close as they'd come to "it." I pulled the vial loose and almost dropped it as I heard a gunshot outside, followed by voices and footsteps pouring into the corridor.

I straightened, heart pounding, and crossed to a store cupboard. I tore the doors open, scattering equipment to the floor until my hands finally landed on the instrument I'd seen Galton using on one of her "assistants."

The *infuser.*

It reminded me of the syringe/gun thing Dr. Montag had used to inject me with a suppressor, all those years ago. One of the last nights of clear memory before the fallout swallowed me up. The thing was shaped kind of like a pistol, with an empty vial in the chamber and a syringe in place of the barrel. I ejected the vial, replaced it with my amber-colored sample of

J_ Thomas, and raced for the door.

In the hall, Mum, Dad and Alyssa had been joined by five scraggly prisoners in hospital gowns. My old neighbors. Alyssa had one of them, Jeremy, wrapped up in a hug.

"Right," said Dad, walking over to meet me. "Where to now?"

I ran a hand down over my beard, stress bubbling up again as I looked at this terrified rabble who had all apparently decided that *Crazy Freaking Bill* was the one to lead them to safety.

I had to lose them. I ran through the tunnel exits in my head: security center destroyed, Shackleton Building impossible, school on fire, mall –

There was a shriek behind me. Alyssa had just released Jeremy from their hug. She was staring, horrified, at her arms. Everywhere she'd come into direct contact with Jeremy, her golden-brown skin was bleached pinkish-white. Stained with Jeremy's own pale skin tone.

"It's okay!" said Jeremy weakly. "It's – I swear it'll go away!"

Alyssa didn't seem to hear. She was clawing at her arms now, trying to scratch the discoloration off.

"Stop it!" I snapped. "You're fine. It won't hurt you. It'll go away."

Alyssa flinched and shut up. She stopped scratching,

but still wouldn't meet Jeremy's eye when he looked at her.

"This way," I said, making my mind up. It was risky, but so was everything. I led them all back the way we'd come, into the little room under the trapdoor.

"You guys go that way," I said, pointing at a door leading up to Phoenix's main office building. "You'll come out up at the other end of the main street. Then run for the east end of town and circle around to the Vattel Complex."

"What about you?" Dad asked.

"I'm – not coming," I said.

I needed to get back to the complex, and I needed to do it *now*. The direct route. Through the hub under the Shackleton Building and out the trapdoor in Aaron Ketterley's office at the north end of town.

The complex would be crawling with security by now. Peter – the other Peter – would be rabidly dismantling the cave-in made by Soren's explosion. But by the time these guys took the long way back, it would all be over and the whole place would be empty. All except for Jordan and, if by some miracle this all worked out, an unstabbed, still-alive Luke.

Dad looked at me, uncertain. "All right, well – thanks, mate. Thanks for everything."

I couldn't help it. I threw my arms around him,

eyes going from zero to bawling in about two seconds. Dad tensed, probably thinking I was about to stab him with the thing in my hand, then relaxed enough to slap me awkwardly on the back.

I released him, turning to Mum. She glanced nervously at Dad, and then reluctantly allowed me to hug her. It was all tense muscles and more awkward patting. But I knew it was my only chance so I squeezed her tight, closing my eyes, taking what I could get.

You did this, murderer.

Don't act like you don't deserve it.

Mum pulled away, deciding my time was up. I wiped my eyes, but the tears kept coming.

"Listen," I sobbed, barely getting the words out. "Both – both of you, listen. When you find out – When this is over and they tell you about me ... You *can't* blame yourselves, okay? Promise me. This wasn't you. None of this was you."

"Sure, mate," said Dad, reverting to his talking-to-crazy-people voice. He moved closer to Mum, just in case I decided to freak out right here at the finish. "Yeah. We'll keep that in mind."

I watched as Dad led the others out of the room. Knowing I could never get my parents back, but hoping that somehow the next hour would make the days ahead a little bit easier for them to handle.

Assuming there *were* days ahead.

I stared down at the infuser, at the sticky orange liquid sloshing around inside the vial, everything blurry with tears.

Last chance, murderer. See if you can do some good before your time runs out.

I shoved open the door and ran.

Chapter 11

BILL

Run, murderer. Run.

Through the tunnels, over the road and into the bush, running and then walking and then limping, chest caving in, everything aching and soaked with sweat.

The shield grid snapped and snarled overhead, like some vicious animal, hungry for blood. I tuned it out, trying to work out where I was going, squinting through the darkness in search of a familiar landmark.

My foot caught on a tree root and I staggered, the infuser slipping out of my hands.

No!

I dived to the dirt. My hands shot out, knocking the thing up into the air and then catching it again, centimeters from disaster. I got up, head spinning, holding the vial up in the moonlight to make sure it was still in one piece. Then a scream split the night and I almost dropped it again.

Georgia. Breathless and hysterical. A guard boomed at her to shut up, but she paid no attention. They were behind me, coming up out of the complex. I'd walked straight past the entrance without even seeing it.

I was halfway back to them before I remembered my powers were gone. Guts churning, I crouched in the bushes, trying to quiet my wheezing breath.

Now what?

Flashlights swept between the trees, most of them pointing away from me, back towards the town. I dropped lower, joints cracking again, and scanned the huddle of faces. Georgia, Mrs. Burke, Cathryn, Soren, Luke's mum, and guards to keep them in line.

No Jordan or Luke. No me.

Georgia wailed again, clinging to her mum. A guard whose name I'd long forgotten stepped up to them, grabbing Mrs. Burke by the hair. "You shut her up right now or I'll —"

"Saunders!" growled a voice from down in the ground, and the guard shut up. Officer Calvin came up through the trapdoor in the grass, a tiny baby in one arm and a rifle in the other. For a second in the low light, I thought his hands were covered in blood, but it was just the red gloves he was wearing.

Calvin turned to the guard holding Cat. "Get them down to the bunker. Find Hawking, she'll let you in."

Cat let out a sob at the mention of her mum's name. The guard's brow furrowed. "Chief –"

"Once inside," Calvin steamrolled on, "you are to put all the entrances under manual lockdown. Remain with the prisoners until I return. Keep them alive and unharmed at all costs."

"What about you, sir?" said another officer, knees buckling slightly under the weight of a half-conscious Soren.

"I'll be back to interrogate the prisoners," said Calvin. He stared down at the baby. "But first, I have this one to deal with."

"NO!" cried Mrs. Burke, breaking her silence for the first time since I'd gotten here. "Calvin, please! He's just a baby!"

Calvin shot her a look I couldn't read. "I think we both know that's not true."

The guard who'd been arguing with Calvin started back towards town. The others fell into line behind him, leaving Calvin standing at the tunnel entrance.

"Tobias!" Georgia shrieked. "No! Give me back my brother!"

Tobias.

The name exploded in my head like a flare. It had been irrelevant to me for so long, just another part of the white noise, pushed aside in my obsession with getting back to Jordan. But now, finally, the pieces started slotting together.

This was what they'd been looking for. First Kara and Soren, and then all of them. The cure for Tabitha. The only way to bring down the Co-operative.

Take Tobias to the release station.

Tobias. Jordan's baby brother.

Seriously?

Georgia's tear-choked screams didn't let up. Calvin stood motionless, watching his men fade away into the night, waiting to make sure they were actually following orders. He muttered something under his breath. Then he turned, striding away through the bush.

Striding straight towards me. No idea I was there, but he'd work it out quickly enough when he trod on me.

I nestled the infuser in the grass and waited until he was two steps away, then heaved to my feet, screaming. Calvin lurched backwards, crying out in shock.

The baby's eyes snapped open.

Calvin swung his rifle around. Too slow. I grabbed his head with both hands, slamming it sideways into a tree. He let out a grunt, eyes fluttering shut, and I swooped down to grab Tobias before he slipped out of Calvin's grip.

Calvin collapsed against the tree, then dropped heavily to the ground.

I slung the strap of his rifle over my shoulder, switching the flashlight on to give myself some light, then scrounged for the infuser.

Still intact.

I raced to the entrance, carrying Tobias with me, but the trapdoor had already rolled shut. I stared down at the low, ragged lines of moldy concrete that ran around the entrance – all that was left of some long-gone building. I traced my free hand around the edges of the ruin. Shackleton's trapdoors all opened by flipping the switches on a fake power outlet. Maybe –

There.

Two little holes, side by side in the concrete. I leaned closer, carefully poking the syringe end of the infuser into one of the holes. There was a tiny hiss and the door trundled open.

I hurried down the winding stairs into an inky-black corridor littered with upturned tables and chairs. I clambered through, frustrated that I couldn't just blast it all away, stopping again as I reached a bed sticking halfway out of one of the doorways.

The whole time, Tobias stayed silent, gazing up at me

with his giant baby eyes. I held him against me, no idea what I was doing. I'd always just seen babies as weird attachments to their mothers, little wriggling things that got hurried across the street at the first sight of me.

I climbed over the bed, into the room on the other side, looking for somewhere safe to ditch him. I took in the kitchen at the far end, ransacked and ripped apart, and the air disappeared from my lungs as I caught a vision of myself, as Peter, tearing those drawers open, scattering their contents, searching for something powerful enough to tear through flesh and bone –

I turned away, dizzy.

There was an old couch in the corner. I laid Tobias on it, tucking him in tightly with cushions to keep him there. His mouth stretched open in a tiny yawn. Even if they got him out to the release station, what exactly was this kid supposed to –?

Not your problem, murderer. You'll be long gone by then.

I tightened my grip on the infuser, ready to run again. But before I had time to leave, the bed in the doorway started rattling with the weight of someone else coming in from outside. Luke. White-faced and panting.

Both of us stopped moving. My hand shook on the infuser, sweat running cold against my skin.

Luke sprung up from the bed, seeming to remember

why he was here. "Where are they? Did you see Calvin? And the others? Did they …?"

"Y-yeah. They're gone. The guards are taking them to that bunker under the Shackleton Building. Calvin's ordered them to put the whole place under manual lockdown."

I tried to subtly pull the infuser around behind my back, but what was the point? He'd already seen it. Plus, I had a freaking rifle hanging over my shoulder, so who was I kidding?

"What about Jordan?" asked Luke urgently.

"She's – fine," I said. "Still down here. Or not up there with the others, anyway."

Do it, murderer.

I moved towards him. Slow.

"I'm sorry," I said. "For – for the murder. All of it. I was –"

"Yeah," said Luke, hardly paying attention, like every second he spent talking to me was more wasted time. "Not your fault."

"Yes it *was!*" I said, suddenly desperate for him to understand me. "Even with the fallout, I was still – Luke! *Look at me!*"

Luke's eyes snapped back from the doorway. He stared at me, scared.

I kept going. "It was *me*, okay? *I* spent my whole life

112

obsessing over her! *I* attacked all those people! *I* put the knife in your chest! Me. I was nuts, but I was still me."

I breathed in. A shudder, wet with tears.

Luke stood there, frozen. Seconds ticked by.

His expression shifted, just the tiniest bit. Not pity or understanding or anything as strong as that, but it did feel like maybe, just for a moment, he was considering the idea that I was still a person.

"Okay," he said, finally. "Okay, well –"

I lunged, latching on to his arm, and his face went right back to petrified.

"No, wait! Bill – Pete – what are you –?"

I hauled him around and threw him onto the nearest bed.

"Let me go!" he demanded, kicking at me. "Peter's still out – *oof!*"

I sat on his stomach, knocking the wind out of him. "Quiet, then. You want to lead him straight to us?"

I reached over our heads, grabbing hold of the make-shift clothesline stretched across the bunks, and tore it down, lashing Luke's arms together against the bed frame. The rifle on my shoulder pressed against his chest as I leaned over him, and he decided to stop struggling.

That decision lasted about ten seconds.

I picked the infuser up from the mattress, checking the vial one last time, and Luke started writhing again, heaving against his restraints. "No! Get that –! I thought you said you were *sorry!*"

"I am," I said, free hand clenching around his face to hold him steady. A tear leaked out of my eye and splashed down onto his cheek. "I really am."

I jammed the infuser down into his arm and pulled the trigger.

Luke gaped down in horror as the serum drained into him, glinting gold in the shadowy half-light of the rifle's flashlight, and then gone, swallowed up by his arm.

"What –?" Luke shook under me but didn't pull away. "Bill, what *is* that?"

I ignored him, counting down in my head.

Four … Three … Two …

"Bill – *Peter*, come on – What are you doing to me?"

One.

I pulled the trigger again and he gasped, eyes squeezing shut as the vial began to refill. Blood. Slightly too thick and slightly off-color, infused with *J_Thomas_Tissue_Modification_Treatment_4-3-0*.

I withdrew the syringe and stood up, leaving Luke thrashing on the bed. He'd given up trying to interrogate me, attention split between writhing free of his restraints and watching to see what I was going to do next.

My hands were shaking again, fingers slippery on the infuser. I sat down on the bed opposite Luke's, begging myself to pull it together.

Deep breaths, murderer. Don't screw it up now.

Something glinted down on the floor. A grimy shaving mirror, sitting in a shoe box of shower stuff. I picked it up and held it in front of me, recoiling slightly at the sight of my own face. I shook it off, stilling my arms the best I could.

And I turned the infuser on myself.

The syringe touched on the soft flesh between my nose and my right eye and I winced, nearly dropping it.

I closed my eyes.

Okay.

Okay, here we go.

I pushed. My skin gave way surprisingly easily and I guided the needle in, dropping the mirror and steadying myself with both hands.

I pulled the trigger and screamed. The infuser pumped the horrible concoction of blood and serum out into my face. I clenched my teeth, forcing my finger to keep squeezing the trigger until the vial emptied out.

I dragged the syringe back out of my face.

And then my face started to move.

I hadn't seen much in my blur of imprisonment down beneath the medical center, but I'd seen enough to know it was a miracle Jeremy Thomas still had any blood left in him. Ever since the Co-operative had first caught wind of his fallout power – the ability to imprint his own skin tone onto someone else's body – Dr. Galton had been hard at work, looking for a way to harness it. Turn it into a weapon.

She'd almost sucked him dry to fuel her research, refining and enhancing Jeremy's "natural" ability, dragging it out of his body and into the Co-operative's arsenal. And now here it was: crude, imperfect, but hopefully, down here in the dark, enough to get the job done.

I cried out, head between my knees as muscles writhed and realigned, teeth jutted through gums, bones shifted under rippling skin. The pain was incredible.

Luke was shouting something – or maybe just shouting. Either way, I couldn't take it in. I was too fixated on the nightmare staring out at me from the shaving mirror lying cracked at my feet. My whole face bubbling up and melting, like I was being boiled alive from the inside.

And then, out of the shapeless sludge, my features began to reassert themselves. Only they weren't my features. Disfiguring scars had given way to smooth fifteen-year-old skin. Brown eyes had turned liquid blue. Even my swollen gums and broken teeth had made some effort to repair themselves.

I gazed down into the broken mirror.

And Luke gazed back.

The real Luke had stopped screaming now. He lay there on his back, chest rising and falling rapidly, a look of dawning comprehension spreading over his face.

Tobias, meanwhile, was staring contentedly at the ceiling, completely oblivious to the crime against nature that had just been committed right across the room.

I stood up, tore off the shredded remnant of my medical gown, and scanned the mess of clothes around the room. I needed something to wear. Something to hide the rest of me, still as mangled and scarred as ever. My eyes landed on a mud-stained tracksuit, and a pair of shoes strewn on the ground. I pulled them on and slung the rifle back over my shoulder.

Luke was still watching me, eyes welling up again. "Peter ..." he began, but then couldn't work out how to continue.

I reached down the back of my underwear, the closest thing I had to a pocket, pulled out Galton's phone and her key card, and dropped them on Luke's stomach.

"Get her home," I said, in a voice that was not quite mine, but not quite his either. "You take those bastards down and you get her home."

I jumped the bed in the doorway and stumbled away down the corridor.

Chapter 12

BILL

Minutes later, I was deep inside the complex, sprinting towards the room of Luke's murder. My insides burned but I didn't stop moving, didn't slow down because every second I wasn't hurtling forward was a second I might lose my nerve altogether.

The rifle bounced against my chest, splashing light across the walls of the passageway, all of it glinting and blurry through the tears.

Just shoot him, pleaded the part of me still screaming for an escape. *Just put a bullet through his head and –*

And what?

Shooting Peter meant shooting *me.* How exactly was that supposed to work?

Forget it, murderer. Keep moving.

For once in your life, be something other than a coward.

I shrugged off the rifle and tossed it aside, then pulled the hood of the tracksuit up over my head.

A few more meters through the dark, and I was there. I crouched at the mouth of Soren's tunnel and felt the dread overwhelm me again. Tears poured from eyes that weren't my eyes, down cheeks that weren't my cheeks. My breath caught in Luke's throat and I swayed on the spot, paralyzed.

Do it, murderer. Move.

I crawled into the tunnel.

I was about halfway through when a bright light flashed in my face. Jordan, flicking on a flashlight. I squinted, pushing forward, over the edge and down into the blood-stained half-room on the other side.

And there she was. Awesome and beautiful and shaking like crazy.

"No!" she said, and for a second I thought she'd somehow seen through my disguise. "Luke, please – *please* – you're not doing this. You can't …"

I kept walking, opening my mouth to speak and coming out with nothing except a wet sob. In a few steps I was close enough to touch her, to breathe in her smell, and for a second, everything else flew straight out of my mind. I met her in the center of the room, hands slipping to her face and her waist, and she didn't flinch, didn't shrink away from it. I pulled her closer, electricity firing through me as our mouths found each other in the dark.

Jordan returned the kiss, all love and desperation, and I knew it was wrong, knew it wasn't meant for me, but it was tender and real, and I drank it all in anyway. She tightened her grip on me, her whole body trembling now.

And then suddenly she was wrenching away from me, throwing herself at the mouth of the tunnel. Trying to get away. Trying to stop it all.

I grabbed at her, but she dropped out of my grip, collapsing to the floor with a groan. It was starting.

I crouched beside her, my body straining with the effort, ignoring her attempts to bat me away.

"*No!* Run! Leave me! I won't let you –!" She twisted into the fetal position, gagging her lungs up. I slipped a hand under her head, trying to calm my own shaking enough to help with hers.

"Please …" she choked.

"It's okay," I said, spluttering up the words. "Just – just try to –"

Her eyes glazed over. "I'm sorry …" she murmured. "I'm so, so sorry …"

Her head slipped through my hands – straight *through* them – and thumped into the concrete.

"No! No, get back! Get back here!" I threw my hands out, but couldn't make contact. Couldn't do anything but watch as she squirmed in agony on the floor.

I kept trying. Trying and failing, again and again until, at last, the seizure passed and she sat up, eyes fluttering open.

"Jordan …?" I croaked.

No response. Jordan stared vacantly across the room, and then slowly got up. I followed, reaching out, only to watch her slip through my fingers again.

And then, as if that wasn't already a perfect enough metaphor for the last twenty years, Jordan started to disappear, fading away in front of my eyes, like all this time she'd been just a hologram and now someone was turning down the power.

She turned on the spot, looking for me. *Looking for Luke.*

"Jordan!" I yelled. "JORDAN!"

Her head jerked around, but not to me. She was staring into the wall. Her eyes dropped downwards, but I couldn't tell what she was looking at.

I grabbed at her shoulders, trying to jerk her around again. "Jordan, *come on!*"

Nothing. Fistfuls of air. I shifted around to face her, getting between her and the wall. She stared blankly through me. What if I couldn't do it? What if I couldn't even bring her back?

"Please!" I cried, breaking down again. "Please –
please – you have to –" I jumped as she reeled back,
finally seeing me. *"Jordan!"*

She reached out, tripped, reached again. Still
nothing.

And then a noise behind me. Heavy breathing,
shuffling hands and knees, and the *chink, chink, chink*
of a knife blade bumping against the concrete.

He was here.

Jordan was still fading, almost invisible now. Her
eyes pierced into me, mouth wide, screaming and
screaming with no sound coming out.

Chink. Chink. Chink.

Peter crept closer. Taking his time, knowing he had
me cornered. Savoring it.

I made another pointless grab at Jordan, barely
breathing now. If he killed me here, before she could
get me into the past, then all of it would be for nothing.

"Jordan!" I gasped, still reaching and reaching.
"Jordan, come on, you need to get me out of here!
I have to go –" My hands crashed into her. "– BACK!"

She was real again. Blurry, semi-transparent, but real.

And I knew it wasn't me. I knew it was Luke that
was bringing her back, that the only reason she could
reach me again was that she thought I was him. And I

was okay with that. Face to face with Jordan's furious love for Luke, the love that had driven me to madness …

And I was okay.

Chink. Chink. Chink.

I glanced behind me again, and then wished I hadn't. Minutes, now. Minutes left to live.

"Please –" I begged, sick with tears. "Please – you have to let me –"

I almost lost her as she lurched backwards, convulsing again. Her body was getting clearer now, more solid, just enough for me to see her eyes lose focus as she started retching.

Chink. Chink. Chink.

"Hurry!" I begged, catching a flash of Peter's knife blade in the flashlight beam. "Please! Whatever you – You have to let me in!"

Instantly, like she was responding to my orders, Jordan started flickering in front of me. Not fading away this time; it was almost the opposite. Like she was filling up with light.

We clung to each other, her terrified eyes boring into me. She grew brighter, brighter, unable to keep it in anymore, her whole body drifting apart, melting into the air.

Chink. Chink. Chink.

I spun around, letting her go.

He was right there. Right behind me.

I turned back, taking Jordan's face in both hands, kissing her again. "I love you," I told her, and it was the truest thing I'd ever said.

There was a *thump* behind me, two sneakers hitting the floor.

Peter Weir. Red-faced and shuddering, dripping sweat. He raised his knife, screaming his throat raw, all of his vitriol and spite finally pointing in the right direction.

You're dead, murderer.

And I was. But not for nothing.

Peter hunched forward, preparing to charge.

I looked him square in the eye. Turned my back on him. And ran.

Into the blinding, blazing light.

Chapter 13

LUKE

We wasted maybe a bit too much time reuniting against the wall of Bill's excavation room.

Everything else pulled back into the shadows, like the whole world had slowed to wait for us. Nothing to do but soak up the impossible wonder of being alive. Eventually, though, the tiny form of Tobias pressed between our bodies was enough to remind us that the day wasn't over yet, and we crept back up the deserted passageway, Jordan's hand locked tight in mine.

I tried to think, tried to focus on everything we had to do, but my mind refused to cooperate. I felt my feet pushing against the stairs and my fingers dragging along the moldy concrete and my skin prickling at the cold and the memory of Jordan on my lips, all of it so vibrant and real and alive, and in that moment, all of the horror up ahead of us felt frail and small next to the awesome privilege of being able to feel anything at all.

"So did he change it or not?" said Jordan, releasing my hand to steady herself against the wall. I watched her move up the stairs ahead of me, just a shadow in the darkness but enough to make my heart feel like it was bursting out of my chest. "I mean, it was still all just a loop, right? Everything happened exactly how we saw it in the video."

"Jordan …"

"But that doesn't – We still chose it all, too. It didn't happen because it *had* to. It happened because – Like, Peter still *chose* to go back there in your place. But then, was it ever even you he was saving, or was he always –?"

"Jordan," I said again.

She broke off, losing track of where she was going. "What?"

"I'm *alive*."

"No, I know, I'm just –"

She smirked, shaking her head. "Right."

I smiled back at her. An actual smile, for the first time in forever. "I mean, please, go ahead, give yourself that headache if you want, but …"

"Yeah," she said, reaching out to squeeze my hand.

"Maybe later."

I felt light. Dizzy.

Peter was gone. Both of them, burned up into the past. One trying to kill me, one trying to save my life, both of them somehow the same person. It was totally confusing and impossible and tragic, but the thing was ...

I was alive.

Alive.

Through the night I'd been running from for so long and out the other side.

The world was still ending and Mum had been kidnapped and my dad was missing on the outside and I was meant to be dead *again* by five o'clock tonight, and yeah, normally I was the king of thinking everything was hopeless. But turns out it's pretty hard to feel hopeless when your life's just been handed back to you.

What was the point of a second chance if I wasn't going to pick it up and run with it?

At the top of the stairs, I killed the flashlight on my rifle and opened the trapdoor. Cool air and the smell of smoke wafted in as I stepped out into the bush.

Jordan slipped an arm around me, holding tight to my hip. I looked down at Tobias, huddled against her chest. He was sleeping again.

The shield grid hummed above our heads, nearly invisible but still oppressive. Smoke hung in the sky but, here and there, the stars were coming out again. It looked like security were starting to get the fire under control, which was bad news for our guys in town.

I stared around at the darkness, pulsing with a kind of wild energy, a need to run out there and *do things*. "Bill said the others have all been taken to the Shackleton Building. To the bomb shelter place underneath."

"We need to get them out," said Jordan. "The longer they're down there –"

"Yeah, but – *How?* He said Calvin's got the whole place under manual lockdown, which means we can't use the key card he gave me. Plus, what about Tobias? We can't drag him into a firefight."

"So, what, we just take him out to the release station and forget about everyone else?"

"No, that's not –" I closed my eyes, head spinning with the weight of it all. "But what else *can* we do? We can't split up. What if you have another vision? – and if we get caught, then –"

"We don't even know where the release station *is*," said Jordan, voice straining. "I mean, it's out there somewhere, but –" Her head snapped up and she broke away from me. "Reeve!"

A white glow shone out from her hand. Ketterley's phone. Reeve had a matching one, taken from another of Shackleton's newly deceased top guys. I shuddered at the memory of pulling the phones from the dead men's pockets.

Jordan hit the call button. She waited, phone in one hand, baby Tobias in the other. A muffled voice buzzed out of the speaker at her ear.

"Reeve!" she said, and I felt a rush of relief. He was alive. "Where are you? Are you okay?"

The voice buzzed again.

"Yeah," said Jordan. "I'm still – Yeah. We're at the complex. Luke's here. But listen –"

She broke off as Reeve spoke over the top of her.

"Yeah, we did. We found him. It's the baby."

Incredulous buzzing from Reeve's end.

"Yeah, I know. But it's – Yeah, we're sure. Long story, but – Reeve, listen, Calvin's been here. He took everyone."

Jordan blinked hard, getting hold of herself as Reeve responded.

"The bunker under the Shackleton Building," she told him. "They're – No, we've got Tobias with us. He's – No, I know. I know, but –"

She sighed, struggling to stay calm. Reeve kept talking. Jordan opened her mouth a couple of times, almost cutting him off. I put a hand on her shoulder –

And then sprung away, whirling around at a crash of bushes behind us.

Jordan crammed the phone into her pocket.

I fumbled with my rifle, flicking the flashlight on and jabbing it out in the direction of the noise.

There was a scream from the bushes and two figures tumbled out, hands above their heads. Amy, our friend with the triple-speed body, and Lauren, the freckle-faced Year 7 we'd rescued earlier tonight.

"Don't shoot!" Amy cried.

I lowered the rifle, heart smashing against my ribs.

Lauren fell back against a tree, shuddering, obviously still traumatized from the gunfight back in town.

"Hey – it's okay," said Jordan, hand outstretched.

"Okay?" Lauren leapt up. "*Okay?* I almost died tonight! It's a *war* out there, and you can't even tell whose side anyone's on! The town is on fire, my family are trapped, my boyfriend is *gone*, and also I'm pretty sure the *world* is ending! *What part of that is okay?*" She slumped back into the tree again, drained by her outburst.

"Yeah, all right. Point taken." I scanned the shadows again nervously as she slumped back into the tree, checking that no one had heard us. "We did kind of save your life, though."

Lauren sighed. "Right. Thanks for that." She smiled sheepishly at Jordan. "Sorry. Kind of a rough night."

"We should get moving," I said, all too aware of the noise we were making.

"Where to?" Jordan asked.

"I don't know. Away." I stepped over a ruined wall of the old Vattel Complex building and we started out into the bush, walking parallel to the town.

"Wait. Where's everyone else?" said Amy.

"Gone," said Jordan darkly. "Taken into town." Then, before Amy had time for any follow-up questions, "Where are have you guys been? It's been hours."

"We ran into more security on the way here," said Lauren. "Had to hide out at my old house for a bit. And then when we went to leave, Amy —" She cut herself short, looking to Amy for permission.

Amy stopped walking.

She slowly turned to face us.

Slowly.

I hadn't noticed it at first — probably because Amy's *slowly* was everyone else's normal — but as she opened her mouth to speak, the realization slammed into me like a truck.

"Your speed," I said. "Your fallout thing. It's ..."

Amy closed her eyes. "I don't know what happened. I was running upstairs to check the street before we left, and then all of a sudden it was like —" Her brow crinkled as she searched for the words. "Like I was treading through water instead of air. Like everything inside me was groaning to a stop. I don't know how, but ..." She spread out her arms. "I think – I think this is me now. I think I'm cured." She didn't sound happy about it.

"When?" Jordan asked, suddenly urgent. "When did this happen?"

Amy took a step back. "I don't know! Sometime –"

"An hour ago," said Lauren quickly. "Like, twenty past two or something. I remember checking the clock on our way out."

"Why?" said Amy. "What's going on? Do you know what happened to me?"

Silence. All except for the hum of the shield grid and the distant sounds of the battle. Everyone stared at Jordan, who shot me a wary look.

I felt my stomach turn over.

Jordan took a breath. "What if it was us?" she said finally. "I mean, we know I started the fallout in the first place, so what if –?"

"Hang on," Amy interrupted. "What?"

"Long story," I said. "Not her fault."

"The fallout was released when the portal collapsed," Jordan pushed on. "Right? The one that sent you and Peter – *Bill* and Peter – back in time. Twenty years ago, when it brought down the complex – That's when it all started. So what if – If the fallout *started* at that end of the portal, what if it *finished* at our end? An hour ago, when that same portal collapsed in the present … What if that was the end of it? What if the fallout started and finished with us?"

Lauren squinted like Jordan was speaking another language.

"So … wait," I said slowly, and it was like a massive weight was creaking up off my shoulders. "If that's true, then it's not just Amy who's been –" I hesitated. "It's not just her who's been 'cured,' is it? It's everyone. It's *you*."

Which would mean no more visions. No more portals. No more spending every waking moment wondering if today would be the day she finally faded out completely.

But then, if the fallout really was gone …

"What about Tobias?" said Jordan, speaking the thought out loud just as it dropped into my head. "If we've all lost our powers, then …"

I felt the weight come slamming back down. If there was no more fallout, then what did that mean for our one hope of saving the world?

Jordan held the baby closer against her.

"We need to get to Shackleton," I said, that dizzy, *how-am-I-even-still-alive?* energy crashing through the fear again before I had time to think the better of it. "Get him to actually talk this time. If Tobias can't stop Tabitha anymore, then we need to find a way to make Shackleton do it."

Jordan's eyes widened, not at the idea but at *me* suggesting it.

"What's going on in town?" I pressed. "What did Reeve say?"

"He told us to stay away," said Jordan, in a tone that said this advice would have zero influence on her decision. "Leave the town to them and focus on getting Tobias to the release station."

"What about our families? Did he –?"

"No, that was the first he'd heard about it." She gazed out towards town again, torn.

Tobias stirred. I watched, imagining him sitting up in Jordan's arms and laying out his plan to save everyone. But he just yawned, his little face screwing up, and settled back down to sleep again.

Jordan turned. She stared into me, gathering herself, like she was still talking herself into whatever she was about to say next. "We should split up," she said quietly. "Now that we can. Now that the fallout's gone and we don't have to worry about me fading out again. One of us should go out to the release station, and one back into town."

"We don't *know* the fallout's gone," I said.

"No, I know, but it makes sense, doesn't it? How else do you explain –?" Jordan faltered, looking sideways at Amy. "Anyway, we've got, what, fourteen hours left?

We're not going to win this thing by playing it safe."

"Sure, but –"

Jordan plowed on. "Think about it: we finally make it out of the complex – which is kind of a miracle all by itself – and we're stuck because we can't split up, and then out of nowhere, here comes Amy, all ready to tell us that whatever the fallout did to her has suddenly come undone. What if that's not a coincidence? What if the reason we ran into these guys is so that we *could* split up without freaking out about me randomly slipping off into another time or –?"

"Whoa," said Amy, holding out a hand to silence her. "Whoa. Do you guys …?"

Lauren shot her a puzzled look, covered almost immediately by a wide, disbelieving grin.

I heard it too. The growl of an engine from somewhere in the distance. Somewhere above us. I looked up, through the haze of smoke and the reverberating cords of the shield grid, and saw a pair of blinking lights drifting across the sky.

"No way," Lauren whispered, and I felt a cold shiver cut my spine down the middle.

It was a plane.

Chapter 14

JORDAN

"They're coming!" said Lauren breathlessly. "They're finally coming."

"Who do you think it is?" Amy asked.

"Who *cares* who it is?"

I tuned them out, hugging Tobias against me, feeling a rush of false hope before the truth came in and tore it all down again.

What were they *doing*?

Luke's eyes were fixed to the sky, his face etched with an expression that said he was thinking exactly the same thing I was. If this was help arriving, if Luke's dad and Kara had actually gotten out alive and convinced the military or whoever to come and rescue us, then why in the world were they trying to get back in here by air? Even before the shield grid went up, there was still –

The plane swooped lower and my stomach went with it. Luke swore.

It was small. Definitely military. Or, at least, definitely not commercial. It roared above our heads, straight over the town center, then sailed around in a wide arc, coming back for another pass.

"Get out!" Luke hissed at the plane. "Get *out*, you idiot. You're going to get –"

"What's it doing?" asked Lauren, somehow oblivious to our panic. "Like, surveillance or –?"

Bright light flashed from somewhere out in the bush, silencing them both, and a low rumble streaked across the sky, almost inaudible over the noise of the jet. Phoenix's automated defenses, kicking into action as soon as the jet was in range.

The jet banked left. The missile swerved with it.

I had just enough time to wonder what kind of insane defensive system involved blowing a target to pieces right over the place you were trying to defend, before the missile hit home and the jet exploded in a brilliant ball of flame.

Exploded, but kept on streaking across the sky.

The missile had struck just as the jet cleared the

town center, but something – the momentum of the jet or the force of the explosion, maybe – kept the wreck hurtling forward, tearing itself to pieces out over the bushland. Right over our heads.

Lauren screamed, darting into the shadows as the jet soared overhead, spilling its guts out behind it. Amy followed, whimpering, sprinting away at what was now her top speed.

Bits of flaming aircraft plummeted towards us.

"RUN!" I yelled, yanking Luke into action. A strangled moan broke out from his mouth. I weaved through the trees, pulling him along behind me until I was sure he'd keep moving on his own, knowing what was holding him back, knowing the question that was flooding his mind.

Had his dad had been on that plane?

I released Luke's hand, holding Tobias in both arms now, racing for the edge of the storm of debris, seeing already that I wouldn't get clear before it hit.

The bushland blazed and twitched as the fire rained down to meet it. Shadows on shadows. I was running blind. My foot collided with the flickering ground and I went sprawling, automatically throwing down my shoulder to shield Tobias from the impact. I landed roughly on my back and leapt up again, ignoring the pain, frantically checking Tobias over. He was okay.

Too okay. The fall had jolted him awake, but it hadn't hurt him, hadn't even *bothered* him. He stared up at me, wide eyes dancing with reflected light.

The light of a giant chunk of flaming fuselage plummeting to the ground, right on top of us. It screamed in like a bird of prey, burning up the night, no hope of escape or even rolling aside before –

CRACK-CRACK-CRACK-CRACK-CRACK!

The sky exploded with a new kind of brightness – harsh, sparking, electrical – as the debris from the jet crashed down into the shield grid. The noise was unbelievable. And it was everywhere. All across the sky, the shield grid sprung into action. Snapping tendrils of electricity shot between the crisscrossed cords of the grid, catching the wreckage, blasting it into oblivion. One moment, flaming debris was tumbling through the air, the next it was melting away like ice on a hot plate.

A little chunk of jet, about the size of my fist, slipped through the fingers of the grid and dropped to the ground at my feet, charred and melted beyond recognition.

And then, a few hundred meters away, with a final, deafening cacophony of sparks, the fiery shell of the jet's cockpit slammed into the grid.

I shuddered for whoever had been on board. Even if they'd somehow survived the missile, there would be no surviving the grid.

Not Luke's dad, I told myself. They wouldn't have put a civilian on a flight like that. Surely.

In seconds, it was over. With the jet destroyed, the grid went dark again, returning to its usual ominous hum, and the world below lapsed into an eerie quiet.

It wouldn't last. Whatever might be going on in town, Shackleton couldn't ignore this. Security would be here in minutes, whoever he could spare.

I looked out through the trees, breathing hard, still half-blind from the light of the grid.

Luke was gone. They all were.

Tobias made a little sighing noise, nose wrinkling. Still not crying, despite the chaos around him. I bounced him gently, unsure whether to feel relieved or worried.

I pulled Ketterley's phone out of my pocket and found Galton's number. *Luke's* number.

He answered almost immediately. "Where are you? Are you okay? I'm so sorry! I didn't even realize you were—"

"I'm fine," I said, smiling. "Tobias too. Are you with the others?"

"Just Lauren," said Luke. I could hear her in the background. She sounded kind of hysterical. Luke hissed at her to shut up.

"Do you want me to come and find you?" I asked.

"No," he said. "I mean, yeah, I do, but if we're just going to split up again …"

Luke's voice was strained, his mind obviously on that plane. On his dad. But there was something else as well. A kind of fierceness, like he was ready to go charging into a burning building or something.

"So that's definitely the plan?" I said.

"Isn't it? You're the one who –" He stopped himself. "Look, I don't like it, but it makes sense. You take the skid from the armory. Get Tobias out to the release station and – and figure out what he's supposed to do. I'll go find Reeve. Work out the rest from there."

I looked back towards town, aching to go after my family, sick at the thought of separating from Luke again after I'd just gotten him back, but there was no way I'd let anyone else take Tobias out to the release station. It had to be me. But then, what if Tobias couldn't even help us anymore? What if we were both better off using the time we had left to find Shackleton and rescue our families?

Do you actually believe that, or are you just looking for excuses?

Hadn't I just been saying we were *meant* to split up?

Peter would've said it was crazy. The old Peter, back when he could still tell the difference. He would've said it was insane to go driving off into the bush, pinning our hopes on a baby, when our families were in danger back in town.

But Peter was gone now. And as it turned out, he was the one who'd died to tell us about Tobias in the first place.

"Yeah," I said heavily. "Yeah, okay, let's do it."

"Right," he said. Then, with a very un-Luke-like confidence: "We'll get them back, Jordan. I know Reeve said it's a mess in there, but we've got to have at least some of the security guys on our side now, right? We'll find Shackleton and get our families out of there. Just – Listen, no dying, okay?"

"Yeah," I said. "You too."

I started walking, but kept the phone to my ear, not wanting the conversation to be over.

Luke didn't hang up either. "Weird that this is the first time I've ever talked to you on the phone," he said, breaking the silence.

"Yeah," I said. "You hang up first."

And for the first time in days, he actually laughed. "Love you, Jordan. Be safe."

"You too."

I stuck the phone in my pocket, glancing up at the smoke drifting out from the town to get my bearings. If Phoenix was over there, then the complex was back that way, which meant –

"Jordan!" puffed a voice up ahead of me, and Amy came staggering out from between the trees. She held her side, fighting for breath. "Oh my goodness. That was – I was so *slow!*" She stared down at herself like she'd just been transplanted into some stranger's body. "Where are the others?"

"Heading back into town. You can probably catch them if you –"

"No," said Amy, cutting me off again. "I'll come with you. If that's okay, I mean. You shouldn't go out there on your own."

"You don't –" I began, then realized how much I really *didn't* want to go out there alone. "Thanks."

I took off in the direction of the firefighting skid we'd stolen from the armory last week, re-energized by having a concrete goal to run toward. Tobias lay quiet and still against me, miraculously and terrifyingly unfazed by having been taken from his mother, dragged out into the bush, and almost flattened by a crashing plane.

"I think you're right," said Amy, crunching through the grass behind me, every step concentrated and deliberate. "What you said before about us being meant to find each other."

"Yeah?" I frowned, still working out how much I believed it myself.

"Down in the complex," said Amy, "back when – When everything was slower – When I was faster,

I mean – I had a lot of extra time on my hands. Like, literally, I had three times as much as the rest of you. All that time to slow down and pay attention. To listen."

"Yeah, I remember you saying." I reached up, shoving a branch out of my path. "Hear anything good?"

Amy was quiet for a minute. I reminded myself that even thinking took more time than she was used to.

"This thing is bigger than us," she said at last. "I don't think –" She paused again, finding the words. "Whatever that *bigger* part is, I don't think it's neutral on how this all plays out. I mean, I'm not saying you should read into every little coincidence, but – I don't know. When stuff feels like it's more than just random, I think maybe that's worth paying attention to."

I opened my mouth to respond, but Tobias beat me to it. He finally let out a heartbreaking cry, his whole body tensing with the effort. The sound carried through the night, so much noise from such a tiny body.

"Shh …" I said, bouncing him as I walked, projecting a calm that was the complete opposite of what I actually felt. "Shh-shh-shh … What's wrong? Do you –?"

Bright light smashed me in the face.

Tobias stopped crying, snapping out of it like nothing had ever been wrong. I stepped back, almost tripping. Headlights. We'd reached the skid, but someone else had reached it first.

"Jordan," said the figure hunched behind the wheel, and I felt the life drain out of me.

It was Calvin. He jabbed a thumb at the cage behind him. "I need you and the baby to get into the –"

"Run!" I shouted, whirling around.

"No!" Calvin leapt down from the driver's seat, ready to give chase. "Stop! Please."

My feet slid to a standstill. *Please?*

Officer Calvin stepped out into the glow of the headlights. He moved slowly, like he was trying not to startle us, arms spread wide in a gesture of non-violence that didn't square too well with the pistol holstered at his hip. Or the fact that he was just about the most bloodthirsty psycho in this whole town.

"Please," he said again. "Don't leave. I realize this will be hard to swallow, but – I'm here to help you."

Chapter 15

LUKE

THURSDAY, AUGUST 13, 3:47 A.M.
13 HOURS, 13 MINUTES

"So, you still haven't told me your plan," said Lauren, jogging along beside me. "How are we going to stop Shackleton? How are we even going to get *in* there? I mean, do you even know how to shoot that gun?" She paused, eyes narrowing. "You do *have* a plan, right?"

I took a deep breath, glad she couldn't see me gritting my teeth in the darkness. "We need to find Reeve."

"Yeah, but how?"

"I don't know," I admitted.

"I mean, if he's not answering his phone –"

"Yeah," I said tightly. "I get it."

She shrank back.

I'd tried to call Reeve a few minutes ago, but he hadn't picked up. Maybe because he was too busy getting shot at, or maybe just because he believed the caller ID when it told him I was Dr. Galton. Texting was a dead end too. If these phones had ever been able to do it, Shackleton had locked the function out.

"Sorry," said Lauren. "It's just – Dad's stuck on security duty and Mum was down in the main prison place. I haven't seen them in weeks. I don't even know if they're …" She couldn't bring herself to finish the sentence.

I pushed through a tangle of undergrowth and something clicked inside my head. "We saw him," I said. "Your dad. Ethan, right? Ethan Hamilton? We saw him a few hours ago, up in the Shackleton Building."

Lauren lit up. "Was he …?"

"Yeah, he was okay," I said. "Still on duty for Shackleton, but he switched sides when the coup started."

Like most of Shackleton's guys, Hamilton was more scared than devoted – strong-armed into submission by the "loyalty room," the cafeteria-turned-high-security-prison where Shackleton held a bunch of their relatives to make sure everyone kept following orders.

The last we'd seen, Hamilton had gone off with Reeve and Tank to help liberate the loyalty room and undermine the Co-operative's hold on its men.

"I knew it!" said Lauren. "I knew he'd stand up to Shackleton. He was just waiting for the right –" She stifled a shriek as I dragged her behind a tree. "What? What's happening?"

I put a finger to my lips and pointed through a gap in the trees.

Movement in the bush up ahead. Not security. Too loud and disorganized. Labored breathing and crunching undergrowth. The sounds of people not used to treading softly through the bush.

I thought about just letting them pass us by. If these were townspeople who'd escaped the fighting, then good for them. They were a lot safer out here than where we were going.

But something about the figure up at the front of the pack made me reconsider. I released my grip on Lauren and got slowly to my feet, flashing on my light. "Hey. Who's there?"

The huddle froze, and I felt a jolt of recognition. It was Peter's parents, both dressed in nurses' uniforms. And five others, all wearing thin hospital gowns.

Mr. Weir was holding a heavy bit of tree branch, wielding it like a club. He turned on me.

"Whoa. Hey!" I said, shifting the light so it shone up into my face. "It's me!"

Mr. Weir let out a heavy sigh, lowering the branch.

"Luke. Good to see you, mate."

I stepped out to meet them, stomach already tensing at the conversation I knew was coming, then felt myself get shoved aside as Lauren exploded past me. She launched herself at Jeremy, a pasty kid at the back of the group, throwing her arms around his neck, kissing him roughly (and noisily) on the mouth.

She kept it up for a good few seconds before a girl with a guard's belt over her shoulder – Alyssa, I think – came up and tapped her on the back. "Uh … guys? I know it's the end of the world, but seriously, get a room."

Lauren broke it off and dragged Alyssa into a hug, leaving Jeremy staring self-consciously at the ground.

"What's happening?" Mr. Weir asked me. "We were coming back to find you all."

"Where's Peter?" asked Mrs. Weir. "Is he okay? Is he still …?"

She trailed off, afraid of the answer. The last time either of them had seen Peter was weeks ago, back before Kara had shown us the murder video, back when Peter was still fairly newly crazy.

I swallowed, trying to work out where to start. But before I had time to even string a sentence together, Lauren and Alyssa broke into our conversation again.

"Luke! Come here!" Lauren held out her arms and I shined the flashlight at her. She looked herself over, like she was checking for injuries or something, then turned to Jeremy, a huge grin on her face. "See? Nothing!"

Jeremy stared at his hands, and I realized what Lauren was talking about. Jeremy's skin thing. His not-so-fun habit of imprinting himself onto anyone he touched. Lauren had had her hands all over him and nothing had happened.

"You're cured!" she beamed.

"You still got me," frowned Alyssa, holding her blotchy arms up to the light.

But Jeremy was still fixated on his hands. *"How?"*

Someone moved behind them and I shifted my flashlight around. Mrs. Lewis, the old school librarian, had reached up to the face of a skinny bald guy. Her brow crinkled. "I think mine's gone too."

There were murmurs from the others. More support for Jordan's fallout theory.

Mrs. Weir put a hand on my shoulder. I stiffened, feeling the tension in it.

I turned to face her again. Searching for the right words. Knowing those words didn't exist. And despite everything, I felt tears spiking at the back of my eyes.

Mrs. Weir let out a sob, seeing the answer before I opened my mouth. Mr. Weir pulled her into his arms.

"He got better," I said finally. "Before he – Before the end. He didn't die sick. He got his mind back. It took a while, but …"

Everyone was quiet now. Listening in. Mr. and Mrs. Weir tightened their hold on each other, but their eyes stayed unwaveringly fixed on me.

"We – we know how to stop Tabitha," I said, and realized that I actually still believed it. "We have a plan. As close as we're going to get, anyway. And that's because of Peter. He died to make sure we got that information. If we win this – if we stop them – it's because of him."

It was true. Not the whole truth, not even close, but true as far as it went. Peter's parents deserved the whole story, and they'd get it. But not now. The rest could wait.

Mrs. Weir stepped out and hugged me. I could feel her shaking. "I'm really sorry," I said. Which was the dumbest thing in the world to say, but also kind of the only thing.

"Thanks, mate." Mr. Weir patted me on the back. "Thanks for looking out for him. I'm sure you did all you could."

Someone grunted next to us, and Mrs. Weir released me. One of the other guys from the medical center was holding a blood-stained shirt up to his arm. He looked awkwardly at the three of us. "Sorry, guys, but can we …?"

"Yeah, sorry, mate." Mr. Weir's face shifted as he forced himself back into action. He bent down, grabbing his branch and pointing it back in the direction of the

Vattel Complex. "This way."

"Wait," I said. "Security know about the complex now. They came for us a couple of hours ago. Took everyone back into town."

"But you guys are meant to be the ones stopping all this!" said Alyssa, like they'd gotten themselves abducted on purpose. "You said you had a plan!"

"Jordan got out too," I said, ignoring her. "She and her baby brother. Tobias. She's taking him out to the release station, this place outside the boundary wall. He's meant to be special. Like, special enough to stop Tabitha. At least, that's – that's the information Peter got for us."

Mrs. Weir pursed her lips, swelling with a kind of miserable pride, imagining Peter as the tragic hero.

"A baby?" said Skinny Bald Guy, looking around like he'd missed the first half of a joke. "*That's* the grand plan?"

"Yeah," I said. "I know it sounds crazy –"

"It *is* crazy."

The others stared at each other, letting it all sink in. Alyssa sighed. "We are so screwed."

"Not yet, we're not," said Mr. Weir, with a very forced-sounding optimism. He set off again, back towards the complex. Then, sensing my unease: "We won't stay long. But Daniel needs patching up, and we need to pick up some tools."

"Tools?" I asked, raising an eyebrow.

Mr. Weir glanced at Mrs. Weir, who handed him something I hadn't even realized she was holding. A dark, amorphous shape, about the size of my shoe.

"Look," he said, "I didn't want to get anyone's hopes up. It's probably not even fixable, but ..."

He stopped walking. "We were right under that jet when it came down. Right under the cockpit. The smaller bits of wreckage all got vaporized by the grid, but the big stuff ..." He shrugged. "A chunk of it dropped down right over Jess and me. Looked like half a storage compartment or something. This was inside. Like I said, probably a lost cause. But I guess those are about the only causes we've got left now, huh?"

I shined my flashlight at the thing in his hands. Charred black, antenna gone, screen shattered, buttons half-melted off. But immediately, I realized what it was. And immediately, Mr. Weir's warning about not getting my hopes up shot straight out the window.

It was the jet's transceiver.

"What do you reckon?" said Mr. Weir, in a voice that said I wasn't the only one ignoring his advice. "Anyone feel like giving the outside world a call?"

Chapter 16

JORDAN

"You're lying," I said, barely keeping my hands steady on Tobias.

"Jordan, please –"

"What are you even saying? That the last hundred days have been just a big misunderstanding?"

My body begged me to run. But some other instinct kicked in, some subconscious *need* to confront him, and I stayed fixed to the spot.

"I know," said Calvin, switching the skid's headlights back off. "I know. It's absurd. And after all I've done, you have every right to just walk away from this. But for the sake of your family –"

"For the sake of my *family?* My family, who you just sent away to be tortured?"

"I sent them away for their protection!" said Calvin, a familiar growl slipping into his voice. "Those officers will follow my orders. They will safeguard your mother and sister until we return." He pressed a red-gloved hand to his injured head. "Or would you prefer them to have been executed, down there in your hide-out?"

"You led those guards down there in the first place!" I said. "If you didn't want to hurt us –"

"What alternative was there?" said Calvin. "Once your friend gave away your location, do you really think there was any stopping Shackleton dispatching a security team? All I had left was to lead them in myself and attempt to contain the damage."

"Yeah, well, brilliant job there," I spat.

Calvin bristled. He gestured at Tobias. "You still have your brother. I believe you know how significant that is."

I pulled Tobias closer against me. "Do you think I'm *stupid?* The only reason I've still got my brother is that Bill took him from you!"

Lies. All of it. The Co-operative knew what a big deal Tobias was. Shackleton had figured it out before we had. That's why he'd burst out laughing last night, back when we were still scrambling to figure out what Tobias even was.

Somehow, in the time since we'd rescued Mum

and Georgia from the medical center, Shackleton and Galton must have discovered something in Tobias that they believed posed a threat to their work.

But if that was true, then why were we even having this conversation? You could always count on Shackleton for a self-indulgent pre-murder chat, but Calvin was much more straightforward. He just pulled the trigger and moved on. So why –?

Like he'd read my mind, Calvin's hand suddenly blurred to his waist, snatching his pistol from its holster. Amy screamed. I twisted around to shield Tobias, eyes shut, legs shaking.

But instead of a gunshot, I heard a muffled *thump* and turned back to see the dark shape of the weapon lying on the ground at my feet.

Amy dropped to the grass and snatched it up. She stood, pointing the pistol shakily at Calvin.

Calvin nodded. "God knows I'd deserve it. But you'd be destroying your best chance at saving the people you care about." He spread his arms wide again. "And trust me when I say you don't want a murder on your conscience. Not even mine."

"Right," I said, "please, tell us all about having a conscience."

But after a moment's hesitation, Amy slowly lowered the weapon.

The shield grid sparked above our heads. Tobias screwed up his face, squinting away from the flash of light. I shifted him around so he was facing my shoulder.

Calvin glanced almost wistfully at the baby. My skin crawled and I clutched Tobias closer to me. Calvin reached to his waist again, unbuckling his utility belt, throwing that to the ground as well. Disarming himself completely.

"Tell me," he said softly, "that day at the airport, weeks ago, when I apprehended you and Luke in an attempt to discover where you were hiding your friend Peter … How did you manage to escape?"

The memory leapt to the front of my mind. Calvin had caught us outside the medical center, where Peter had just been kidnapped by Tank, Cathryn and Mike. Calvin thought we'd done it, so he'd dragged us out of town to the airport, where he'd be free to interrogate and murder us without interference. But just as Calvin had been about to pull the trigger on Luke, I'd dived at him. Somewhere in the scuffle, my thumb had ended up slipping into Calvin's mouth, and then …

Calvin smiled grimly, spotting the gleam of recognition in my eyes. "That was the first time I felt it. Empathy, as I'm sure you've realized, has never been a strong suit of mine. But in that moment – I felt it all. Everything you felt. Your fear for Luke, for Peter, for your own life. Your worry for your family. Your darkest nightmares about the end of humanity. Your rage at the Co-operative. Your rage at *me*. I felt all of your pain and frustration and hurt as though the feelings were my own, and it … it was …" His voice cracked with the memory.

Almost as soon as he'd bitten me, Calvin had stopped struggling. He'd scrambled away from me and fled the airport, sobbing like a child.

"At first, I thought it was something *you'd* done," continued Calvin. "But then the symptoms began to recur."

Another memory. Two weeks later. Calvin and his men had stormed my old house back in town to abduct Mum and Georgia. Luke had thrown himself at Calvin, and Calvin had recoiled in spontaneous, irrational fear. *Luke's* fear.

So what? I thought fiercely, pushing against the doubt creeping in around the corners of my mind. *A couple of random freak-outs. What does that prove? They wore off, and he went straight back to being evil.*

"Soon it was everyone I touched." Calvin held up his hands, indicating the gloves. "My condition was so severe that Shackleton pulled me from duty. He felt he couldn't trust me to carry out my orders. He questioned my loyalty to the ideals of the Co-operative." Calvin's arms slumped back to his sides. "He was right to question."

Amy raised the pistol again. "It's a trick," she said skittishly. "Jordan, you know it is."

I wanted to agree with her. I *did* agree with her, mostly. But the harder I tried to just shake Calvin's story off, the more it needled at me. I'd never known Calvin to be an actor or a con man. He wore his depravity on his sleeve. Point and shoot. Simple. Even if this was all some elaborate deception, it was still a side of Calvin I'd never seen before.

But why bother? Unless there was something I was missing. Some reason he needed me alive and on-side.

"Even if it's true," said Amy, and even in the dark, I could see the gun shaking in her hands. "The part about him feeling your emotions or whatever. Even if that's true, the fallout's *gone* now."

Calvin glanced at me for confirmation, clearly thrown by this news. "No," he said, voice not quite steady. "I am not – There's no going back. The fallout may be gone, but my guilt isn't." His eyes pierced through me, shining in the moonlight. "I am not claiming to be a new man. And I am certainly not expecting you to forgive me. But, at least in some small way, I know how you feel. I've *felt* it. I can't just ignore that. Not even if I wanted to."

I knew what Luke would tell me: that this was no time to be putting our trust in a man who'd only ever tried to kill us. That we should hold out for a plan that didn't involve acting like naive hitchhikers in a bad horror movie.

But he'd still come with me.

Tobias stared up at me, like he was waiting for me to make a decision. Again, Georgia's drawing popped into my mind. Calvin and Tobias and that huge, haunting smile.

That's what the baby wanted a picture of.

All right, kid, I thought, crouching to pick up Calvin's belt with my free hand. *I hope you know what you're doing.*

I started towards the skid. Immediately, Amy rushed in to block me. "Jordan, no! You can't be – It's a trick! You can't trust him!"

"I know I can't, but we need to get out there and right now, he's our best shot. Remember how well it turned out the last time I tried driving one of these things?" I said, handing Amy the baby so I could climb into the open-topped storage cage at the back of the skid. I shot a warning look at Calvin, who kept his distance. Then I swung inside the cage and took Tobias back. "I'm not asking you to –"

"I'm coming," she said, gun trained on Calvin again as he returned to the driver's seat. "You think I'm leaving you alone with him?"

On either side of the storage cage were little platforms with non-slip treads where passengers could ride standing up. Amy jumped up onto one of them, holding the cage with one hand and keeping the pistol determinedly fixed on Calvin with the other.

"You can put that down," said Calvin without turning around. "I give you my –"

"Just drive," said Amy.

Calvin started the ignition and the skid rattled to life underneath me. Tobias let out a gleeful little squeak. I stared down at him, trying not to read anything into it, and crouched in the cage, wishing there was some safer way to strap him in.

We rumbled slowly through the bush, headlights off. I looked up, watching the dark cords of the shield grid slip past above our heads, trying to visualize the quickest route to the edge of the bush.

"How are we even supposed to get over the wall without that shield thing burning us to bits?" Amy asked, jolting as the skid rolled through a bush.

"We can't," said Calvin. "Shackleton has already locked down the controls, and any attempt to penetrate the grid by force would be pointless. There may be another way, but it will require a detour to the armory."

"For what?" I asked, my suspicion ratcheting back up again. "If you try to hurt anybody –"

"I hope it won't come to that," he said, in that unnerving new introspective tone of his.

"Then *what?*" said Amy impatiently. "If we can't get over the wall by force –"

"We're not going over the wall," said Calvin, veering through a gap between two enormous trees. "We're going *through* it."

Chapter 17

LUKE

THURSDAY, AUGUST 13, 4:22 A.M.
12 HOURS, 38 MINUTES

"You're *WHAT?*"

"Shh!" said Jeremy. He and Lauren glared at me from their lookout at the bedroom window. I looked back apologetically, then slipped out onto the landing.

"Jordan, this is –"

"I know," her voice crackled in my ear. "I know what it sounds like."

"It sounds like you've got a death wish!"

"I know, but –"

"Is he making you say this?" I asked, fingers tensing on the phone. "Does he have a gun to your head or –?"

"No. Actually, we've got one to his," she said, with enough confidence for me to believe that at least *she* thought she was safe. "Did you get on to Reeve?"

"Jordan –" I began, not ready to change the subject.

"I'm *fine*, Luke. Really. It's under control. Now did you get on to Reeve or not?"

"Not yet," I said, pacing over to a window. "That's kind of why I called. We've made it into town. We're hiding out in a house for a bit, but –" I paused, my attention snatched away by a gunshot from somewhere out on the street. "Listen, it's pretty crazy out there. Wherever Reeve is – I mean, we can't just walk out there and look for him."

I stared out the window. We were right up against the center of town now, but it was still pretty hard to get any real sense of the fight – except that we were losing it.

It didn't seem like there was any kind of organized attack going on at all; just pockets of resistance from the few people who'd made it out onto the streets. Now and then, we'd hear an explosion of gunfire or see someone scuttling through the shadows, but it looked as though the majority were still trapped in the Shackleton Building.

Instead of the glorious overthrow of the Co-operative we'd been dreaming of last night, it seemed like our coup attempt had just littered the streets with a bunch of scared civilians with guns. And now we only had a couple of hours left until the sun came up. If we hadn't found Reeve by then, we could pretty much give up on finding him at all.

"Let me try him," said Jordan.

"Yeah," I said, tracing a finger along the windowsill, thick with dust after all these weeks of abandonment. "That's what I was thinking. Reeve knows you've got Ketterley's phone. He might answer for you."

"Right. Let me know if you get anywhere with – with the thing," she said, avoiding the word *transceiver* in Calvin's hearing.

"I will," I said. "And look, just be careful, okay? You know who you're dealing with. If you can get him to do what you want, then great. But make sure you can get away when you need to. Don't –"

"Don't die," she said. "Got it."

"Don't *trust* him."

"That too. Okay, I'm calling Reeve. Be safe."

She hung up and I headed downstairs.

I passed the front door and felt the insane impulse to just walk straight out.

We were wasting time. Hours left until the end and we were sitting around like we were waiting for someone to come in and tell us what to do. If I was going to find Shackleton and free Mum and the others, it wasn't going to be with this group.

Fifteen minutes, I told myself, glancing up at the

clock on the wall. If Reeve hadn't called back by then, I'd push on without him.

I walked into the family room, feeling like I'd just drunk ten cans of Red Bull, still jittery with the shock of being alive. Mr. Weir was hunched over the coffee table, tinkering with the broken transceiver. The others crowded around. Alyssa had a flashlight pointed down at the table, shielded by her hand to keep the light from reaching the windows.

Mrs. Weir stood at the other end of the room, looking out onto the empty street. Theoretically, she was keeping watch, but one look at her face told me she was somewhere else altogether. I caught Mrs. Lewis's eye, and she went to take over.

"Anything?" I asked, taking her place in the circle.

Mr. Weir held the transceiver right up to the light, pulling a screwdriver from his mouth and levering off a half-melted bit of casing to reveal the circuitry underneath. His eyes grew very slightly wider, and I felt a flicker of hope. But before he had a chance to speak, a buzz in my pocket pulled me away again.

"Luke!" said Reeve as soon as I picked up. He sounded a bit out of breath. "Sorry, mate, didn't realize it was you. Where are you? Jordan said you'd made it into town."

"Yeah, we're behind the security center. Where are you?"

"On the move," he said. "We're back out of the Shackleton Building, but – Hold on a sec." I heard another voice at his end of the line, and then Reeve said, "Yeah, okay, but check around the back first." He turned his attention back to me. "Sorry. Bit of a situation. Can you get down to the south end of town? I'll send someone out to meet you."

"Um … yeah, probably," I said. "We're –"

"No, still coming. Maybe a block behind," said Reeve to whoever was with him. Then to me: "Get down to the bike tracks. We'll – Hang on, mate. I think –"

He broke off, and I heard a frantic shuffle of footsteps. Someone shouted. Then a burst of gunfire echoed through the speaker in my ear and the line went dead.

JORDAN
THURSDAY, AUGUST 13, 4:27 A.M.
12 HOURS, 33 MINUTES

"Okay," I said, hanging up on Reeve, my voice raised over the rush of air as we tore along the road out of Phoenix. "Start talking, Calvin. What happens when we get out there? What does he actually have to do?"

Visions were spiraling through my head of the

moment when Tobias and Tabitha finally collided. Visions of defeat, Tobias hanging limp in my arms, failed by the fallout. Visions of victory with Tobias dead anyway, the price of saving the rest of us.

Stop it, I ordered myself. *You know that's not how this ends. Whatever the plan is, it has to be better than that.*

I stomped it all down and focused on interrogating Calvin, thinking wistfully that I could really have used an *actual* vision right about now.

The trees flew past the skid, a blur of shadows. Tobias took it all in with gleaming eyes, eerily unfazed by the cold or the crackling sky or the jolting of the skid.

He still hadn't cried for a feeding. That wasn't right. Not *normal,* anyway. But then, we were talking about a baby who'd reached full term after only three months in the womb. Abnormal had been written into his life from the very beginning.

And isn't that what you're counting on? Don't you need *him to be abnormal?*

"You going to answer me?" I pressed.

Calvin kept driving, like he hadn't even heard me speak. I grabbed him from behind. "Hey! *Listen –*"

The skid swerved, throwing me sideways against the cage. Tobias murmured but still didn't cry out.

"Enough!" Calvin growled, steering us back on track again. "Unless you believe running us all off the

168

road is a productive use of your –"

"TELL ME WHAT HE HAS TO DO!"

"Pull over," said Amy, black hair fluttering behind her as she clung to the side of the cage. The words didn't have much force behind them, but she made up for it by raising Calvin's pistol again. "We're not going any further until you tell Jordan what she wants to know."

The skid slowed just enough to soften the roar of the wind in my ears.

"It's better if you don't know what's coming," said Calvin, not turning around.

I sneered at the back of his head. "How about you let me decide what's –?"

"Better for humanity," said Calvin, "even if not for you."

"You know what, Calvin?" I said, almost laughing. "I'm not sure you're actually the most qualified person to make that call."

"Perhaps not. But I am the one who knows what is coming, and I cannot risk losing your cooperation at this late stage."

"You don't think you might be risking that *now*?" I said, shoving aside my apprehension at his words.

"No," said Calvin. "I don't. I know you, Jordan."

"You don't –"

"I know enough. I know that with half a day left

until the extermination of humanity, you are not simply going to abandon your one hope of putting things right."

I straightened angrily, the cold wire of the cage digging into my back. I wanted to argue with him, to bite back, put him in his place. To jump out of the moving skid and prove I couldn't be so easily manipulated.

Instead, I just slumped back down to the floor of the cage. He was right. I couldn't leave without knowing. Which meant that as long as Calvin kept me in the dark, he was pretty much guaranteeing my cooperation. Amy glanced back at me, her right hand still stretched out towards Calvin's head.

"Mmm," said Calvin approvingly, taking my silence for agreement. "You are a person of incredible moral integrity, Jordan. It is only recently that I've come to appreciate what a great strength that is."

"Yeah, well, thanks for the compliment, chief," I said, gritting my teeth. "That means a lot, coming from you."

The skid roared up to full speed again. The wind swirled around my head, throwing my ratty dreadlocks up against my face. Tobias gazed up at me with something oddly like a searching look. Like he'd heard what Calvin had said and was trying to work out if he agreed with him. He yawned, closing his eyes, and I shoved the idea aside.

"I won't let you hurt him," I said after a minute.

Calvin kept driving.

"Is that what this is?" I asked. "Is he going to have to, like, go in there and get injected or something? Because I won't … I won't let you …"

I trailed off, the confidence I'd just been preaching to myself getting shaky again. My baby brother, going up against a virus powerful enough to exterminate humanity; surely that wasn't going to happen without a cost.

And still Calvin refused to speak.

"Calvin!" Amy snapped.

"It won't kill him," said Calvin finally. "It shouldn't –" He glanced back, frowning like he'd heard something, then turned his eyes back to the road.

"Jordan, I have no doubt that you will try to do what is right," he went on. "But if there's one thing that might persuade you to compromise that cast-iron conscience of yours, it's your family. Which is exactly why –"

Light exploded behind us.

Calvin barked in shock, and the skid swerved, throwing me to the floor on my back. I rolled over, looking back through the cage, and saw headlights bearing down on us.

BLAM! BLAM!

Calvin jolted in his seat, and the skid unit spun out of control. I wrapped both arms around Tobias, curling into a ball to shield him from the impact. Amy shrieked, lost her grip, and disappeared, thrown to the ground. The skid kept spinning, stars and shield grid blurring together above my head, so eerily like slipping into one of my visions that I almost believed I'd been wrong about the fallout being over. Then, with a nauseating jolt and a spray of gravel and dirt, we dropped into the ditch at the edge of road.

The skid lifted onto two wheels, sending me sliding across the bed of the cage, and then crashed down onto its side, scraping along through the bush, before finally hammering to a stop against an enormous eucalyptus. Somewhere through the dizziness, I took in a glimpse of fading lights and the noise of an engine rumbling off into the distance.

I stumbled out of the cage, beat up and dizzy but otherwise okay. I held Tobias to the moonlight, heart in my throat, checking him for injuries. He was fine. Conscious. Nothing broken.

"Oh my goodness." Amy came limping in through the bush, holding her side, the pistol still clutched in her other hand. "Oh my goodness. What was *that?*"

"A delivery truck," grunted Calvin, peeling himself off the seat of the skid. "Probably headed for the same place we are."

He rose to his feet, apparently uninjured, and scowled at the skid's front tires, torn apart by the gunshots. My heart sank. No way was that getting back on the road again.

"Who were they?" Amy asked. "Were they Shackleton's or –?"

"It doesn't matter who they were," said Calvin. He reached into the back of the upended skid and grabbed his utility belt. "They're gone, and so is any prospect of reaching the armory before sunrise."

I watched him fasten the belt around his waist, suspicion trickling through my mind again. Had this been his plan the whole time? To strand us out here in the middle of nowhere? To lure us off to some secret Co-operative facility where he could torture us in peace?

Get a grip, I told myself. *You're starting to sound like Luke.*

In a place like Phoenix, though, Luke's paranoid hunches had an unfortunate habit of being right.

Calvin pulled a compass from his belt. He threw our ruined skid one last resentful glance, and then jogged away through the trees. "This way."

"Now what?" Amy breathed, coming up behind me.

I wavered for just a moment longer, then sighed, setting out after him. "Now we run."

Chapter 18

LUKE

I snapped the phone shut, resisting the urge to shout in frustration. Still no answer.

"Give it a rest for a bit," said Mr. Weir, crouching next to me. "That battery won't last forever."

I stuck the phone in my pocket. I hadn't heard from Jordan in almost an hour. I'd tried her ten times since, and every time, the phone just rang and rang. I'd even tried calling Calvin's number, but he wasn't picking up either.

I shifted in the undergrowth, working out a cramp in my leg. In the end, only the Weirs and I had come to meet Reeve. Everyone else had lost their nerve when I'd told them the part about my phone call ending in gunfire. Apparently, creeping through a war zone to meet with a guy who might have just been killed was not their idea of a good time. And the longer we waited out here in the cold and the dark, the harder it was to blame them.

The transceiver still wasn't working, but Mr. Weir seemed confident. Seemed *determined* anyway. While Mrs. Weir had shrunk down inside her grief, Mr. Weir seemed to be channeling his outward, like he'd forged some connection in his mind between fixing this thing and honoring the death of his son.

I gazed up through the shield grid at the stars.

What did it mean? A hundred days without even a hint of rescue, and now suddenly we had a jet getting shot down right on top of us.

Surely this had something to do with Dad. He had to have gotten out. He *had* to. And surely, I told myself with as much conviction as I could, *surely* Dad couldn't have been on board that jet. If the military were mounting some kind of rescue mission, they wouldn't send a civilian in on their first —

I shook my head, fighting to get a grip on myself. This was pointless. Assuming Dad *was* still alive, the best I could do to keep him that way was to focus on getting hold of Shackleton.

I gazed out through the trees at the town. Where would he be?

Please not in the bunker.

Please nowhere near Mum and the others.

No, I thought firmly. Surely he had more important things to worry about. He must have realized by now that the fallout was gone. And surely he had to be at least as freaked out by that as we were.

So, what then? The medical center? Would he risk moving out from the Shackleton Building? *Could* he risk it even if he wanted to? If the bunker was still locked down, maybe he was just –

Wait.

My hand shot to my pocket, a dangerous idea flaring to life inside my head.

"Luke," Peter's dad said wearily, as I pulled the phone out again.

"I'm not calling Jordan," I said, scrolling shakily through the list of names, a shiver flashing through me as I found the one I was looking for.

Noah Shackleton.

I hit *call* and brought the phone up to my ear, a weird out-of-body feeling rippling over me.

I flinched as the ringing cut out, replaced by a howling, agonized scream. I heard hurried footsteps, and then a door slammed shut, muffling the poor man's cries.

"Who is this?" hissed Shackleton. There was a fire in his voice that I'd never heard before.

I took a breath. "It's me."

A moment's pause. I shuddered as another muted scream echoed in through the closed door.

"I'll kill you," Shackleton spat. He was breathing hard. "I don't know *how* you've managed this, you miserable ulcer, but whatever else results from your actions, I *promise* to repay you with an excruciating end."

I dropped a hand to the ground, steadying myself. Not that I'd been expecting Shackleton to be thrilled to hear from me, but usually he kept all that buried under layers of calm, grinning menace.

"Come on, then," I said, surprising myself by getting the words out the first time. "Where are you? Tell me where to –"

The guy through the door screamed again, louder still, freezing the words in my throat. The noise intensified, raw and guttural, grinding through my insides. Finally, it choked itself out. Silence fell on the other end of the line.

I heard a door clunk open again. *"Well?"* Shackleton demanded of whoever had just come out.

A woman's voice. Dr. Galton? "He's dead. Negligible resistance to the pathogen."

"Get another one," Shackleton seethed.

"Noah, we've already lost –"

"Get another one! A woman. Get downstairs and ..."

Shackleton kept talking, but I'd zoned out for a second. *Downstairs.* He was back in the Shackleton Building. Probably somewhere up on the top floor.

Mr. and Mrs. Weir were both staring at me now, frozen in place. How much could they hear?

"… you can inform Melinda that if she does not have the bunker back open by the time I return, it will be *her* on the table."

"Of course," said Galton stiffly.

The door banged shut, and I felt a glimmer of relief. Whoever they were mutilating up there, it wasn't any of our guys from the complex. Not yet, at least.

There was a scuffling sound as Shackleton pulled the phone back to his ear. "You will not die with the others," he spat. "I will not afford you the dignity of succumbing to Tabitha. Before this day is over, I give you my word, I will spill the life from you myself."

The line went dead. I pulled the phone away from my ear and stared at the display until the light flashed off, my heart pounding like I'd just run a lap of the town.

Shackleton couldn't possibly *know* that Jordan and I were the ones who'd killed the fallout – we barely even knew it ourselves – but clearly that wouldn't keep him from pinning it on us anyway. And whatever sick experiments he and Galton were doing up there, it didn't seem like they were filling him with confidence.

What did it mean?

What would happen if the clock ran down to zero now? Would *anyone* survive? And what would Shackleton do if he found out the answer was *no*?

"Well?" whispered Mr. Weir. "You gonna tell us what he –?"

I jolted as a boot crunched in the dirt nearby. Mr. Weir's hands rushed to the rifle I'd given him – then froze as the muzzle of another weapon came down between our heads.

"Nope," grumbled the weapon's owner. "Not a smart idea."

Mr. Weir slowly lowered the weapon and lifted his hands to his head.

"Better," said the man, taking a step closer.

I glanced down at a muddy boot and the black leg of a security officer's uniform. The guard flicked on his flashlight, throwing my shadow out in front of me.

"Luke Hunter," he said gruffly, coming around to face us.

I squinted into the light. The guy was tall (or seemed like it from down here, anyway), with massive shoulders, a shining bald head and a scar running down from his eye to his chin.

"Listen," said Mrs. Weir, "we're not –"

But the guard was already lowering his weapon.

"Lazarro," he said, stretching out a hand to pull me up. "Reeve sent me."

Mr. Weir's hands shot towards the rifle.

"No, wait!" I said, the guard's name clanging in my head. Lazarro had been working behind the scenes on Reeve's coup. "He's okay! He's on our side!" I lowered my voice. "You *are* on our side, right?"

"You're still alive, aren't you?" said Lazarro, ignoring Mr. Weir's distrustful glare. "You guys coming or not?" He flicked off his flashlight and trudged away through the bush.

"Is Reeve okay?" I asked, striding to catch up. "What happened?"

"He's fine," said Lazarro. "Just a little run-in with an escaped civilian with a gun. Lucky for us, he didn't have much clue how to fire it." He frowned at the darkness ahead of us. "Now, how about we cut the conversation until we get where we're going?"

Peter's mum and dad fell tentatively into line behind us, and we crept out around the southwest corner of town. Somewhere along the way, it started raining. The shield grid sparked and spat with it, but most of the water still seemed to make it through. Not heavy, but enough to feel it through my clothes.

After jogging down several blocks, Lazarro took us behind a row of blacked-out houses and waded through the knee-high grass of a backyard, up to someone's back door.

He crouched down, pulling a bit of paper from his pocket and slipping it under the door. There was a tiny rustle as someone on the other side picked the paper up, then the handle turned and the door clunked open.

Reeve stood in the doorway, grinning broadly. "Hey, guys. Good to see you." He ushered us inside. "Sorry I never returned that call. Battery was already on the way out when we spoke the first time."

We padded down the hall, into a family room identical to the one we'd left behind an hour ago. Three men sat hunched around the coffee table, weapons resting at their sides.

"Wilson, Hamilton, Chew," said Reeve, and the officers all nodded or waved halfheartedly.

The one called Wilson had a pile of chopped-up T-shirts sitting on the table in front of him. He stood up, bringing over a handful of what looked like bracelets or something: strips of blue, red and black fabric, braided together.

"Here," he said, handing one to each of us.

"What's this?" I asked.

"Friendship bracelet," smirked Chew from back on the couch. "I think he likes you."

"Rebel ID," said Wilson, flipping a casual middle

finger over his shoulder at Chew, reminding me forcibly of Peter. "So we know who's one of us." He patted his own arm, tied with a woven band up near the shoulder.

"Wilson loves his braiding," said Chew, still grinning. "He wants to be a hairdresser when he grows up."

"Nice to know at least one of you has plans to grow up," said Lazarro dryly. "Get rid of them. Stupid idea. Might as well sew a target to our chests."

"So, what's going on?" I asked, handing the band back to Wilson, who stared down at it, dejected. "How come you guys are back out of the Shackleton Building?"

Reeve's expression darkened. "Shackleton Building's not such a fun place to be right now. We lost the loyalty room not long after we took it. Got a few of the prisoners out, but not many. Not enough. And now they're out on the streets, and Shackleton's locking the town center down again. He's setting up a perimeter around the Shackleton Building to deal with anyone who tries to get back in."

"Where's Tank?" I asked, dreading the answer. I turned around, like I might have missed him the first time. "And Officer Miller. Are they …?"

"Still inside," said Reeve. "There's a few of them still in there. Lying low, or posing as Shackleton's men again."

"Or *actually* Shackleton's men again," said Lazarro gruffly.

"Or dead," said Chew.

"Better dead than back in Shackleton's pocket," said Lazarro, shooting Chew a penetrating look.

Chew shrank back in his chair a bit. Lazarro had been working with Reeve for weeks now, but the rest of these guys had only switched sides a few hours ago. It looked like the trust was still pretty shaky.

"Chew, why don't you head upstairs and take over the watch?" said Reeve, moving to break things up before they had a chance to escalate.

Chew rolled his eyes and stood up.

"I spoke to Shackleton," I said, as he disappeared upstairs. Mouths dropped open around the room. I pulled out my phone and they all relaxed a bit. "We need to get back into the Shackleton Building. He's up there with Galton, running some kind of –"

Reeve held up a hand. "You'll get no argument from us, mate. But we're not getting in there with a handful of rifles – which is why we've got four guys out at the armory, picking up some supplies. When they get back, we'll figure out what we've got to work with."

"*If* they get back," Lazarro muttered.

"They will," said Reeve. "Kirke and Ford are solid, and this place is in more than enough chaos for the guys on duty out there to believe Shackleton's sent them in as reinforcements."

"It's not Kirke and Ford I'm worried about," said Lazarro.

"Look," said Reeve, "I know the other two are inexperienced, but we don't have a whole lot of –"

"Yeah," said Lazarro, far from convinced. "Best we can do."

"It'll work," said Reeve.

Lazarro slumped down onto a couch, face twisting up like he had a bad taste in his mouth. "Just as long as no one tries anything stupid."

Chapter 19

JORDAN

"Stupid," spat Calvin, squatting beside me in the mud. I twitched as he thrust an arm at me, but he was just handing over his binoculars. I took them from him, casting him an uneasy look before peering through the dripping undergrowth at the scene unfolding at the armory.

I knelt in the wet grass, one hand on the binoculars and one cradling Tobias as I focused on the entrance. There was a truck parked outside – the one that had shot our tires out. It was open at the back, with a ramp to the ground and boxes piled up inside. Guns and ammunition and who knew what else. And in front of it all, strapped down just inside the roller-door, another skid unit.

It looked like the guys guarding the armory had been helping load it all up. Not anymore.

As I watched, a guard dragged a scraggly-haired officer out of the armory at gunpoint and threw him to the ground next to a pair of others.

"The one with the hair is Ford," said Calvin. "The two with him are Kirke and Green."

My ears pricked up. Ford and Kirke were two of Reeve's guys.

"And I take it at least one of those two morons lying unconscious on the ground is yours as well," Calvin continued.

"Huh?"

"Inside," he said.

The sun was rising by now, a faint glow creeping in through the blanket of gray clouds. I peered back through the gaping doors of the armory and spotted two figures sprawled out on the concrete. A metal canister lay on its side between them. Sleeping gas, like the stuff we'd used last night at the Shackleton Building.

They had them fooled, I thought, passing the binoculars along to Amy and squinting out at Reeve's three remaining men, kneeling in the dirt while Shackleton's guys paced around them, shaking their rifles. *Reeve's people told the guards they were here to pick up supplies for Calvin or Shackleton or whoever. And they bought it. But then some idiot decided to try knocking them out with the sleeping gas.*

Amy gasped next to me and I jolted. "What is it?"

She pointed at the ramp leading up to the armory's second level. The roller-door at the top was clattering shut, and another security officer was swaggering down, rifle in hand.

"It's him," she said.

Officer Reynolds. The last time we'd come out here, he'd put a bullet in Amy's leg.

I watched as he made his way casually down the ramp. For whatever reason, the rest of Shackleton's guys seemed hesitant to pull the trigger on their old colleagues, but I had a feeling Reynolds might not be quite so discerning.

"Do something!" said Amy, suddenly panicked. "If you really are here to help us –"

"Stay here," hissed Calvin. He strode out into the clearing, eyes on the ramp. "Reynolds!" he barked.

Reynolds froze. The other two guards turned, raising their weapons, then saw who it was and dropped them again.

Calvin waved Reynolds down, and they converged on the spot where Reeve's men were lined up in the mud. Calvin glanced down at them, then turned to the officers standing guard. He started speaking, but I couldn't hear a word of it over the rain.

I hoisted Tobias up off my lap, holding him against me, ready to move at a moment's notice.

Amy flinched next to me as the guards abruptly stood back from the men on the ground. But then Reynolds thrust a hand at the scraggly-haired guy, Ford. He stepped back, helping him to his feet. The others followed suit, and in ten seconds, all three of Reeve's guys were walking off towards the truck, looking over their shoulders like they couldn't figure out what was going on.

A minute later, they'd retrieved their unconscious friend from the entrance, piled back into the truck, and peeled out onto the narrow dirt road back to town.

"Huh," said Amy, like it was about the only word she could manage.

I nodded vaguely. "Yeah …"

Calvin watched until the truck was out of sight, then started towards the armory. His men fell into line behind him, and they disappeared inside the enormous, gleaming building. The heavy double doors trundled shut, sealing them in.

Tobias gurgled happily.

"What do you think?" I asked.

Amy lowered the binoculars, raised them, and lowered them again, still experimenting with the new speed of her body. She turned to look at me, long hair clinging to her face and shoulders in the rain. "I don't know. I mean, up until right now, I would have said we should get out of here as fast as we could, but ..." She shrugged. "I don't know."

I wished Luke was here. My hand was halfway to my pocket to call him before I remembered it was pointless. Twenty minutes into our walk here from the wrecked skid, I'd felt around for my phone and discovered that it was missing. Left behind in the crash.

I'd asked Calvin for his, but he'd refused. Said he didn't want to waste the battery unless it was something important.

I got to my feet. The rain was getting heavier now, pasting my sweater down to my arms and back. I leaned over Tobias, doing my best to keep him out of it.

We waited.

Eventually, Amy got up from the bushes and stood beside me. She opened her mouth, then bit her lip, like she'd decided not to say whatever was on her mind after all.

"What?" I prodded.

She sighed heavily, almost shuddering. "I hate him," she said at last. "I mean – I *hate* him. He abducted me. He took away everything – everything I ever –" She sighed again. "I haven't seen my family in *months*. I don't even know if they're *alive*, and now ..."

She faltered, tears filling her eyes. I waited, giving her a chance to finish. Amy had hardly ever spoken about her family, these past few weeks.

"And now *this*," she said bitterly.

"You don't trust him," I said.

"No, that's –" Amy twisted in frustration. "That's the thing. I don't *want* to trust him. I want to keep hating him because that's what he deserves. But then he goes off and does all this –" she waved a hand at the armory "– and I just don't know what I'm supposed to *do* with that. How am I supposed to feel when the guy who's always been the bane of my life turns around and does something that might *save* my life?"

I stared back at the armory, thinking of Peter: crazy, violent, abusive. Murderous. A killer who'd died to save Luke from a murder of his own creation. Emotion surged in me. Everything, all at once. I held it back, pushing it down the way I'd been doing all morning. No time for it. Not now.

But now here was Calvin, murderer in chief, pulling the same change-of-heart trick, and this time it wasn't just one life at stake. It was everyone's.

"I don't want to trust him either," I said in an undertone. "You're right, it's like betraying everything we've ever fought for. But if he really is trying to help us, if the fallout really did change him, then we can't just turn our backs on that. And listen, if you're right about – If this really *is* all headed somewhere, if there's a purpose to it … What if that purpose is big enough to include even him?"

Amy frowned. "I was afraid you were going to say something like that."

"Look, I'm not saying you have to *like* –" I began, but then a faint clatter from the armory put an end to the conversation. I looked up to the top of the ramp and saw the door rolling open again. A shiny new skid unit rumbled out, the cage at the back piled high with wooden crates.

"He's alone," said Amy, handing me the binoculars.

Calvin was at the wheel, guiding the skid carefully down the ramp, a new rifle slung over his shoulder. The roller-door closed behind him as soon as he was clear.

Calvin steered onto the dirt road, idling just out of sight of the armory.

As we splashed through the wet bush to meet him, my eyes hovered over the crates stacked up in the cage. Before long, I was close enough to read the black writing stamped across the sides. They were all the same. Explosives.

My mind shook with stark, bright images of another skid, rigged up with C-4, tearing through

Phoenix, veering into the security center, swallowing it up in a ball of smoke and flame. Mike, blindly sacrificing his life out of misguided allegiance to a deranged monster who cared about nothing but self-preservation.

And as I clambered up over the side of the cage and found a seat in between the boxes of explosives, for all my talk of meaning and purpose, a part of me couldn't help wondering if I was being just as blind as he was.

Chapter 20

LUKE

"I saw them," said Reeve, fiddling absently with an old tennis ball he'd found in one of the bedrooms. "Katie. And Lachlan, my kid. They're alive in the Shackleton Building."

I swallowed the last of a stale cracker from a package we'd found in the kitchen. "They see you?"

We were down at the back of the house, sitting on opposite sides of the floor in the hallway, still waiting for Reeve's guys to return from the armory. Chew had gone out to the edge of town to meet them and bring them back. Assuming they were coming back, which seemed more doubtful all the time.

Reeve shook his head. "It was just a glimpse. Just as we were leaving. Back of their heads." He bounced the ball off the wall and caught it again. "I just hope –"

He jerked upright as a creak of wood signaled the arrival of someone outside.

I got up, holding my breath, and a wet bit of paper appeared under the door, words scrawled across it in half-dead pen:

Officer Wilson is a fairy princess.

I showed it to Reeve. He rolled his eyes and pulled open the door. "That's *not* the password," he said wearily, as Chew stepped through the door, followed by two more guys in guards' uniforms.

"I like mine better," Chew grinned, and Reeve looked too relieved at their arrival to push it.

"Kirke and Saunders are waiting back at the truck," said one of the new guys. He had wild hair and a look of complete bemusement on his face.

"Everything okay?" Reeve asked.

"Mate," the guard smirked, slapping Reeve on the back and moving up the hallway, "have I got a story to tell you."

But before he could even get started, a head popped out of the family room. Mrs. Weir, looking more alive than I'd seen her all day. "It's working!"

We raced into the kitchen, where Mr. Weir had been working on the transceiver. One of the newcomers dumped a backpack on the floor. The others were already crowded around, except Wilson, who looked longingly over from his watch at the window, and Lazarro who was somewhere upstairs.

"It *should* be working," Mr. Weir corrected, holding up the transceiver, a Frankenstein's monster of looping wires and spare parts he'd scavenged from stuff around the house. "Won't know until we turn it on."

He was holding the thing just a little bit too tightly, and again, I got the sense that this project was all that was keeping him from melting down over Peter.

"So what are you waiting for?" asked Chew, pushing to the front.

Mr. Weir flicked a switch. Two lights, one green, one red, started blinking at the top of the transceiver, and the cracked screen flashed to life.

"That's good, right?" said one of the new arrivals.

"Bloody miracle is what that is," Mr. Weir beamed, tapping something on the screen. "Now, I've left it at the frequency it was transmitting on when the jet crashed, so with any luck, we should still ..."

He tapped at the screen again. Static crackled out of a speaker, and I felt my breath catch in my throat.

Mr. Weir held the speaker tentatively up to his face. "Hello?"

Static.

Mr. Weir tried again. "Hello? Is anyone there?"

More static. And then –

"Who is this?" a gruff voice demanded. "Identify yourself."

The kitchen hummed with stifled noise. Everyone grinning and staring at each other, fighting to contain their excitement.

"This is Brian Weir," said Mr. Weir. His hands were shaking. "I'm a prisoner of the Shackleton Co-operative."

The voice at the other end was silent for just long enough to make me think we'd lost the signal, then: "This is a restricted frequency. How did you –?"

"We found your transceiver," said Mr. Weir in a rush. "When your jet came down. I pulled it from the wreckage. It was damaged, but I –"

"Shh!" I hissed, grabbing Mr. Weir's arm, pulling the transceiver closer to me.

I'd heard something. Another voice. Muffled, distant, as though the speaker was across the room from whatever they were transmitting with.

"*Stop*," the voice demanded. "Let me go. You're being –" He broke off, regaining his composure, and I almost lost mine completely as I realized who it was. "Listen. *Listen* to me, I know you have your protocols, but this is –" He grunted again, still struggling. "I'm telling you, I know that man. He's a *friend*."

And finally, I found my voice. "*Dad!*"

"Luke!" he called back, closer this time, or maybe just louder. "Luke, are you all right? What's happening out there? Where's –?" He growled at whoever was holding him. "Enough! Please, I just want to –"

"Oh, for goodness sake," snapped a third voice, sharp and impatient. "It's his *son*, you jackass. He's fifteen. How much harm could he possibly be?"

It was Kara.

Alive. Both of them. They'd made it out.

There was what sounded like a scuffle for control of the transmitter, and then Dad's voice cut through the static again, louder and clearer. "Luke! Are you okay?"

And without warning, all the trauma and the exhaustion finally caught up with me and I disintegrated into tears. Mr. Weir handed over the transceiver and I held it up to my face, unable to speak, staggering over to lean on the sink for support.

"Luke …" said Dad, his own voice breaking. "Talk to me, mate."

I took a breath, pulling myself together enough to get words out, painfully aware of the huddle of security officers standing over me. "It's – it's a mess, Dad. Jordan's on her way out to the release station now, but –"

"You've found Tobias?" said Kara, cutting in.

"Y-yeah, but I don't even know if –"

197

"Where are you?" asked Chew from behind me, losing patience. "Who are those people you're with?"

Through the static, I heard Dad sigh. Whatever was coming next, I had a feeling I wasn't going to like it.

"We're with the military, in a temporary facility outside of Alice Springs. They're mounting a rescue effort, but there's been some … difference of opinion," Dad said carefully, "about how to go about it. About how much of what we've told them is actually reliable."

"What – what do you mean?" I said. "What about all that video Jordan took?"

"They've watched it," said Dad, his voice crackling with static. "And obviously they can't deny that there's some kind of hostage situation going on in there. What they aren't so sold on is Tabitha. Their surveillance hasn't shown any sign of –"

"Enough!" barked the military officer. "That information is –"

"Their *surveillance* just got blown out of the sky!" I said. "Tell them I *saw* it! Tell them if this isn't fixed by five o'clock –"

"I know," said Dad bracingly. "I know. And I'd love to tell you they'll be quicker to trust us on Tabitha than they were on Shackleton's defenses, but I hon–"

His voice cut out, and the static went with it.

"No …" I breathed. At first, I thought the connection

had been cut at his end. But then I held the transceiver away from my face. Lights, screen, everything dead.

Mr. Weir pulled the transceiver out of my hands.

"What happened?" the scraggly-haired guard asked. "What did he do?"

Mr. Weir didn't answer. He was too busy poring over the transceiver.

I spun away, pushing out of the circle.

"Mate, I didn't mean …" the scraggly-haired guard began, but Reeve held up a hand and said, "Leave him."

I stumbled back into the hall and slumped on the carpet, grabbing for my phone, needing to talk to Jordan, not even to tell her about Dad, just to know she was still out there, but again, the phone just rang and rang. I tried Calvin's number, expecting nothing and getting it, and by the time the call rang out, my tears had evaporated into stony anger at the guards in the other room.

I could hear their hushed tones, probably griping about all the time I'd wasted crying to Daddy when we should have been exchanging information. Like any of them could lecture me on not having my priorities straight. Like they hadn't wasted *months* fighting on the wrong side of this war.

Not helpful, whispered the rational part of my brain. I got to my feet. No point dwelling on dead ends.

We had to get out of here, out to wherever they had this truck and –

"Back from the windows!" hissed Lazarro, thundering into view down the stairs. "Everybody down!"

"Where are they?" asked Reeve, appearing in the doorway, already armed. "How many –?"

He dragged me down just as a spray of gunfire tore into the house, splintering the front door off its hinges.

"Don't want to alarm anyone," said Lazarro from the stairs, taking aim at the half-destroyed doorway, "but I think they might have found us."

JORDAN
THURSDAY, AUGUST 13, 7:26 A.M.
9 HOURS, 34 MINUTES

"It is *not* moronic," Calvin insisted as we roared along the road. "It is the most extraordinarily sophisticated surface-to-air defense system on the entire planet."

"Sure," I shouted over the wind in my ears, "except for the part where it gunned down that jet over the place it was meant to be defending."

Calvin's shoulders arched up a bit. "That was your fault, not ours."

"*Our* fault?"

"We have protocols in place to ensure that our automated systems are not disrupted by the movement of our own aircraft," said Calvin, wiping the rain out of the goggles he'd pulled from under the driver's seat. "Protocols which were disregarded completely last week when your people commandeered one of our helicopters."

I rolled my eyes, sinking into the wall of boxes at my back. "How thoughtless of us."

Amy was hanging on to the side of the cage again, shivering in the wet and the wind. Silent since we'd left the armory. She still glared disparagingly at Calvin, but she'd given up pointing the pistol at him.

"The system *should* have been manually recalibrated as soon as Officer Barnett was notified of your escape," Calvin continued. "Yet another duty he mismanaged in my absence, it seems."

"Why didn't you just shut the whole thing down while you were in the armory, then?" I asked.

"The controls aren't in the armory," said Calvin. He slowed the skid down, eyes drifting to the right side of the road. "Now that the security center has been destroyed, they can only be accessed from Shackleton's office, and my removal from active duty has made sneaking in there somewhat more difficult than it might once have been."

"Of course it has," I grumbled, shifting Tobias as my arm started to cramp. He lay there, all bundled up, shivering occasionally but still never complaining, never crying out.

Which would have been unnerving enough without the eyes. I watched them swivel in their sockets, tracking my face with an intensity that no baby should have been capable of, and tried to convince myself I was just imagining things.

What could possibly be going on inside that tiny head of his?

My mind burned with a swirl of sickening visions of what might be waiting for him outside the wall. I shook them off, readjusting Tobias's covers again. Calvin had found Tobias a waterproof blanket in the armory to replace the dirty towel he'd been wrapped in before. What was that? An actual gesture of humanity, or just Calvin protecting his interests? Clearly, he needed Tobias alive for *something*, but –

The skid slowed as Calvin turned off onto a faint dirt trail leading off into the bush. I realized I'd seen this area before, way back in the beginning, when Luke, Peter and I had come trekking out to the wall, following a map scrawled in a library book by Crazy Bill.

We'd known *nothing* back then. No idea who we

were really following, or where he was taking us.

And now, after everything, after all we'd learned, here I was, riding out to the wall again. Just as lost and confused as ever.

The skid splashed down into the wet bush, onto what was not even a real path. Just a winding trail worn into the grass and the mud. We'd known since our first trip out here that there must be a way through the wall – how else had Reeve brought us back from the outside in a van? – but we'd never actually been out here to see it.

Calvin's hand slipped from the wheel. His head tilted down in the direction of his pocket.

I sat up. "Who is it?"

Calvin's eyes shot back out to the road.

"*Calvin,*" I snapped. "Who's calling you?"

"No one," said Calvin. His hand returned to the wheel. "I was checking the time."

"He's lying," said Amy, drawing her pistol. "I saw the caller ID. *Victoria Galton.*"

"That's Luke," I said. "Give me the phone."

"We do not have time for distractions," said Calvin, swerving to avoid a fallen tree.

"Give it to me," I said. "It could be important."

"More important than saving the world?" Calvin asked. "Worth running down the last of my battery? He has been calling for hours, Jordan. And he is *still* calling, which means that whatever's happening to him, it isn't –"

Amy leaned over, pressing the pistol into the back of Calvin's head. "Give it to her."

"Put it away," said Calvin.

"Give it to her!"

"I think we've established by now that you're not going to –"

BLAM!

The skid screeched to a halt, spraying muddy water, almost smashing into a clump of trees. I grunted in pain as a box of explosives thumped into the back of my head.

"Oh my goodness," said Amy shakily. "Oh – Oh my goodness."

I clambered to my feet, shoving the dislodged boxes back into place.

Amy was frozen, clinging one-handed to the side of the cage like it was the only thing keeping her standing. The pistol was pointed straight up into the air above her head.

Calvin stared back at her, face twisted with fury. He thrust out a hand. "Give me that!"

Amy shakily lowered the weapon and pointed it at Calvin. "The phone," she said. "First, give Jordan the phone."

Chapter 21

LUKE

The firing stopped and for a second the world went quiet. Nothing but the spatter of rain coming down on the roof.

Gray dawn light broke in through the bullet-riddled front door, gleaming down across our faces. I pushed up from the ground, disentangling myself from Reeve, then froze as the light began to move. A shadow rose up over the carpet. Someone was coming.

"I'd stay outside if I were you!" called Lazarro from the stairs, rifle still aimed down at the doorway. "We got plenty of guns in here, and some guys too incompetent to know when to hold their fire."

"Nice working with you too, mate," said Chew from somewhere in the family room.

Lazarro turned to Reeve. "I counted two out the front. Another one coming around the back. We've got the numbers for now, but –" He fired a short burst into the wall above the door. "I said *get back!*"

A scream pierced the gunfire. "Please – I'm unarmed!"

A woman's voice. Reeve sprung up from the ground like he'd been electrocuted. "Katie!"

"*Matt!*" the voice called back.

"Stand down," Reeve told Lazarro. "Let her in."

Lazarro didn't budge. "It's a trap."

"It's my *wife*," said Reeve.

"Yeah," said Lazarro. "Just out for a walk, is she?" He barked into the family room: "One of you clowns feel like getting out here and watching the back door?"

I jerked sideways as something vibrated at my leg.

Galton's phone. Someone was calling me.

Reeve started down the hall. "Katie! Are you okay?"

"Enough!" snapped a voice from outside, stopping him dead. "All of you, out the front door! Hands behind your heads!"

I dug my hand down into my pocket, shuffling out of the way as Chew and Wilson appeared in the hall, slipping out to the back of the house.

"That you, Justin?" Reeve called, his voice strained.

The guard hesitated. "This isn't personal, Matt. I'm just doing my –"

"You have a gun on my wife!"

I stood, checking the caller ID.

Bruce Calvin.

"Matt, please," Katie begged, "you have to do what he says! They've got Lachlan!"

I slid the phone open. "Luke!" said Jordan, and it was like something dead inside of me had come back to life.

"*Jordan,*" I hissed. "We're surrounded. They've got Reeve's wife. They're using her to –"

Reeve took a step towards the door, and I lost my train of thought.

"Don't," Lazarro warned. "Don't do it, Matt. You know that doesn't end the way you want it to."

"I'll give you thirty seconds, Matt," called the guard. "Tell your men to stand down and get their arses out here or I shoot your wife and we start again with the kid."

Katie let out a desperate wail.

I turned my attention back to the phone call. "Jordan?"

No answer. I heard rain, frantic voices, the rumble of an engine.

"Listen to yourself!" Reeve shouted back through the door, voice cracking. "Listen to what you're saying! He's a *kid*, Justin. He's three. Are you seriously going to –?"

"This – this isn't about me, Matt," said the guard. "It's just orders. Twenty seconds."

"Jordan!" I hissed. "What's –?"

"Luke," said a stony voice at the other end of the line. Sweat prickled at the back of my neck. It was Calvin.

"Ten seconds," said the guard.

"Turn on your speakerphone," Calvin ordered.

"Nine."

"Why?" I said.

"Eight."

"Do it, Luke!" Jordan called in the background.

"Seven."

I pulled the phone away from my ear.

"Six."

Scanned the keypad, trying to figure out where the speakerphone button even *was*.

"Five."

Reeve lurched towards the door.

"Four."

Lazarro dived, thrusting a hand between the railings on the stairs.

"Three."

He grabbed at Reeve, fist clenching on his collar.

"Two."

I ducked under his outstretched arm, thumb finally coming down on the right button.

"One –"

"– DOWN!" Calvin roared, managing to sound

loud and commanding even over the tinny speaker. "REPEAT: STAND DOWN!"

Stunned silence, broken only by muffled sobbing from outside. I crept to the door, cranking up the volume as high as it would go.

Finally, the guard called Justin spoke up. "Chief ...?"

"I'm sending Luke Hunter out with the phone," said Calvin. "Ensure that he is not harmed."

"Jordan?" I whispered, switching off the speakerphone for a second and holding the phone to my ear.

There was a pause as Calvin handed the phone back.

"It's okay," said Jordan, clearly trying to sound more convinced than she actually was. "Do what he says."

I looked back at Reeve, still in Lazarro's clutches, tears streaming down his face. He nodded.

"O-okay," I said, steeling myself, turning the speaker back on. "Okay, I'm coming out. Nobody shoot anyone."

I shoved the wreck of the door aside and stepped into the doorway. A woman with dark, curly hair stared back at me, red-eyed, white-faced, shaking in the grip of a heavy-set guy with a pistol jammed up under her chin. Two more guards stood out in the rain, aiming rifles through the family room window.

"Matt!" Katie screamed, catching sight of Reeve. "Don't let them –"

"SILENCE!" Calvin demanded.

I scanned the street. So far, it was just the three of them (plus maybe one more around the back), but the gunfire would attract others.

"Sir," said the guard holding Reeve's wife, "Officer Collins speaking. Shackleton's orders were to find these men and return them to base for questioning."

"Do you think this is news to me, Collins?" Calvin asked.

"No, sir," said Collins quickly. "I – I just didn't realize you were back on duty."

"I am ordering an emergency meeting of all security personnel," said Calvin. "Return to the Shackleton Building immediately."

Collins stared at me, bewildered. He wasn't an idiot. He could see that something about all this wasn't adding up, but he knew better than to question Calvin.

The two other guards edged closer to the house, straining to listen in.

I held my breath, waiting for it all to fall apart.

"Sir," said Collins, "I have Officer Reeve and a number of his fellow rebels here with me. If you would be willing to send in some additional forces –"

"Officer Collins," said Calvin fiercely, "if I find myself in need of your tactical advice, I will ask for it."

"Y-yes, sir." Collins glanced back at his companions. They shrugged back at him, confused and frustrated.

And then, just in case we didn't have enough men with guns around, I spotted three more figures in black emerging from a side street, over the road. Half a minute, and they'd be right –

BLAM!

The window shattered behind me, showering the verandah with glass.

Officer Collins staggered. Blood poured from the side of his head. He crumpled to the ground, pulling Katie down with him. I dived behind them as the guards on the lawn returned fire, their rifles pointed back up at the family room. Katie cried out in horror, crashing into me as she scrambled from the limp form of Officer Collins.

Calvin's voice was still bellowing out of the phone, but I couldn't make out a word of it. I twisted around, deafened by gunfire, and caught a blur of movement as a little metal canister came sailing out of the window. It bounced off the railing and clanked back down onto the verandah.

I cringed away, thinking it was a grenade or something, but the explosion never came. Instead, with a loud hissing sound, the thing started spewing out thick black smoke, rattling around on the ground with the force of its own spray. Smoke filled the verandah, spilling out in all directions, across the yard and through the house, pouring into my eyes and nose and mouth.

Someone was still firing. The noise ricocheted in my head, everywhere at once.

Katie brushed past me, already on her feet. "Matt!"

I staggered up after her, blind, eyes streaming. But the upside to a town full of identical houses was that it was pretty easy to find your way through one in the dark. I ran inside, ducking for cover, and stumbled down the hallway.

"Everybody out!" bellowed Lazarro, still somewhere above me. "Go! Go! Go!"

I kept going, through the house and out the already-open back door, almost tripping down the steps. Smoke billowed out after me, clouding the yard, but it was thinner here, a gray haze instead of total darkness.

A figure stalked through the murk at the other end of the yard. It turned, catching sight of me. I dropped onto all fours, just as –

BLAM! BLAM!

The bullets whooshed past, swirling the smoke above my head. There was a shout from the house and someone else returned fire. How could they even tell who they were shooting at?

I shrank down, crawling away through the long grass, not stopping until I reached the back fence. I looked back. Someone was coming. I jumped up, vaulted over the fence, and ran.

Chapter 22

JORDAN

He's okay, I told myself, like thinking it could make it true. *He's okay. He got out.*

But the sound of gunfire still rattled in my head. Luke hadn't called back, and I hadn't called him for fear of giving up his hiding place, or running down the battery.

I trudged through the mud, trying to busy my mind with the work of carrying explosives.

The wall was bigger than I remembered. A massive expanse of concrete, stretching forever in both directions, towering over our heads. It encircled the town, a line marking out the reach of the fallout. Towering bush on this side, barren wasteland on the other.

Last time had been easy enough. We'd just climbed

a tree and thrown a rope over the side. But now that the shield grid had come bursting out of the wall, electrified cords slashing and burning through any tree tall enough to get in their way, things were a bit more complicated.

The sun was brighter overhead now, the shield grid even more ominous for being able to see it clearly. Dark lines crisscrossed the gray sky, making this whole place feel, if possible, even more like a prison. The rain had eased off a little bit, but we were all so soaked through by now that it didn't really make any difference.

I picked up another box of explosives, lugging it through the rain towards a pair of gleaming silver doors: the hidden access point Reeve and the others had used to run their patrols to the outside, back in the day.

Calvin crouched in front of the giant doors, mounting explosives and connecting wires. Once upon a time, he could've just keyed a code and popped the doors open automatically, but somewhere along the line, Shackleton had locked him in with the rest of us.

He took the box from my hands, and I felt a twinge of something that felt bizarrely like solidarity.

"Thanks," I said. "For trying to get them out of there. That was …"

Calvin nodded slowly and then got back to work. I went back to the skid for the last box, an unwelcome thought gnawing at me. I was starting to trust him.

How was I starting to trust him?

Amy was in the driver's seat, taking care of Tobias. After the incident with the gun, Calvin had decided that that was the best place for her. Amy had been too shaken up by the whole thing to argue, and I was more than happy to actually get up and *do* something.

"How is he?" I asked, leaning in to check on Tobias.

"Yeah, fine," said Amy. "Sleeping."

"Listen, thanks for –"

"What do you think he's going to have to do when we get out there?" Amy cut in. "I mean, what *can* he do? *Sleep* Tabitha to death?"

"I don't know," I said.

"But you really believe Calvin's going to show you."

I grabbed the final box of explosives from the cage, flicking my head to shake back a stray dreadlock. "I don't know."

I returned to the wall, dropped off the last of the explosives, and watched as Calvin set them in place.

What if this really was all just wishful thinking? What if my desperation to get out there and save the world had blinded me to some crucial detail that might have let me in on what Calvin was *really* doing here?

Or what if it was even simpler than that? What if Shackleton was just running down the clock? With only hours left until the end, what if he'd just sent Calvin out here to keep me distracted until it was too late?

But if that was true, why *Calvin* of all people? And why even bother when he could have just shot me or taken me prisoner? What wasn't I seeing?

"We're going to have to leave her behind," Calvin said, without looking up at me.

"What?"

"Amy," he said. "Once we get the doors open, we're –"

"No. We're not." I crouched down, glancing back to make sure she hadn't heard. "She's coming with us."

Calvin bent down lower, plugging something into one of the wads of explosive. "She's too unpredictable."

"*She's* too unpredictable?"

"You and I have a job to do –"

"Right, that secret job you won't even –"

"– and we cannot afford to take unnecessary risks," Calvin steamrolled on, finally stopping to look at me. "I will not allow the integrity of this operation to be compromised by a reckless rogue element."

"By someone who might shoot you, you mean?"

"And what if I *had* been shot?" Calvin snapped. "What then?"

"You weren't," I said. "And you won't be. She was just trying to get your attention."

"Are you sure of that? Are you willing to stake the lives of all humanity on her cooperation?"

I opened my mouth to defend her and found that I couldn't get the words out. How was it that I was having a conversation with Calvin about whether someone *else* could be trusted with the future of humanity?

"Do you think you're safe from this?" Calvin asked. "Do you think your *family* is safe if we fail today? If the effects of the fallout have truly been undone, what does that say for your immunity to Tabitha?"

A chill ran through me, deeper than anything the rain or the cold could reach. The question had been there all along, but I'd mostly managed not to let myself think about it.

"I don't know," I said.

"Neither do I," said Calvin. "And I would prefer not to find out." His eyes were filling up with what looked amazingly like genuine compassion. "Amy is as safe here as anywhere. We'll pick her up on our way back. And by then, with any luck …" He wiped his hands on his pants and stretched upright. "Come on. We're ready here."

He started back towards the skid, apparently assuming he'd talked me around. And maybe he had. I fell into step behind him, still conflicted, but no longer convinced he was wrong. I told myself it wasn't a question of loyalty. I'd back Amy over Calvin every single time. But as long as they were together, there'd be conflict. And Calvin was right: we couldn't afford it.

Amy got up from the driver's seat as we approached, handing Tobias back to me. Calvin jumped behind the wheel and threw the skid into reverse. "Follow me. Everyone get back to a safe distance."

I took one last look back at the wall and hurried after him.

Calvin parked the skid, leapt out, and bobbed down behind it, pulling out a little remote-control thing. I crouched behind one of the giant front tires, draping Tobias's blanket over his face and crossing my arms around his back.

"Stay down," Calvin warned, flipping a little cap up from the detonator.

He pushed the button, and the whole wall vanished in a hurricane of orange light. The explosion roared through the bush, fierce, bloodthirsty, devouring everything with churning flames and a rushing wind, scorching my rain-drenched skin and hammering me into the ground and rocking the skid so hard I thought it was going to roll over on top of us. Debris rained down, exploded trees and hunks of wet earth.

And then it was over.

I sat up, ash and dirt cascading from my body, and pulled back the blanket to check on Tobias. He just yawned at me, like he did this kind of thing all the time.

"You call that a safe distance?" Amy grumbled.

Calvin ducked away to see what was left of the wall. I brushed the worst of the dirt off Tobias and jogged to catch up.

Twenty meters in, we reached the clearing created by the explosion. Light glowed through the smoke as the trees around the edge crackled with flames. The ground was uneven, ripped apart by the blast. I tried to make out how much damage had been done to the shield grid, but everything I could see was still intact.

Calvin squinted at the smoke, which was finally beginning to clear. A gust of wind whipped by, clearing a path in front of us, and Calvin stepped back like he'd been slapped. He swore under his breath, and I felt dread crash through me with even more force than the explosion.

"No way …" breathed Amy, coming up behind us.

The doors were still there. Scorched black, but still looming over us. Undamaged. Unmoved.

Nine hours until the end of the world, and our last hope of saving it had just gone up in smoke.

Chapter 23

LUKE

I stretched above the low line of the picket fence, risking a glance out at the bush, and then dropped back down again, heart pummeling my chest. The darkness was long gone now, and every movement I made felt like taunting death.

Mrs. Weir knelt in the grass beside me. She was the only one I'd found since abandoning the house. I'd run into her behind the primary school and almost smashed her over the head with a tree branch.

Together, we'd made our way down to the south end of town, agonizingly slow as we dodged the pairs of guards who were combing the streets, rounding up escapees. That was definitely not good news. If security were free enough to start sending out search parties, then we had to be pretty much back to square one in the Shackleton Building.

Already, whatever resistance there'd been out across the town was now nearly stamped out, everyone lying low or escaped into the bush or recaptured or worse. I thought of Lauren and the others we'd left behind this morning. What would happen to them when security came knocking?

"We should never have left you," murmured Mrs. Weir, eyes to the ground.

I turned to look at her. A cold breeze swept through, rustling the grass around our shoulders.

Mrs. Weir sniffled, the ratty nurse uniform she was wearing still sticking to her skin with the rain. "The night at the medical center," she said, "when Brian and I got ourselves captured. We *knew* Peter was sick. We knew he needed us, but we ran off on that fool's errand and look where it got us."

My insides squirmed. What was I supposed to say to that? What words could possibly make any kind of difference to someone who'd just lost their kid?

Dad would know. Somehow, he always knew what to say in situations like this.

"You were trying to help," I said. "You were doing what you thought was best for all of us, *including* Peter."

"It was reckless," she said. "Stupid. Trying to spy on Shackleton when our son was sick and imprisoned. If we'd just stayed behind, we could have …" She sank lower in the grass, eyes red.

"No," I said. "You couldn't – I know you love him. But even if you were there … No one could've stopped what happened to Peter. And like I told you, he did get better. Before – before the end. He was better."

I bobbed up again, no idea if she'd taken anything in. No idea if I'd actually said anything *worth* taking in.

Mrs. Weir didn't move. She'd been like this the whole time. Dazed. Sluggish. One foot in reality, and the other one a thousand miles away.

"C'mon," I said, sweat pricking the back of my neck. I pulled her up and we started into the bush, heading for Reeve's truck and whoever was still alive to meet us.

"How did it happen?" asked Mrs. Weir. I could see her steeling herself for the answer. "How did he …?"

She faltered, unable to finish, and the storm in my stomach intensified. There was no right answer. Nothing that would even come close to capturing the convoluted mess of the last twenty-four hours.

"He was brave," I said, surprised by the sudden flare of emotion as I said the words. Whatever else he'd been, Peter had started out as a friend. "He died trying to do what was right. He stood up to maybe his worst enemy in this whole place, and he was – he was killed. Murdered. But it wasn't for nothing."

Mrs. Weir nodded, a kind of miserable gratitude on her face.

"I know that's not a whole answer," I said. "It's all – I don't know if I'll ever be able to explain it all completely. But I'll try. When all this is over, I promise I'll answer as much as I can."

I flinched as Galton's phone started buzzing in my pocket.

Bruce Calvin.

"Jordan?" I said, sliding the phone open.

A sigh of relief at the other end of the line. "What *happened* back there?"

"Someone started shooting," I said, the sound of her voice calming my nerves a bit. "But we're out now. At least –"

"Is everyone okay?"

"I don't know. We got separated. I'm heading back now to see if I can find the others. Where are you guys?"

"We're at the wall," she said. "Calvin tried to blow open the exit, but it didn't work, and now –"

Calvin barked something at her, but I couldn't make it out over the sound of the engine behind them.

"Need to be quick," said Jordan. "Phone's going to die any minute." Her voice was steady, but I'd learned to hear when she was trying not to panic. "We can't get through the wall. Calvin says the only way out is over. We need you to shut down the shield grid."

I looked up at the sky, at that massive, kilometers-wide structure that could shred military aircraft into smoke and rubble. "How exactly …?"

"Shackleton's the only one with access to the control systems," said Jordan. "You're going to need to get up onto the roof of the Shackleton Building and physically bring it down."

"The roof of the Shackleton Building," I repeated.

"I know. I know it's crazy, but –"

"It's all crazy," I said. "Yeah. I'll try."

"Did Reeve's guys in the truck make it back to you?" asked Jordan. "Have you got any explosives or anything?"

"I don't know," I said. "Probably."

"Okay, good. Calvin says the only way to knock out the grid by force is to destroy that antenna on top of the Shackleton Building that holds all the cords togeth–"

The phone beeped in my ear. She was gone. Battery finally dead.

Mrs. Weir glanced over at me with the closest thing to focus I'd seen since we met up. Then a shout up ahead ripped her attention away again.

"Jess!" Mr. Weir charged out, almost knocking Mrs. Weir over in a ferocious hug.

There were others milling around behind him, gathered together in a little clearing in the trees. Reeve had gotten his wife out. The two of them were deep in a hushed conversation with Lazarro. Chew and Wilson were here too, and Hamilton, Lauren's dad, plus two new faces – the guys who'd been back here guarding the truck, I guessed.

"Any sign of the others?" I asked Mr. Weir. "There should be like three more of us, right?"

"Not anymore," he said darkly. He forced a smile, clapping a hand to my shoulder. "Glad you're okay, mate."

"Yeah. You too."

I turned away, crossing the clearing to talk to Reeve. He saw me coming, whispered something to Lazarro and Katie, and they backed off, leaving us alone.

"Mate," said Reeve, pulling me out of earshot of everyone else. "I need you to tell me exactly what's going on out there with Jordan and Calvin." He stared at me with absolute focus, like hearing the answer was the most important thing in the whole world. Maybe it was.

"I don't know," I said uneasily. "I mean, they're trying to get out to the release station. Jordan says Calvin's trying to help them."

"And you believe that?" said Reeve.

"No," I said automatically. "I mean, of course I don't. But –"

"But how else do you explain what happened back at the house?" Reeve finished. "And how do you explain him letting our guys go free when he caught them out at the armory?"

"Right," I said. "Wait. What?"

"Kirke's been telling me what happened out there," said Reeve, nodding at one of the guards I hadn't met yet. "Crazy story about Calvin ordering his men to stand down and let them go. Anyway, you were saying …"

"They're at the wall," I said. "Calvin tried to blast through, but I guess it didn't work. He needs us to take down the shield grid so they can get over the top."

Reeve's gaze drifted up to the grid.

"We're going to do it, right?" I said. "I mean, we have to. If Jordan doesn't get out there by five …"

Reeve frowned, dark shadows under his eyes. It had been way too long since any of us had slept. He caught Lazarro's eye, cocking his head out at the bush. Lazarro nodded and started rounding everyone up.

"My gut still says Calvin can't be trusted," said Reeve finally, leading the way out of the clearing. "But you're right. We're down to the wire here. We might not have the luxury of only working with people we know we can trust."

We'd reached the truck. Reeve and Lazarro did a quick circuit to make sure we were alone, and then

Kirke rolled open the back door of the truck.

I peered inside. The truck was pretty packed, but it was hard to make out what was in there past the skid unit parked inside the door. Reeve's eyes widened. He climbed inside and twisted past the skid, making his way into the back to take stock.

"Uh … question," said Chew, raising an eyebrow. "You know this skid unit you have here? This smaller, faster, more maneuverable vehicle with the handy cage at the back for transporting equipment? Any reason why you didn't just –?"

"Didn't have a whole lot of choice," said Kirke, who apparently had about as much patience for Chew as Lazarro did. "The boys at the armory were suspicious enough when we showed up unannounced. Had to make things look as routine as possible."

"Any more stupid questions?" Lazarro asked. "Or shall we get to work?"

"Right," said Reeve, reappearing from inside before the bickering could take off. "We've eaten up too much time already." He dropped down in front of the skid, legs dangling over the side of the truck, and clapped his hands together. "Here's what we know: five o'clock tonight, Tabitha gets out and the whole world bites the dust. Maybe us as well. Shackleton knows we're out here, but he also knows there's nothing we can do about Tabitha while the shield grid's still up."

"And nothing we can do about the shield grid while we're stuck out here," I said.

"Exactly," said Reeve. "Which means smart money for him is on just hunkering down in the Shackleton Building and running out the clock."

"So we're screwed," Chew summarized. "Yeah. We knew that already."

Reeve rubbed his eyes. "Not quite. Way I see it, we've got two shots left, and I reckon we've got to take them both at once. First, we get to the roof. Take out the shield grid. Free Jordan up to get out to the release station and deal with Tabitha."

I shot him a grateful look. A few other glances fired around the circle too. We hadn't actually *told* the rest of Reeve's men that Jordan and Calvin were road tripping out to the release station together, but it looked like some of them were starting to fill in the blanks.

"Second," Reeve pushed on, "we go after Shackleton. Make him turn the countdown back himself."

"You really think that's going to happen?" said Wilson.

"Not without a fight," said Reeve, "which is why we have to play it smart. Retake the loyalty room first. Use that to leverage more support to our side. There's enough of us now, we should be able to hold it."

"Hang on," said Hamilton, "where's the part where

we rescue our families?"

"I've just told it to you," said Reeve. "Listen, we've all still got people we care about in there, but if we're going to do this, we need to do it right. Blindly running in and grabbing our families gets us nowhere unless we get the rest done first."

"Okay, sure, but aren't we getting a bit ahead of ourselves here?" asked Chew. "I mean, as much fun as all that sounds, how are we even planning on getting inside in the first place?"

"Calvin's locked down all the tunnels," I said. "We're not getting in that way again."

Reeve nodded. "I think we might be past taking the subtle approach. If we want to get in there, I'd say we're gonna need to be a little bit more direct this time. Straight in the front before they see us coming."

"One more stupid question," said Chew, raising his hand. "As genius as walking in through the front doors might sound, isn't there an outside chance someone might think to shoot us full of holes on the way in?"

"Yep. That's why we won't be walking." Reeve reached behind to pat the giant tire of the skid unit. "This time, we're taking the car."

Chapter 24

JORDAN

I glared up at the wall, hands pressed against the wet concrete, shaking with the frustration and the cold, adrenaline charging inside of me with nowhere to go.

The others were behind me with Tobias, still in the skid. We'd driven around to what Calvin had decided was a safe distance from the site of the explosion, then pulled up to wait for Luke to knock out the shield grid.

Calvin had suggested that Amy could take the skid back into town to investigate his progress. Amy had suggested that Calvin could go screw himself. Since then, there'd been silence.

It had been hours. At least, it had *felt* like hours; Calvin's phone had been our last way of keeping track of time. I'd paced. I'd punched the wall. I'd climbed trees and watched the shield grid vaporize anything I threw into the gaps. Anything to work out the nervous energy, to keep pretending I still had some kind of control over the situation.

None of it helped. This was out of my hands, and I knew it.

And, worse than that, with the end of the fallout, I felt like I'd lost the one thing that had ever given me any kind of edge in this fight.

For so long now, I'd been carried along on the strength of the visions that the fallout had handed down to me. Visions that had seemed almost handpicked to nudge us along in the right direction, to keep us crawling forward towards some kind of solution to all this.

The fallout was what had brought us all out here in the first place. If I had my time-travel paradoxes straight, the fallout had even brought *itself* out here, using the portal-creating abilities it had given me to disperse itself over Phoenix, way back in the beginning.

It was the fallout that had caused Calvin's (alleged) miraculous change of heart. And it was the fallout that had brought Tobias into the world six months ahead of schedule, holding him up as the cure against the end of humanity.

But now the fallout was gone. And all the freakish

mutations it had created were gone with it.

Where did that leave us? Whatever Tobias was meant to do, could he even still do it?

I dug my nails into the concrete. A cable as thick as a tree branch arched over my head – one of the cords that made up the shield grid. You saw the hugeness of the thing in a whole new way at this distance.

Luke is dealing with it, I told myself. *We're going to get out there. We're* meant *to get out there. Tobias is still the answer. He has to be.*

But if there really was some greater purpose at work here – something that, like Amy had said, wasn't neutral about how this all played out – then why had it let *any* of this happen in the first place? The only reason the world needed saving was that Shackleton had been drawn out here by the same fallout that had caused all the rest of it.

I started pacing again.

"Save your energy," said Calvin from his perch on the skid. "You'll need it if the grid comes down."

"*When* the grid comes down," I said. But I did what he told me, abandoning my march along the wall and coming over to take back Tobias.

He smiled as I picked him up and I felt my chest tighten with anxiety. Who *was* this kid?

How many hours had it been since Mum had fed

him back at the complex, and all this time he was just perfectly content with not being fed or changed or even shielded from the rain?

I sat down against the wall, knees bent, propping him up in front of me.

"He'll have to be killed," said Calvin.

My head snapped up, terror exploding like a grenade.

"Shackleton," Calvin clarified, seeing the panic on my face. "Whatever else happens, if we succeed, Shackleton has to be taken care of."

I let out a shaky breath.

"And what about you?" Amy asked, getting to her feet behind him. "What should we do with *you* when this is all over?"

"Whatever you think best," said Calvin, that mournful tone coloring his voice again. "You're right, of course. I am every bit as guilty as he is. But I'm not talking about justice. I'm talking about ensuring that this doesn't happen again."

He returned his gaze to me, like for some reason he thought I was going to be the one who'd be making that decision. "You can't imprison Shackleton. He's too well-connected on the outside. A prison sentence might as well be an acquittal for all the time it would take him to free himself. And then he'll be back on his feet, ready to start all over again."

"No he won't," I said. "I mean, even if all that's true … Phoenix is a one-off, right? He can't recreate the fallout."

"The fallout was a gift," said Calvin. "A shortcut. But Shackleton's dream of a better world stretches back far beyond his discovery of this place. That dream will not die here. Not unless he does."

Amy leaned over the side of the cage, face hidden under her streaming hair. "Brilliant."

It took a minute to even get my head around it. However impossible it had seemed that we might actually *succeed*, in our minds, the end of Tabitha had always been The End. It had never even entered my head that it could drag out beyond that.

But what should have plummeted me to a whole new depth of exhaustion and despair felt strangely like the best news Calvin had shared with us since we ran into him.

Because what if *that* was the answer to the question I'd just been asking? What if Shackleton's discovery of Phoenix was no accident? What if he was *meant* to find this place – *this* place, out of all the other places and plans he could have come up with – not so he could exterminate humanity, but so he could *fail?* So that *we* could beat him?

What if we really could still win this thing?

Tell me that makes some kind of sense, I thought, lifting Tobias up so we were face to face. *Tell me I'm not just going crazy.*

Tobias gazed blankly back at me.

I mean, apart from the bit where I'm trying to communicate telepathically with a baby.

Tobias stared at me for a moment longer, nose wrinkling as a raindrop splashed into his face. Then he yawned and closed his eyes, drifting off into sleep.

Chapter 25

LUKE

"This is insane," said Chew.

"We've done insaner," I said. Then I took another look at what we'd done to the skid unit. "Actually, no we haven't."

"It's kind of like the Trojan horse," said Wilson.

"Right," said Chew, "because no one's going to suspect a thing when this rolls up to the door."

"You don't want to come?" said Lazarro. "Feel free to stay back here and guard the trees."

"Oh, I'm coming," said Chew. "I just want it on record that I think this is insane."

"Noted," said Reeve. "Get in."

We piled into the cage at the back of the skid. Ten

of us: the Weirs, Reeve and Katie, Hamilton, Chew, Wilson, Lazarro, Saunders, and me. All armed with rifles and utility belts.

I felt the weight of the weapon in my hands. Reeve had pulled me aside and showed me how to fire it, but even *holding* the thing felt wrong to me.

Could I do it? When the time came, when someone got between me and where I needed to be, could I actually pull the trigger on another life? And what did it say about me if I could?

I twisted sideways as Lazarro pressed in next to me, a black metal tube thing perched over his shoulder. It was the centerpiece of our plan: a shoulder-mounted missile launcher. Shackleton Co-operative designed, sleek and compact and hopefully just powerful enough to take down the shield grid.

"Oi!" said Chew, as the back of the launcher swung past. "Careful, mate. You could put an eye out with that."

Lazarro rolled his eyes. "Don't tempt me, Chew."

Bodies crushed in all around me, and I felt the skid dip under our collective weight. This was definitely not what this thing was built for.

Kirke slammed the back of the cage shut behind us. He came around the side, to where four large riot shields were leaning against the side of the skid.

"How come we've never seen the Co-operative use these before?" I asked, as Kirke started passing the shields into the cage.

"Never had a riot," said Kirke. "Not a smart move to bring these things out until you really need them. People see a bunch of guys suited up in riot gear, they tend to rise to the occasion."

Reeve, Chew, Wilson and Hamilton held the shields together above our heads, creating a kind of makeshift roof over the cage.

The rest of the skid was as well-protected as we could make it. We'd roped whatever bits of wood and metal we could scrounge to the sides of the cage, and mounted another riot shield to the front of the skid to protect Kirke as he drove.

The engine rumbled to life beneath my feet. We turned in a slow circle, struggling only slightly under the weight of our oversized cargo, and surged off in the direction of the road.

The rain might have eased up a bit by now, but the cold still reached all the way down to my bones. I held on to my rifle, everyone pressed in close around me, and watched the trees slide past overhead, warping out of shape through the plastic of the riot shields. I might have been crammed in here like a battery hen with all the others, but I felt more alone than I had in weeks. It felt so unnatural to be going into something like this without Jordan standing next to me. Like half of me was missing.

"You okay, mate?" asked Mr. Weir behind me.

"Yeah," I lied. "You?"

"Not my best day ever," he said, a rough edge to his voice.

The skid dipped, emerging onto the main road. Kirke slowly brought us around, pulling to a stop just short of the south end of town. My nerves were stretched to breaking point. I pictured myself edging to the top of that first enormous hill on a roller coaster. Nothing to do but hold on and wait for the drop.

Kirke glanced back, waiting for Reeve's okay.

"Stay together," said Reeve, nodding at him. "We stay together and we keep each other alive in there."

"Friends forever," said Chew. "Got it."

Kirke stomped on the accelerator and the skid lurched forward, engine roaring. We shot up the road, bushland melting into a green-gray smear, bodies crushing into each other as we were thrown to the back of the cage.

The town raced up to meet us. We rocketed over the threshold where the trees gave way to houses, straight up Phoenix's only asphalt road, town center dead ahead.

Past my old street, past the house where Jordan and

I had hidden out all those weeks ago, all of it blurring together the same way it did in my head. I held my breath, waiting for the first gunshots.

The park whooshed past on my left, and suddenly we were threading the gap between the medical center and the exploded shell of Phoenix Mall, the Shackleton Building towering over all of it. Our skid bucked and swerved as Kirke dodged the worst of the wreckage and plowed straight over the rest. Bits of debris kicked up from the tires, bouncing off the riot shields.

The second we cleared the medical center, rifle fire surged from somewhere out of sight. Hamilton cried out as the bullets sprayed across his shield, cracking the plastic right in front of his face.

"Hold!" Lazarro barked.

He was okay. The gunfire hadn't made it through. Not this time, anyway.

SMASH!

The skid charged straight into the razor-wire fence guarding the entrance to the Shackleton Building. My head jolted up, smacking into the thing on Lazarro's shoulder. More gunfire, from multiple shooters now. I heard gasps and screams, but we were too packed together to tell if anyone had actually been hurt.

The skid shuddered against the fence and then finally pushed through it, dragging down a whole section and rampaging over the top. Kirke swerved around the fountain on the other side and punched the accelerator, speeding us towards the steps of the Shackleton Building.

And finally, I caught a glimpse of one of Shackleton's men. He peered up from a flower bed at the bottom of the steps, lining us up with his rifle.

"Kirke!" Reeve shouted, spotting him. "On your left!"

Kirke's head twitched to the side, but it was already too late to change course. Cracks splintered across the riot shield at the front of the skid as the guard pulled the trigger. Kirke jolted in his seat, but held the wheel steady. The skid's massive tires hit the steps of the Shackleton Building and started roaring up them.

Then disaster. The guard fired again, attacking from the side as we hurtled past him. Blood spattered the inside of Kirke's shield. He slumped over the wheel. The guard kept shooting, and the skid rocked violently as a tire exploded under my feet. Chew's riot shield flew from his hands, disappearing behind us.

The automatic doors at the top of the steps slid open as we approached, but didn't get ten centimeters apart before they were smashed to pieces. Glass rained down on us. The skid veered, tipping onto two wheels, smashing through a table and a couple of benches and crashing sideways into a row of portable toilets before winding up on all fours again, still moving, spinning out of control, until we finally crunched to a stop against the wall.

"Out!" Reeve shouted, pushing open the back of the cage. "Everyone out!"

I looked up to the front of the skid. Kirke was gone. Left behind somewhere in the crash.

I turned to get out, but then Chew shoved past me, almost knocking me over. He leaned out over the side of the cage, raising his rifle.

The noise ripped through my ears.

Back at the entrance, a man fell to the ground, dead. The guard who'd shot Kirke had been coming back for the rest of us.

Chew looked ready to throw up. "Harris, you dumb idiot. What'd you make me do that for?"

He knew him, I thought, falling out of the cage, shaky but miraculously uninjured. *Of course he did.*

Twenty-four hours ago, they might have been on duty together. They might have been friends.

I ducked next to Katie, but she didn't even register that I was there. She was too fixated on her husband, already weaving his way across the giant, high-ceilinged foyer-turned-concentration-camp, holding up his riot shield in one hand and unclipping something from his belt with the other. Wilson and Hamilton were right behind him, zigzagging through the sea of tables and chairs that had all been quickly abandoned when the explosions started going off last night.

"No," said Katie, as I stood to go after them. "He said to wait here."

"But –"

BANG!

At the far end of the foyer, a set of double doors flew open and a half-dozen guards leapt out. The sound of a terrified crowd spilled through the doorway behind them. The people of Phoenix, crammed together inside the town hall with who knew how many armed men keeping them under control.

Shackleton's guys spread out, opening fire. Reeve and the others kept moving, while Lazarro, Chew and Saunders all jumped up from behind the skid to help cover them.

There was a strangled cry from across the foyer and one of Shackleton's men collapsed, clutching his leg.

"Idiot!" Lazarro snapped at Chew. "Any minute now, we'll be asking them to *join* us. Don't shoot them unless –"

"Unless *what?*" said Chew. "And it wasn't even me! It was Saund–"

He looked sideways just in time to see Saunders jolt

243

back and crumple to the floor. I leapt out of the way as he fell, heart thumping into my throat. He was gone.

Lazarro swore. He fired again. Across the foyer, I saw Shackleton's guys digging in, taking positions behind whatever cover they could find.

Reeve stopped maybe twenty meters out from us. He dropped down behind a table, pulling his whole body in behind his barely intact riot shield, and hurled a silver canister over his head at the guards. It was a smoke bomb, like the one they'd used back at the house. Hamilton and Wilson followed suit, and in seconds, a murky black cloud was spreading out across the foyer.

"GO!" Reeve shouted out of the darkness. "GO! GO!"

"You heard him!" said Lazarro. "MOVE!"

I jumped up, almost knocking over Mrs. Weir, who was supporting Mr. Weir over her shoulder. It looked like he'd twisted his ankle or something in the crash.

"More coming!" said Katie breathlessly, looking back at the front steps as the smoke began swirling over us.

"Get out of here," Mr. Weir grunted, shooing me away.

I ignored him, rushing to his other side and helping Mrs. Weir steer him around the skid unit. I almost dropped him again as someone came charging through the smoke towards us.

It was Reeve. He dashed past, throwing an arm over Katie, covering her with the riot shield, then glanced at

Mr. Weir, taking in his injured leg. "Are you guys –?"

"We're great," said Mr. Weir. "C'mon, I'll race you."

We hobbled as fast as we could, barely dodging tables and benches and random other obstacles as they loomed up out of the smoke. Reeve and Katie tried to hang back with us, but it wasn't long before we lost them.

Gunfire blazed around us, flashes of lightning in the swirling cloud. I flinched every time, expecting the bullets to come tearing through me, throwing me to the ground in a bloody heap, just like Kirke, and Saunders, and the guard across the foyer, and the one back at the school, and –

An agonized scream rang out across the room, then stopped. Another one. Gone.

"Keep going," Mr. Weir urged. I hadn't even realized I'd stopped.

We limped around the last couple of tables and either the smoke was thinning out or we were getting to the edge of it because when the doors to the town hall burst open again and another armed guard came barreling out in front of us, I had no trouble seeing him.

"Steve!" said Mr. Weir, locking eyes with the guard. He straightened on his good leg, pulling his arm from my shoulder to reach for his rifle. Too slow. "Steve – C'mon, mate. You don't want to –"

The guard raised his own rifle and Mr. Weir froze.

He stared at us, stony-faced — then almost jumped out of his skin at a sudden burst of shrieks and gasps behind him.

A huge shape blurred through the doors, body-slamming the guard to the ground. The figure sprung back to his feet, grabbed Mr. Weir, and threw him over his shoulder. Then he bolted along the back wall in the direction of the elevator. "This way!"

It was Mr. Burke. Jordan's dad.

Mrs. Weir and I stared at each other, still trying to work out what had just happened.

A flash of movement inside the hall snapped me out of it. More guards coming. I grabbed Mrs. Weir's arm and sprinted for the elevator.

Chapter 26

LUKE

"Come on, come on, come on, come on!" said Wilson as we tore up the last few meters to the elevator. He and Reeve were standing at the doors, shields up to guard everyone inside. They split apart, letting us in, and then Reeve hammered the close button.

The elevator slid shut, muffling the noise from the hall. From the sound of it, some of the other prisoners had taken Mr. Burke's breakout as their cue to do the same.

Reeve hit another button and the elevator jolted upwards. I did a quick head count. Ten of us, counting Mr. Burke. We'd managed not to lose anyone else since the smoke bombs went off.

"Thanks for the lift, mate," said Mr. Weir, as Mr. Burke lowered him to the floor. "And listen, sorry for leaving without you last night. You know we would never have –"

"Of course," said Mr. Burke. "Where are the others?"

"Most of us were captured," I said, breathing hard. "Taken down to Shackleton's bunker."

"So that's where we're heading?" he said.

I hesitated, not wanting to be the one to tell him no. Mr. Burke was the most gentle, kind-hearted guy you'd ever meet, but he was also huge and imposing and fiercely single-minded about the safety of his family.

"It's on the list," Reeve jumped in. "First we need to disable the shield grid, then we need to get to the loyalty room, *then* we can see about –"

"We should split up," said Lazarro. "While they're still reeling. Won't take them long to get the crowd back under control, but while they're doing it, we have an opportunity."

"Up to the top first," Reeve insisted. "We need that shield down. Until we're sure we can –"

"I'm sorry," Mr. Burke broke in, sounding the complete opposite of sorry, "but if you expect me to cooperate with a plan where my wife and kids are priority number *three* –"

He silenced himself as we slowed to a halt at what was allegedly the top floor. There was a clatter around the elevator as everyone grabbed hold of their weapons.

Reeve and Wilson hoisted their shields back up in front of the doors. I squeezed the handle of my rifle, just needing something to hold on to.

The elevator doors opened to reveal the reception area. Wide hallways ran out to our left and right, leading off to offices for all of Shackleton's top guys. Everything was silent. Abandoned. Reeve and Hamilton stepped cautiously out onto the carpet, shields up.

"That way, right?" said Mr. Burke in a whisper, getting out after them and pointing down the corridor to our right.

Katie nodded. She and Mr. Weir had worked up here, back in the day.

The elevator we'd been in only ran from here to the ground floor. To get up to the roof or down to the bunker, we'd need to take the *other* elevator – the secret one outside Shackleton's office.

"We won't get to the bunker that way, though," I breathed, knowing what Mr. Burke was really asking. "That elevator was locked out from the basement level last night, so unless anything's changed since then ..."

"Let's get the shield grid sorted first," said Reeve, voice low. "Once that's out of the way –"

"Doesn't take ten of us to navigate an empty corridor," said Lazarro, joining them outside. "Come on, Matt. Waste of time for us all to go up there."

"You know what *else* is a waste of time?" said Chew, getting jittery. "Standing around talking while –"

"I might be able to override the elevator," said Mr. Weir. "If I can get to a computer …"

"We'll need numbers to take the cafeteria later," said Reeve, still talking to Lazarro.

"You need *soldiers*," said Lazarro, rolling his shoulder under the weight of the missile launcher. "Numbers are only good to you if they know their way around a gun. Look, I'll take these guys – Luke, the Weirs, and the Incredible Hulk, here. We'll deal with the grid, then see what we can do about getting into the bunker. Every chance Shackleton will be down there, anyway. You guys head for the cafeteria."

Everyone shut up, waiting for Reeve's decision. Gunfire rattled up through the floor beneath our feet.

"Okay, yeah," he said finally. "Go." He turned to his wife. "Did you want to –?"

"No," said Katie, eyes set. "I'm with you."

"Right," said Reeve. He and the others stepped back into the elevator, and the Weirs, Mr. Burke and I started down the corridor with Lazarro. "See you all soon."

The doors slid closed. I felt a ripple of fear as they disappeared, knowing I might never see them again.

We headed towards the other elevator, down the all-too-familiar corridor lined with the creepy red-brown abstract artworks Shackleton painted in his spare time.

"How did you get out?" whispered Mr. Burke, running a hand through the tangle of dark, curly hair that had overtaken his formerly shaven head. "If the others were all captured …"

"Long story," I said. Then, deciding it was going to come out soon enough anyway: "Jordan got out too. She's gone out to the wall with –"

"Shh!" warned Lazarro, coming to a sudden stop.

Muffled voices, somewhere out behind us. I couldn't see anyone yet, but –

"In here!" hissed Mr. Weir, pushing open the nearest door. The word *PRYOR* was stenciled next to the handle.

The room was almost identical to Pryor's principal's office. Giant wooden desk with a computer in the corner, an ornate rug underneath – but this office had a huge oil painting of a phoenix in place of the tapestry she'd had back at school.

"Here, hold this," murmured Lazarro, unstrapping the missile launcher from his shoulder and thrusting it into my hands. He stood back from the door, rifle raised, the scar on his cheek folding in as he smirked at the look on my face. "Don't worry. Won't hurt you with the safety on."

I stood to the side, hefting the launcher against my chest, straining to hear as the voices outside drew closer.

"Yes, ma'am," said a nervous voice, "I understand that. But those were his orders."

"To lock down a facility you are not even authorized to access unaccompanied? To compromise our ability to navigate the town at this critical hour?"

The voice was sharp, aggressive and all too familiar. Ms. Pryor. We had chosen the *wrong* office.

"Ma'am, you have to believe me," said the first voice, closer now, and I realized it was Officer Cook, one of Calvin's guards from the Vattel Complex this morning. One of the guards who was *supposed* to be keeping Shackleton away from Mum and the others. "I realize how it sounds. I had my own doubts about the orders, but –"

"But you still did what Calvin told you," finished Pryor.

"Ma'am – It was *Calvin,*" said Cook, exasperated. "If I'd kept arguing –"

I held my breath as the footsteps padded closer. There were more than just two of them. Whoever the others were, they weren't speaking. Probably more guards. I doubted Pryor would be going anywhere without an escort today.

My hands grew slippery against the missile launcher, my mind flashing down to the bunker. What was going on in there? If Cook was up here chatting with Pryor …

The footsteps stopped, just outside our door.

Mr. and Mrs. Weir raised their weapons. Mr. Burke stood behind them, unarmed, but still just as menacing. None of it made me feel any better. They had at least as many guns as we did. We weren't getting out of here without a blood bath.

"You are extremely fortunate that Mr. Shackleton is too caught up at the medical center to come after you for this," said Pryor, in a voice that said she was feeling pretty fortunate about that herself.

"Y-yes, ma'am," said Cook uncomfortably.

I felt a tiny trickle of relief. A bucket of water on a house fire. If Shackleton was across town in the medical center, then at least he wasn't doing anything to hurt –

But then, what if that's exactly what he *was* doing? What if he'd hauled Mum or Mrs. Burke or Georgia out there to interrogate them or experiment on them or …?

"Get back down there," said Pryor. "Keep the prisoners in line until he comes for them. Keep *Louisa* in line. Give Shackleton every reason to forget this morning's mistakes. And give me no reason to remind him."

"Yes, ma'am. Understood," said Cook, and I heard his footsteps fade back out the way we'd come.

I watched the door, waiting for it to move. Waiting for the tiny creak of the handle that would make this whole place erupt in fire and blood.

Instead, I heard more footsteps. They were fading.

Continuing up the corridor towards Shackleton's office.

The corridor went quiet again.

I waited, still hardly daring to breathe, not ready to believe that they were really all gone. But the silence stretched out.

Finally, Mr. Burke started towards the door.

"Give it a minute," said Lazarro, holding out a hand.

Mr. Burke glared down at him, obviously in no mood to be taking orders from a guy in a security uniform. But he backed off, rounding on me instead. "You said Jordan was out at the wall. Why? What's going on out there?"

"She's with Calvin," I whispered. "And Tobias. They're –"

"With *Calvin?*"

"No, it's okay," I said, hoping I was telling him the truth. "He's helping her. Well, he seems to be. He hasn't hurt her, at least."

"It does sound like he and Shackleton aren't on the same page anymore, doesn't it?" said Mr. Weir, jerking a thumb out at the corridor.

Mr. Burke still looked far from convinced, but Mr. Weir's reassurances seemed to sink in deeper than mine did. I guessed they'd formed a pretty tight bond after all those weeks trapped in the camp together.

"And this Tobias," said Mr. Burke stiffly. "Who's he?"

I glanced sideways at the Weirs. I kept forgetting how long he'd been out of the loop. "He's … he's your son," I said, and watched his face transform in a second. "Mrs. Burke had the baby last night, right before the guards found us. Jordan and I got out, and we brought Tobias with us, and …" I paused, struggling to even get the words together. "Mr. Burke, we think Tobias can do something to stop Tabitha. That's why they're out there. Calvin says he knows what Tobias has to do."

Mr. Burke looked like he'd been hit by a truck. He stared at me, open-mouthed. Then slowly, he nodded. Not like he understood, but like it was all he could get his body to do.

"We should get moving," said Mr. Weir, glancing at the computer on Pryor's desk. "I'll head down the hall and see if I can find a safer place to override the elevator controls."

"Ben More's office?" I suggested. "He was killed last night. Shouldn't be anyone in there."

We split up and I headed for the secret elevator with the others, stopping at the big metal door opposite Mr. Weir's old office. I shifted my grip on the missile launcher, which Lazarro still hadn't taken back, and swiped Bill's key card against the wall.

The door swung open. We stepped through, and I hit the button for the elevator. The doors didn't open right away. Instead, I heard the heavy mechanical clunking of the elevator coming down to meet us.

"It was upstairs," said Lazarro in a low voice. "There's someone up there."

"Pryor," I said, steeling myself, "and the guards, or whoever was with her."

"Hopefully too busy to notice us coming," Lazarro said. "Don't worry. We'll deal with them."

The doors sprang open. We got inside and I hit the button for the basement, just to be sure we really were locked out.

The elevator didn't move.

I pressed the button for the floor above us, and the doors slid shut.

"Here," I told Mr. Burke as we trundled upward, shrugging my shoulder to indicate that he should take my rifle. He was just pulling it away from me when the doors opened onto the secret top floor, a big open-plan office with floor-to-ceiling glass running along one side.

Lazarro opened fire as soon as the gap was wide enough. The noise roared around us, drowning the shouts of the security guards as they ducked for cover.

There were two of them. One was dead before he hit the ground. The other dived behind a desk, twisting around to return fire.

Behind them, Pryor abandoned the filing cabinet

she'd been searching through and dropped to the floor.

I dived behind a desk and started crawling towards the door at the back of the room, dragging the missile launcher awkwardly along beside me.

The surviving guard fired his rifle, tearing up the wall behind me, and Mr. Burke thumped heavily to the ground on my left. He rolled over, unhurt.

Lazarro was behind us. He fired again, blasting a giant hole in the glass wall. The wind swirled in, scattering paperwork and chilling the air.

A computer monitor exploded above my head. I hurried forward, throwing myself across a walkway between two desks.

And suddenly, there was the guard.

He turned, spotting me, whipped his weapon around in my direction – and then jerked backwards, shuddering with the impact of a dozen bullets from Lazarro's rifle. He collapsed against the wall behind him, streaking the glass with blood as he slid to the ground.

An eerie quiet swept through the office, broken only by Lazarro's cautious footsteps and the rustle of paper in the wind. Where was Pryor?

Lazarro crept up to join us, rifle sweeping through the air ahead of him. "Stay behind me," he muttered.

I kept low to the ground, my eyes jittering around the room. Where *was* she?

"This it?" said Mr. Burke as we reached a locked door in the back corner of the office. I nodded, and he jumped up, smashing the door handle to the ground with the butt of his rifle. Then he flinched and dropped to the floor again, just as –

BLAM! BLAM!

Two neat holes pierced the door, right where his head had been.

"GO!" said Lazarro, returning fire. "Get up there!"

I grabbed the bottom of the door, yanked it wide and scrambled through, finding a flight of steep metal stairs on the other side. I started climbing, still heaving the missile launcher.

More gunshots. Two from Pryor's pistol, and then a burst from Lazarro's rifle. A shrill scream cut through the air.

Lazarro came racing up the stairs behind me, followed by Mr. Burke.

"Hurry!" said Mr. Burke. "I don't –"

BLAM!

He cried out, and I heard a dull thud as he hit the stairs.

Lazarro swore. "No!" he shouted as I turned to look. "Go! Keep going!"

He fired back down the stairs.

I kept staggering up until I came to another door.

Unlocked. I pushed it open and an icy wind blasted me in the face.

Lazarro caught up again, practically throwing me out onto the roof. "Quick!" he said, shrugging off his rifle. "Take this. Give me the –"

BLAM!

Lazarro fell silent. His mouth opened and closed, a trickle of blood spilling down the side of his chin.

He fell to the ground.

Chapter 27

LUKE

Clank. Clank. Clank.

The footsteps were heavy and uneven. Pryor was still coming, but she wasn't having an easy time of it.

I stood there, stunned, unable to drag my eyes away from Lazarro's body. Twelve hours ago, I could barely have told you who he was, but now ...

Clank. Clank. Clank.

The wind was ridiculous up here. It blasted into me like a cannon, spraying me with rain, almost knocking me off my feet.

Clank. Clank.

The panic finally overtook my paralysis and I stumbled backwards, away from the door. I broke into a run, lugging the missile launcher across the giant expanse of the roof, but where was there to go? Those stairs were the only way down.

The only way down you could survive, anyway.

The antenna loomed over me, so much bigger than it seemed from the ground, thicker than the oldest trees in the bush and impossibly tall. I circuited around it, ducking out of sight just as Pryor emerged at the top of the stairs.

Antenna in front of me. Edge of the building behind, way too close for comfort.

The missile launcher shifted in my hands, slippery with rain. I hoisted it onto my shoulder, staggering sideways as a particularly savage gust of wind blew past, realizing what I was going to have to do.

My hands found the twin grips on the underside of the launcher, one index finger slipping around the trigger. My eyes twitched between the antenna and the edge of the roof behind me and the single bulbous missile sticking out of the front of the launcher. I had one shot. One chance to knock out the shield grid. And about ten seconds to make that shot before Pryor came and finished me off.

I edged backwards, putting as much distance as I could between me and the antenna. There was a little plastic targeting thing half-hanging from the launcher.

I pulled it down and stared through the cross hairs.

What are you doing? I thought, body screaming at me to run. *You don't know how to fire this thing! You're going to blow yourself off the side of the building!*

I shoved it aside. No other choice. I had about five hours left anyway if the grid didn't come down, and failing now meant dooming everyone else in the world with me.

No way was I going out like that. If this really was a one-way trip, then I was at least going to make sure the ending counted for something.

I dropped to one knee, feeling the bone scrape against the concrete as I angled the launcher up at the antenna. A bizarre sense of calm fell over me.

Maybe Jordan was right after all. Maybe there really was a bigger picture here, even if it wasn't the one I would have painted. Maybe I hadn't been saved from getting murdered just so I could run off into some happily-ever-after.

Maybe I'd been saved for *this*.

I aimed high, pointing the cross hairs to the top of the antenna. With any luck, it would take out the electrified cords without –

A breathless grunt from behind me shattered my focus. I whipped the launcher around and the sights locked on to a pale and bleeding Pryor.

"Drop it," she coughed, staggering out from the antenna, one hand pressed against her bloody side.

I panicked, pulling the trigger on the missile launcher. *Click.*

Nothing happened.

Pryor smiled weakly and took another lunging step.

The safety, I realized. How did you –?

Pryor raised a shaky hand, pointing her pistol at my head. She swayed, almost losing her balance in the wind, and then –

Whump.

I had barely registered the sound of running footsteps before the blurred figure of a man in black threw himself into Pryor, knocking her off her feet.

BLAM!

The gunshot went wide as they flew through the air together, crashing down precariously close to the edge of the roof.

Time slowed. They were still moving, rolling over each other. The guard's face came into view and I realized it was Lazarro, still alive, and with enough energy left to –

No.

He latched on to Pryor, and together they rolled over the side.

I dropped the launcher, stretching over the edge on

my hands and knees just in time to see them thump down against the Shackleton Building's front steps. It was surprisingly quiet.

Pryor tumbled limply down the stairs, rolling to rest on the walkway. Lazarro lay sprawled on his back, gazing up at the sky. Both of them just bodies now. I started retching, hacking violently, as shouts echoed on the ground. Shackleton's men rushing over to see what had happened.

When my gag reflex subsided, I backed off from the edge, fumbling for the missile launcher. I dragged myself back to the other side of the antenna, looking the launcher over, trying to figure out where the safety was. My eyes landed on a little switch above the trigger. I flipped it, and lifted the launcher back over my shoulder.

Then came the voices. Reinforcements arriving downstairs. Discovering the mess and the bodies in the office. Spotting the open door up to the roof ...

I readjusted the little targeting lens, cross hairs back up on the antenna.

And I hesitated.

It wasn't just the antenna that looked bigger from up here. The crisscrossing cords of the shield grid were enormous too, thick as my arm and rippling with electricity. What was going to happen when I brought them all crashing down on top of us?

Clank-clank-clank-clank.

The sound echoed up the stairwell behind me. Boots on metal.

Now or never.

Clank-clank-clank-clank.

I dropped down on one knee again.

Clenched my fists, struggling to keep the launcher steady.

Clank-clank-clank-clank.

I aimed high. Fixed the cross hairs up where the lowest cords converged on the antenna.

Felt for the trigger. Felt it give slightly under the weight of my finger.

Clank-clank-clank-clank.

"HEY!" demanded a voice behind me. "DROP –!"

I closed my eyes and fired.

Chapter 28

JORDAN

Bright orange light exploded in my peripheral vision.

I whirled around, almost losing my balance on the tree branch. I was climbing again. Not because I thought it was going to get me anywhere. Mostly just because I couldn't keep still. And because from up in this tree, level with the top of the wall, I could see the top of the Shackleton Building peeking up between the treetops.

My heart was already pounding before my brain had time to catch up with what was going on. An explosion. Something had just detonated in the air above the Shackleton Building.

A huge fireball rose up from the roof, brilliant against the gray sky. I squinted into Calvin's binoculars, but it was all too far away. In seconds, what little I could see had been enveloped in a cloud of roiling charcoal smoke.

"Guys!" I shouted, fists tight on the branches as I peered down at the others. "I think –"

But the rest was choked out by a gasp as the shield grid began to shudder above my head, sending sparks raining on top of me. I dropped down a couple of meters, half-climbing, half-falling through the branches.

They'd done it.

The thundering above me grew more violent, the whole grid rolling like someone shaking out a blanket. I looked up, grabbing a branch above my head and leaning out to see better.

"Keep moving!" Calvin called up. "Get down here!"

The grid creaked and hissed, sparks still cascading down all around me. I dropped down to the next branch, losing my footing in the wet and only just catching myself in time to avoid falling the rest of the way.

And then a new sound. A low, echoing rumble that seemed to come from somewhere deep inside the wall itself. I turned back and saw the cord nearest to me slithering back into the top of the wall, like a power cable getting sucked up into a vacuum cleaner.

The grid was coming down – but not *straight* down. The cords were shrinking away again, unlacing from each other, retracting the way they'd come.

It was a safety mechanism. Of course. Shackleton was cocky, but he wasn't stupid. He'd clearly put a lot of faith in his shield grid, but if it *did* come down, he couldn't have it crushing his precious town. As usual, he had a contingency in place.

I looked down. Still maybe five meters to the ground. The cords might have left the town untouched, but they weren't going to do the same to the treetops. I could already hear them rustling back through the branches, flailing like the tentacles of some hideous sea monster.

Amy screamed as the cord above me suddenly crashed down into the tree, whipping past only centimeters over my head. I ducked, slipping from branch to branch, falling again, jarring my shoulder as I shot out an arm to catch myself, the whole tree shaking with the writhing of the cord. I caught a glimpse of the end of it, ragged and frayed from the explosion, snaking towards my tree.

"Jump!" Amy yelled.

I hesitated, judging the distance, and took her advice. I dropped to the ground, bending my knees to absorb the impact but still jarring both legs. I landed awkwardly on my back just as the cord pulled clear of the tree and out of sight.

For a few seconds, everything was silent. A hand shot out in front of my face. Calvin, coming to help me up.

I grabbed on, skin still crawling a bit at his touch, and he hoisted me to my feet.

"He did it," said Calvin with just the hint of a smile.

I looked up at the sky, wide open again.

"Here," said Amy, handing Tobias back as soon as I was upright. She'd rearranged his blanket while I was up the tree, tying the corners together to create a little sling. "For the climb."

Calvin turned on her. "You're not coming."

Amy took a couple of steps back.

"She's coming," I said.

"We can't trust her," said Calvin. "When we reach the release station –"

"We can't trust *me?*" said Amy. "I'm sorry, but –"

"Yes, well done, you've noticed the irony. Be that as it may," said Calvin, pulling a coil of rope from the back of the skid, "I cannot allow you to jeopardize the success of this mission. You are staying here."

"If you think you're just going to tie me up and –"

"I don't," said Calvin, slinging the rope over his shoulder. He tracked across to the wall, sizing up nearby trees, picking one out not far from the tree I'd just been climbing. He reached up, hoisting himself up off the ground, and got to his feet on one of the lower branches. "This is as far as I climb until Amy agrees to remain behind. If the two of you believe you can stop Tabitha without my help, then by all means, continue on without me. If not …"

He let the sentence hang in the air, a look of infuriating calm on his face. He had me, and he knew it. And so did Amy.

I reached out to her. "Listen –"

"It's *fine*," said Amy.

"It's not," I said. "None of this is fine. But if we want to have any shot at stopping –"

"Yeah," she said, shrugging my hand off her shoulder. "I get it." But then her expression softened a little. "Sorry. I just … It's been kind of a big day."

She peered down at Tobias. He stared back at her, smiling. "I think he can do it," she said. "I mean, I don't know *what* I even think he can do, but – I don't think we're wrong about Tobias. I really think he can fix this. Don't trust Calvin. Not for a second. But if you can get Tobias out there …"

Again, my mind shook with images of Tobias's grisly death. And again, I pushed it all aside.

"I'll get him out there." I reached out to hug her, and this time she didn't pull away. "You just stay safe until we get back. Keep hidden. They're sure to come looking for us, now that the shield's down."

"Yeah," she said as I released her. "And listen, if

they have a Coke machine at the release station …"

I half-smiled, stomach grumbling at the thought of some actual food and drink. "Back soon."

I checked Tobias's sling to make sure he was fastened as securely as he could be, and then grabbed hold of the first branch, following Calvin up into the tree.

LUKE
Thursday, August 13, 11:45 a.m.
5 hours, 15 minutes

BOOM!

I'd barely even felt my finger come down on the trigger before the missile exploded away from me, setting the sky on fire. The launcher slammed against my shoulder, but not nearly as hard as I'd worried it would. Fire and smoke blasted out behind me and I staggered, somehow managing to stay upright.

The explosion swelled, blinding, deafening, drowning me in its heat, filling my nostrils with the smell of my own singed hair. Gravel-sized bits of exploded antenna rained down on top of me.

With a terrified glance out at the edge, I lurched to my feet, eyes readjusting as the explosion passed.

There were guards at my back, but they didn't seem

to be in a hurry to grab me. They looked on, stunned as I was, as a massive section of the antenna came plummeting out of the smoke.

I ducked pointlessly as it tumbled overhead, staggeringly huge, catching the corner of the building on its way down, smashing through the concrete and sending shockwaves across the roof. I lost my footing, landing hard on my hands and knees.

Somewhere far below, the giant bit of antenna hammered into the ground with an earth-shattering crunch.

I'd done it.

I hung there, head between my arms, struggling to even process it. The whole scene seemed to drag to a stop, everyone frozen in place, until the sound of someone else climbing the stairs woke me up again. He paused at the top, let loose with a long string of expletives, then snapped at the guards. "What are you doing? *Grab* him, you idiots!"

The two guards latched on to me from behind, hauling me to my feet, and I saw who was handing out their orders. Arthur van Pelt, the weedy little guy who used to run Phoenix Mall. I'd only ever seen him once or twice, but I knew he was another one of Shackleton's inner circle.

"This is a disaster," he muttered, pushing his glasses

back up onto his nose. He stared through the clearing smoke at the shield grid, which was collapsing rapidly. Not down onto the town, but back out to the wall, like it had just been switched off rather than blown up.

The guards dragged me towards the stairs, and again, I felt that weird sense of calm drift over me. If they were going to kill me, there was nothing I could do about it. And if they weren't …

Then I might just have found myself a way into the bunker. From there, I could find Shackleton and –

"Where's Melinda?" van Pelt demanded, suddenly up in my face. "Ms. Pryor. Your principal. Where is she?"

"She's dead," I told him, and watched his face turn pale.

He spun away from me, barking at his guards. "Quickly! Take them away!"

Them? I wondered, as the guard shoved me down the stairs ahead of them. But then a shout from downstairs answered my question.

My heart lifted. It was Jordan's dad. He was alive.

I stumbled back out into the office and saw Mr. Burke glaring darkly at two very nervous-looking guards as they cuffed his hands together behind his back. His right sleeve glistened red with blood.

"I know what you're thinking," said van Pelt, slipping into the room behind us. He advanced on Mr. Burke, jabbing a finger at his chest. "But let me warn you, an escape attempt would be unwise. We've been ordered to keep your friend," he jerked a thumb at me, "alive for questioning. We've received no such orders for –"

Van Pelt swore as Mr. Burke landed a sharp kick between his legs.

"Oi!" snapped a guard behind Mr. Burke, tugging backwards on his enormous arms. Mr. Burke gasped at the strain on his wounded shoulder.

One of the guards pushed past me, drawing his pistol.

"No!" I shouted. "Leave him!"

"Not –" van Pelt winced, grabbing himself as he leaned against a desk. "Not yet. Take him down with the others. If he wants to see his family again, he'll be sure to cooperate." He limped determinedly up to Mr. Burke. "Won't you, Abraham?"

Mr. Burke sneered but didn't bite back, and the guards hauled us through the mess of our gunfight to the elevator. As we passed the giant, shattered window, I looked down at the fallen antenna stretched out across the street, cracked concrete snaking out around it.

The shield grid had completely retracted by now. Nothing but cloudy sky all around.

As we squeezed into the elevator, one of van Pelt's men hammered the bunker button. "Bloody lockdown," he muttered, when the elevator wouldn't budge. "Sir, I thought Shackleton got inside already. Can't you just call and ask him to let us down this way?"

"Would *you* like to call him?" said van Pelt, pulling a phone from his jacket. "He's only working furiously to save all of our lives. I'm sure he wouldn't mind hearing from an insolent security officer with a complaint about his orders."

The guard's eyes flickered. "Why don't we just take the long way around?"

"Yes," said van Pelt, returning the phone to his pocket. "Why don't we?"

The elevator brought us down to the floor with all the Co-operative heads' offices. The two guards on Mr. Burke shoved him outside, steering him towards the other elevator. I moved to follow him, but van Pelt clamped a hand down on my shoulder. "I'm afraid not, Mr. Hunter. We've made other arrangements for you."

He nodded at the two remaining guards, and they started dragging me off in the opposite direction.

Mr. Burke twisted around to see where they were taking me. His two guards freaked out, shoving him into the wall, shattering a painting of some rust-red animal. Mr. Burke cried out at the pain in his arm. He jerked back his good elbow, catching one of them in the face.

"Get him under control, will you?" van Pelt snapped, straightening his glasses again, and my two guards ran off to help. But before I could even think about making a run for it, I felt the cold muzzle of van Pelt's pistol pressing between my shoulder blades. "This way, Mr. Hunter."

He marched me up to the end of the corridor. I realized where we were headed seconds before we got close enough for me to read the name on the door. The noise of Mr. Burke's scuffle with the guards seemed to fade into the distance. My legs went numb, stumbling to a stop, like they'd suddenly lost their connection to my brain.

"*Move,*" snarled van Pelt, pushing me forward again.

My eyes hovered over the name on the door and whatever warmth my body had left drained away.

"Oh, don't worry," said van Pelt, stretching up to whisper into my ear. "I know I said he was busy, but I'm sure Mr. Shackleton will be *extremely* pleased to see you."

Chapter 29

JORDAN

"What if they find her?" I said, as we jogged up the gentle slope through the rocks. "We *know* they'll be coming after us – How could they not? And she's just sitting out there, waiting for –"

"Yes, Jordan, I do understand the situation," said Calvin impatiently. "Whatever else I might be, I'm not a fool. And as I've already said, she's far safer there than we are here. Whoever Shackleton sends after us, they won't come climbing over the wall. They'll go through the gates. They won't get within half a kilometer of her."

"Unless they see the rope we used to get over the wall," I said.

Calvin stopped, catching his breath. "Jordan, please,

try to keep this in perspective. We are out here in an attempt to *save the world*. Amy may be your friend, but I will not stake the lives of billions on −"

"Who are *you* to decide what happens to the lives of billions?" I spat bitterly. "You're the one who −!"

"I'm the one who can show you how to save them," said Calvin. He turned his back on me and continued up the slope.

It was just over an hour since we'd touched down on the outside of the wall. It had been terrifying scaling the side with Tobias, but we'd both reached the ground in one piece.

The wasteland stretched all around us. Just rock and dirt and the occasional scraggly plant. Still no sign of the release station.

We'd made it far enough from Phoenix now that I could see the curvature of the wall and the wasteland stretching out behind it on both sides. It was so weird to be *outside* it all − to see all of the past hundred days, everything we'd been through, sealed off in its own little world within a world.

"What about me?" I asked Calvin, holding my side as we reached the top of the rise. "If you're so worried about *rogue elements*, then what am *I* doing here? Why didn't you just take Tobias and do it all yourself?"

"Because I *can't*," said Calvin, voice cracking. He

slowed again, gazing down the hill. "I cannot do this on my own. I need you here with me in case …"

"In case what?" I said, but something about the sudden shift in his body language made the fire drain out of my voice.

"I did plan to come alone, at first," said Calvin, slipping back into creepy-introspective mode. "Last night, when Shackleton first learned of your whereabouts, my priority was to extract your brother and bring him here as quickly as possible. And I almost managed it. But then I was attacked by – by the man you call Crazy Bill."

"But you *had* us," I said, pushing aside sudden, swirling images of Peter. "When you ambushed Amy and me out at the skid, you could have just –"

"I couldn't," said Calvin, voice even softer now. "I couldn't take him. After everything I'd already inflicted on you …" He sighed deeply, staring out into the distance again. "I am not accustomed to making emotional decisions. But I made one then. I felt you deserved the opportunity to come out here and see this through for yourself. But then you informed me of the apparent disappearance of the fallout. And however I might have responded at the time …"

I looked up, ready to prod him to continue, and was startled to see tears welling in his eyes. And it was more than just sadness or regret or whatever. I could see it all over his face: he was scared.

"The fallout was –" Calvin swallowed hard. He wiped his eyes, pulling himself together, and tried again. "Whatever change you see in me – Whatever *good* you see … This is not something I chose. I did not summon up this change of heart from some deeply hidden store of my own inner goodness. You of all people know what I was before. I was dead. The fallout dragged me out of that. It gave me back my humanity."

He stared down at his hands, still covered up by the same Phoenix-red gloves he'd found to keep from soaking up everyone else's emotions.

"And now the fallout's gone," I said, feeling suddenly cold, "and you don't know what the rules are anymore. You're worried that it's all going to go away again. So you've brought me out here to – to make sure you actually see this through."

Calvin drew his pistol, holding it out to me. "And for as long as I am able to, I'll do the same for you."

I took the gun.

It was so unnerving, seeing him like this. An actual human with actual vulnerabilities. But even worse was the thought that he might just lose all that and revert to his same old evil self.

"Okay," I said, sticking the pistol down into the

back of my jeans, "okay, but look, if we're doing this, then you need to *tell* me what we're actually out here to do."

"I will. When we get there."

"Calvin, if you're that worried about me flipping out and –"

"Shh!" he said, dropping behind a boulder, eyes back out the way we'd come. He rested his rifle on top of the rock.

I crouched behind him, one hand on Tobias, and whipped out the binoculars. I could hear it too, now. The hum of an engine, faint, but getting louder.

I swept the binoculars back in the direction of the wall. *There.* A pillar of dust, trailing out from the oversized tires of a skid unit as it streaked across the wasteland towards us. One guy in the driver's seat, and a few more hanging on at the back.

I jumped as Calvin suddenly let loose with his rifle, opening fire right next to my ear. Tobias flinched. I honed in on the skid again just in time to see it crunch down on its side in a cloud of dust and smoke.

I stared at Calvin. "How on *earth* did you do that from all the way up here?"

"That was not my first time firing a weapon," he said, getting up from the rock, looking uncharacteristically shaken by what he'd just done. He started walking again, down the far side of the hill.

"They'll keep coming," he warned. "The ones who still can. Today more than ever, they know what Shackleton will do if they fail him."

I hurried after him. "It's too late though, right? They're not going to catch up to us on foot."

Calvin nodded. "Not far to go now."

I trod carefully down the slope, both arms tight around Tobias, my mind running back over what Calvin had said about the fallout.

I tried to reassure myself. Whatever other fears he had, he still believed Tobias could do what he needed to do out here. That, or he was just clinging desperately to the same shred of hope that I was.

"What I don't get," I said, more to fill the silence than anything else, "is how you guys were *expecting* all this to go. I mean, if you knew about the fallout, then surely you must have known what it was going to *do* to us. Did you really think people would just turn a blind eye when their neighbors started randomly developing superpowers?"

"Of course we didn't," said Calvin, who for all his apparent changed ways was still weirdly defensive of the solidness of the Co-operative's plans. "Do you honestly think we would have bothered to construct the whole elaborate facade of the town if we'd *known* these things were going to happen?"

"But that was the whole point!" I said. "I mean, wasn't it? Wasn't the fallout *supposed* to change us? Isn't that why we were all chosen in the first place? Isn't that what a genetic candidate *is?*"

"The point," said Calvin, "was to create a society that could survive the release of Tabitha. And to that end, yes, candidates were selected for their genetic susceptibility to the effects of the fallout. Over the course of one hundred days' exposure, we knew the fallout would render such candidates immune to Tabitha. We were also aware that the fallout would boost your immune systems and accelerate your bodies' natural healing abilities. What we did not expect were the *other* side effects."

"How could you not have expected them?" I said, picking up my pace as the ground leveled out again. "What about Bill? What about *Galton?*"

"We learned about Bill's abnormalities at the same time you did. The night out at the airport. His *outburst* –" Calvin winced at the memory "– was our first indication that the fallout was doing more than we'd anticipated. We didn't know about Galton's powers until days after –"

"But she's Shackleton's *daughter!* How could you not have known she was …?"

Calvin narrowed his eyes, like he thought I was messing with him. "What?"

"Are you serious?" I said.

"Galton isn't Shackleton's daughter."

"She is! She lived here as a kid with the Vattel Complex people! Shackleton adopted her when the complex was destroyed because he *knew* something was up with her. She's how he discovered the fallout in the first place!"

Calvin shook his head, taking it all in. "If that's true," he said slowly, "then why was Shackleton as surprised as the rest of us when he found out about her telekinesis?"

I thought back to our first real run-in with Dr. Galton, under the medical center. She'd strode into the room with complete calm, lifting up furniture and people and hurling them at the walls, every movement so smooth and perfect. So controlled. Definitely not the first time she'd used her powers.

And in that vision I'd had last week ... A teenage Dr. Galton, out in the bush with a ten-years-younger Shackleton. She'd gotten all antsy as soon as he'd started talking about what the fallout had done to her body, and then weirdly relieved when –

When she realized he was just only talking about the small stuff.

She was hiding the rest of it, I realized. *She knew she had other abilities. Way back then, she knew. But she was keeping them from him.*

And she'd kept *on* keeping them from him. All this

time. All through their plotting and planning for the end of the world. Right up until – when? The day Dr. Montag started blood-testing everyone in town?

"Just up here," said Calvin, apparently taking my silence as an admission that I'd been wrong about Galton.

I looked where he was pointing, but all I could see was more rocks and dirt.

Movement against my chest. Tobias was stirring in the sling. I brought up an arm to cradle him through the blanket, thoughts still wandering back to Dr. Galton.

Why hadn't she told him?

Shackleton had obviously brainwashed her enough to help him with his plan for world domination. Tabitha might have been his idea, but Galton had been the one who'd created it, and she'd never been anything but fully committed to the cause.

Or had she? Was there some part of her that still clung to that old resentment, that knowledge that Shackleton wasn't her true father, that he was just using her the way he used everyone else? Had she *wanted* him to fail?

Or was she too scared of what he might do to her if he knew she could throw him across the room with her brain?

Calvin stopped in front of me.

"What's wrong?" I asked. We'd come to the top of a little hill. Not even a hill. Just a slight rise in the ground, low and circular, like the top of a giant ball poking up from the dirt. Still nothing but wasteland all around.

Calvin crouched at the top of the rise. He pulled off his gloves and started clawing at the ground with both hands, scratching away the dirt. There was something under there. Gleaming silver, like Shackleton's tunnels under the town.

I looked back out over the rise we were standing on and couldn't believe I'd missed it: the perfect, symmetrical roundness; the complete absence of rocks and plants. This wasn't a hill. It was a bunker.

Calvin continued brushing away the dirt, revealing a square panel set into the metal. He slid back the dirt-encrusted cover to reveal a single silver button beside a little round hole.

Out of nowhere, Tobias started squirming against me, like he was trying to fight his way out of the blankets.

Calvin pulled his gloves back on. His hand slipped into his pocket, coming back with a plastic vial filled with what looked horribly like blood.

He looked up, smiling grimly. "We're here."

Chapter 30

LUKE

I waited.

Hunched over, hands cuffed around one arm of an enormous wooden chair that looked like it had been swiped from a museum. I was wrung out. Sick with fear. Dripping sweat. Beyond exhausted, beyond anything but the nightmarish visions of what Shackleton was going to do when he finally came for me.

His office was immaculate, everything just as creepily neat and tidy as Shackleton himself. A giant desk stretched out in front of me, empty except for a computer and a little stack of journals topped with a fountain pen. Behind the desk hung another one of Shackleton's paintings. The same weird, abstract brushstrokes, like finger painting almost. The same dull red.

The walls on either side of me were lined with books – history, poetry, philosophy, art – all painstakingly arranged and ordered. I realized that every one of them was authored by someone who was either dead or about to be.

A clock ticked loudly, somewhere out of sight. Like Shackleton had hidden it there, just to torture me with the noise of it.

How long had it been now? An hour? More?

I hadn't heard a gunshot in ages. I hadn't heard *anything* except the clock and the murmuring of the guards outside and the low hum of Shackleton's air conditioner blasting the room with an oppressive, unnatural heat.

Where were Reeve and the others? If they'd taken back the loyalty room, then why hadn't anyone come for me? And if they hadn't taken it back…

Then the quiet outside was not a good sign.

I looked down to where I'd tried to saw through the arm of the chair with my handcuffs. I'd kept it up for about twenty seconds before the guard came in and told me to knock it off, and in that time I'd done a whole lot more damage to my wrists than I had to the chair.

What if this was it?

What if he just never came?

What if I just sat here cuffed to this fancy chair

until Tabitha swept in and twisted me inside out?

No. It couldn't end like that. Even trapped here in Shackleton's office, I couldn't believe the world was just going to fall apart without me even fighting it.

Jordan was still out there. She was probably halfway to the release station by now.

Jordan, Calvin, and a magic baby.

What could possibly go wrong?

I tensed, my wrists jarring painfully against the handcuffs as the door suddenly burst open.

Shackleton came striding into the office, as dressed-down as I'd ever seen him. He was still wearing his usual shirt and suit pants, but his jacket and tie were gone, his top button undone, his sleeves rolled up to the elbow. Red splotches spattered his white shirt and stained his hands and forearms.

I felt a cold surge of adrenaline. Whose blood was that?

"Please," Shackleton grinned, staring down at my raw wrists, "don't get up."

He was back. Whatever little blip of fear or uncertainty I'd heard on the phone before had disappeared without a trace, covered over again by his usual smiling calm. And something else: a kind of gleeful anticipation on his face, like whatever was coming next, he was planning on enjoying it.

Shackleton padded across to a little side table and poured himself a glass of water from a silver jug. He crossed back to his desk, taking the seat behind it as though this was just another business meeting. He held the glass to his thin lips, took a tiny sip of water, and then sighed loudly, pulling a coaster from somewhere under the desk and setting the glass on it.

"I tell you," he said, arms crossed in front of him, "I've had quite a time this morning. These things never seem to work out quite as cleanly as one imagines at the outset, do they, Mr. Hunter?"

He paused, giving me room to respond, then pushed on, just as happy to carry the conversation by himself. "The disappearance of the fallout on today of all days!" he said, like it was all one giddy adventure. "It gave us quite a scare. Imagine, making it this far in, only to have it all come to nothing in the final few hours."

My eyes dropped to Shackleton's water glass, smudged red where his fingers had pressed against it. His hand slipped down, picking it up again.

"Thankfully," he went on after another sip, "it appears our fears were unjustified. Dr. Galton and I took a small sample group to the medical center this morning. The fallout may have dissipated but, evidently, the protection it afforded our candidates has not." He lifted the glass up to eye level, frowning at the smudge marks. "The same,

I am sorry to say, does not apply to their healing abilities."

I clenched my fists together, shaking but trying not to show it. *A small sample group.* Like our guys in the bunker? Was that Mum's blood splashed across his –?

No. The bunker had still been locked down when I'd called.

But that was hours ago now. Anything could have happened since then.

Shackleton smiled again, guessing what I was thinking but not giving anything away. His gaze slipped up over my shoulder, and the ticking of the clock seemed to swell to fill the room.

How long left until the end?

Shackleton's eyes returned to mine, piercing through any attempt to cover up the terror flashing through me. I stared back, forcing myself not to look away. Sweat slithered across my skin, sticking my clothes to my back.

Shackleton chuckled and took another mouthful of his drink. "I'm almost disappointed you won't be around to see it," he mused, running his finger in a slow circle around the rim of the glass. "You're an intelligent young man, Luke. I know in time even you would have seen the beauty of what we are about to accomplish here."

"Right," I said, finally taking the bait, "because slaughtering humanity is exactly my idea of –"

291

"*Salvaging* humanity," Shackleton corrected, like I'd said the wrong word by accident. "Grasping hold of what little is left before the whole enterprise disintegrates completely. Or would you have us continue down the path of blind self-destruction until we tear ourselves to pieces entirely?"

"You *want* to tear everyone to pieces!" I said, handcuffs grinding into my wrists again. "That's your exact plan!"

Shackleton shook his head patiently. "Not everyone. And not because I take any joy in it. I am no monster, Luke. However, one need take only the most cursory survey of the history of the human race to discern the trajectory on which we are currently traveling."

He looked like a kid at Christmas.

"The present humanity is a cancer. A hulking, self-destructive scourge, unguided and ungoverned, stubbornly incapable of rising above its primordial origins. Its only hope," he paused, leaning forward, "is leadership. The singular vision of a guiding force with the courage to see the crisis for what it is and the prescience to set a course toward true human flourishing."

"By *murdering* us all?" I said. "How is that –?"

Shackleton chuckled darkly. "As if you were not already accomplishing as much on your own! The entire planet teeters on the precipice of complete environmental collapse and still you forge merrily onward, gorging yourselves into oblivion as if the next generation were an enemy to be slaughtered. You make a sport of inequity and waste, turning a third of your own food production into landfill, while every two seconds another child dies of starvation."

The clock ticked loudly overhead.

"Meanwhile, not content with the two hundred and thirty-one million butchered in the insipid wars of the past century, you continue the proliferation of weapons powerful enough to render this entire planet uninhabitable and obliterate whatever slender hope of recovery you might delude yourselves into believing you have left. How long before it all boils over, Luke? How long before the last threads snap and the whole human enterprise vanishes into the darkness of a blind, indifferent universe?"

I opened my mouth and closed it again.

"You could not be setting yourselves a more exacting course towards self-annihilation if you were doing it on purpose," said Shackleton. "Humanity does not need my help to die, Mr. Hunter. That much is well in hand already. Humanity needs my help to *live*."

"Yeah, well, no offense," I said, finding my voice, "but I vote *not you* for that job."

"Oh?" said Shackleton, eyes glinting again. "Go

on, then. Tell me I'm wrong. Plead humanity's case. After countless centuries of chaos and depravity, tell me with a straight face that *yours* is the generation that will spontaneously pull itself up by its bootstraps."

I sat back in my chair, caught off-guard by the question and, worse, by a fresh jolt of the same nagging feeling that had gripped me in the depths of Mum and Dad's divorce: that if humanity was the best the universe had to offer, then maybe we really *were* all screwed.

"Mmm," Shackleton nodded, before I had time to answer. "So you admit –"

"No! I don't – That's not the point!" I exploded, reeling but still convinced I was right. "Who are *you* to decide any of this? What gives you the right to –?"

"The right?" said Shackleton, excruciatingly calm, the smile back on his lips. "Right is what we make it, Luke."

"That's crap!" I said. You don't just get to *decide* –"

"And in any case," he pressed, holding up a hand, "the matter is now closed. Your second attempt at a coup has proven even more ill-conceived than the first, and your reckless destruction of my shield grid has gained you nothing. Even if Officer Calvin had not been eliminated at the armory this morning, and even if you were somehow able to penetrate the release station without my being present – which, let me be clear, you cannot – the dissipation of the fallout certainly does not bode well for an infant's chances of besting the most sophisticated weapon ever devised."

Shackleton studied me intently, waiting for a reaction. But instead of caving under the weight of such a comprehensive list of all the ways we were done for, my brain latched on to the one chink in Shackleton's armor. Calvin hadn't been *eliminated*. Not at the armory, anyway. Where was Shackleton getting this from?

"You didn't know?" said Shackleton, misreading the confusion on my face. "Yes, I'm terribly sorry. And just when you might have found yourselves an ally with some hope of assisting you," he shrugged, face twisting in false sympathy. "Your dear friend Jordan and her newborn brother – Tobias, is it? – were apparently not with Officer Calvin at the time, or else my men at the armory might have made a clean job of it.

"Not to worry," he said with a slight grunt as he pushed back to his feet. "I have dispatched a team to address the situation. The two of them will, I expect, not live out the hour. All that to say," he continued, sliding his chair under the desk, shrugging off murdering a baby like it was no worse than butchering a pig, "that despite today's unforeseen obstacles, despite any lingering philosophical objections, and despite your

295

incessant efforts to the contrary, Phoenix will survive."

I wanted to shout back at him, to kick and curse and rattle my chains, but what would be the point of any of it? He had me. And he knew it. And any reaction I gave would only be another victory for him.

"So what am I doing here?" I asked, as Shackleton paced across the room again, disappearing somewhere out behind me. "If you've already won – If I'm just going to get vaporized in a few hours anyway –"

"I read a fascinating study earlier this week," said Shackleton casually, as though he hadn't even noticed I was speaking. "A pair of Dutch researchers, investigating the human experience of pain."

I shifted, trying to see what he was doing, but the stupid high-backed chair blocked him from view.

"The study sought to apply a numerical value to the intensity and severity of various causes of pain," said Shackleton, in a voice like an English teacher trying to get me excited about a new class novel. "The idea being that one could then rank those experiences against one another."

I heard a *clack* of wood on wood, and another little grunt as Shackleton bent to lift something.

"The finer details of their research methodology were a little over my head," said Shackleton, moving back into view. "I must ask Victoria to walk me through it all sometime. But some of the findings were truly eye-opening."

He stopped on my side of the desk, snapping open the thing in his hands. An easel, holding up a blank white canvas.

"There was one particular pain experience that stood out to me," said Shackleton, pulling open another drawer. "An experience the study ranked far higher than I ever would have thought, higher even than *childbirth*. You'll never guess what it was."

He leaned forward, both hands on his desk, like he was actually expecting me to guess.

I stared back at him, at the blood splattered across his shirt. It had still been wet when he came in here, but in the sweltering heat of the office, it was quickly drying out, turning the same dull rust color as –

Cold realization washed over me as Shackleton reached into the open drawer and pulled out a glinting, silver-handled knife.

"Accidentally severing a finger," he said, advancing on me, "ranked as one of the top *five* pain experiences measured by the study." He grinned incredulously. "Can you believe that? I understand it has something to do with the unusually high concentration of nerve endings in that part of the body."

I shuddered audibly, finally unable to contain the fear.

Shackleton's smile broadened. He stopped at the easel, tracing his free hand along the top of the canvas. "This is a momentous day, Mr. Hunter. You may not survive to see the end of it, but have no fear." He rolled the knife handle slowly between his fingers. "I will not let you disappear without leaving your mark."

Chapter 31

JORDAN

"Whose blood is that?" I asked, holding Tobias with both hands while he wriggled around like there were bugs on him.

"Shackleton's," said Calvin, giving the vial a little shake and then pulling the cap off. "He and Galton are the only ones who still have access."

I lifted Tobias up against my chest, finally giving up on keeping him in the sling, and crouched beside Calvin. Tobias kept squirming, like he was trying to flip himself over and see what Calvin was doing. A squeak of frustration escaped his throat and, feeling somewhere between stupid and terrified, I spun him to face the ground.

Calvin's hands hovered over the little panel in the dirt. "If this doesn't work …"

"*Make* it work."

He pressed the button. Something blurred out of the little hole next to it and then back in again. A needle. Calvin upended the vial, sending Shackleton's blood dribbling down into the hole.

"Trust him to make this as disgusting as possible," I muttered, as the excess liquid bubbled up over the side.

"Careful," said Calvin holding out his arm. "Don't –"

The ground jolted under my feet and I lurched into him. He got up, dragging me back from the square-meter section of the bunker that had started sinking into the ground. A trapdoor, like the ones under the town. Light shone up from inside.

"Thanks," I said, shaking Calvin off and readjusting my hold on Tobias, who seemed to have calmed down a bit now that he could see what was going on.

The trapdoor rolled aside, revealing a set of shimmering silver steps. Calvin sighed heavily as he stepped inside, and I felt my breath catch in my throat. I looked back at Phoenix, the top of the wall peeking up over the rise behind us. "There'll be more, right? More than just the guards from that skid. If Shackleton knows we're out here, he'll throw everything he's got at us, won't he?"

Calvin paused on the stairs. "If Officer Reynolds has done his job, Shackleton thinks I'm dead already. He will be far less concerned than he should be."

"But Reynolds didn't even –" I broke off, figuring it out. "You sent him back to tell Shackleton he'd killed you. But you had him wait until after we left."

Calvin nodded. "You doubted me enough as it was without seeing me order him back into town."

"What about the explosion at the wall? Surely they must have seen that from town."

"With any luck, Shackleton has assumed you were acting alone," said Calvin, continuing inside. "It certainly seems that way, judging by the halfhearted approach he's taken to coming after us."

He slipped out of sight and I rushed down after him, into a narrow passageway, gleaming silver on all sides, as spotless and pristine as all the buildings back in town. As all the buildings back in town *used* to be, anyway.

Tobias squeezed his eyes shut against the light, and I raised a hand to shield his face.

As soon as the door hissed closed overhead, the fear that had been pressing in since last night suddenly lunged at me, biting down like an animal. I was shocked by the force of it.

The stairs continued down and down, a lazier spiral than the one running down to the Vattel Complex, like we were circling around and around some giant structure in the middle.

"So," I said, pulling myself together enough to get the words out, "how about you tell me what happens when we get to the bottom of this thing?"

Calvin kept walking.

I sped up, closing the gap between us. "Calvin –"

"Almost there," he said.

I backed off, startled by the emotion in his voice.

Just keep going, I told myself over and over again as we plunged into the ground. *Whatever this is, Calvin already told you Tobias isn't going to die. He can't. That's not how this is meant to end.*

But then what was Calvin so freaked out about?

Finally, the stairs ran out and we emerged into a big round room, almost completely empty. Every surface was the same Shackleton Co-operative silver, glinting under bright white lights.

In the center was an enormous pillar, maybe three meters across. The pillar ran straight up for about ten meters, then spread out like a giant kitchen funnel until it was as wide as the room itself.

Mounted to the side of the pillar at head height was a monitor like the one I'd seen last night, up on the top floor of the Shackleton Building. Two digital countdown clocks:

Final Lockdown Procedures
00:00:00:00
Tabitha Release
00:03:29:57

"Come here," said Calvin, pulling a biohazard suit from a cupboard built into the wall. "Put this on."

I took the suit from him, willing my hand to keep steady. "What's this for?"

"Just in case," said Calvin, taking down a second suit for himself.

"In case *what?*" I said. "I thought you knew what was down here!"

Calvin gestured at Tobias. "Make sure he's in too."

I squeezed my eyes shut, letting it go, lowering Tobias back into the sling. He kept still this time, like he somehow knew this was important. I pulled the biohazard suit on over the two of us, one arm in the sleeve and the other one guarding Tobias.

Calvin finished zipping up his suit and pulled what looked like a tool kit out of the cupboard. He pushed the door shut and the cupboard disappeared into the wall again.

I jumped as his voice crackled through a speaker in my ear. "This way."

Go, I thought, turning after him. *See it through. What else is there?*

I followed Calvin clumsily out across the huge open floor, still getting used to moving in the suit, which felt somehow too big and too small at the same time.

It was freezing in here. Or maybe that was just my nerves kicking into overdrive. Tobias started wriggling against me, his agitation rising again after the momentary lapse.

We reached the pillar. Calvin circled around to the far side and crouched down. He opened his tool kit, pulled out a screwdriver, and started undoing one of the silver panels.

I stood back, expecting an alarm to start blaring or something. Instead, as soon as the panel came loose, there was a deep, echoing hiss, and the air around Calvin began to distort, like heat rising off a hot road.

Calvin froze. It was some kind of gas, almost invisible. I held my breath as it swam up around my head.

Tobias tensed against me, a tiny groan escaping his throat. I looked down, but all I could see was the little bulge of his body inside our suit.

The hissing sound cut out. Slowly, the gas began to dissipate.

Calvin breathed again, the sound rasping in my ear.

I stared down at him. "Was that …?"

"No. Not Tabitha. A last line of defense. At least, we should hope it is the last." Calvin leaned in with the screwdriver again, returning to work. "Tabitha is still inside, housed within a containment capsule at the core. All automated access was locked down the moment the hundred-day countdown was initiated. I'll need to get inside and remove the capsule manually." Calvin said all this without looking at me, like he was trying to distance himself from whatever was coming next.

"And then what?" I asked.

The last screw clattered to the ground and Calvin pulled the panel away. The opening was as wide as a doorway and half as high – big enough for Calvin to squeeze through in his suit.

I don't know what I'd expected to see inside. A computer console, maybe, or a mess of circuitry. Not this.

The pillar was completely hollow. Empty, except for a set of metal rungs on the far wall, running up towards the roof and down into the darkness below.

"Wait here," said Calvin, moving to crawl inside.

I grabbed the back of his suit. "No. No further. Not until you tell me what happens next."

Finally, he turned to look at me. The face staring out from behind the glass of his helmet was more real than I'd ever seen it before.

"Wait here," he said again, "and I'll tell you."

I released him, clenching my teeth to stop the chattering. He crawled inside and started down the ladder, taking himself even deeper into the ground.

I slipped my other arm into the chest of the suit, cradling Tobias against me. "Start talking."

Calvin took a couple of heavy breaths, already out of sight but coming in loud and clear through the speaker in my helmet. "The Co-operative has known about Tobias for some time now. Not by that name, of course, but we caught our first glimpse of your brother's true nature at the same time you did."

"The night at the Shackleton Building," I said, shivering at the memory. "When we broke in to contact Luke's dad."

It was the first of many narrow escapes from being murdered by Calvin. We'd made it out alive, only to find Mum and Dad stumbling to the medical center in the dead of night, crying out for help, their unexpected pregnancy suddenly a whole lot more unexpected.

Dad's voice rang in my head. *There's something wrong with the baby!*

"Exactly," said Calvin, snapping me out of it, voice punctuated by the steady *clank, clank, clank* of footsteps as he continued down the ladder. "Over the days that followed, we began to understand how your brother's condition fit into the bigger picture of all the *other* changes befalling the residents of Phoenix. We identified as many cases as we could and brought them into the medical center for testing."

"You kidnapped my family, you mean?"

Calvin was silent for a long moment. When he spoke again, I could hear the tears in his voice. "Jordan, when this is all over, I promise you, I will sit down and confess to every crime I have ever committed here. I will make whatever amends I can, and accept whatever punishment is handed down to me. But cataloging the full extent of my guilt will be a lengthier process than even you can imagine, and right now we do not have the time. You have asked for an explanation. May I continue to give it to you?"

I didn't answer.

After a few seconds, the clanking of Calvin's footsteps echoed in my helmet again. Slower now. Quieter. He'd reached the bottom of the pillar.

"You and your friends managed to break into the medical center and free your captured family members before we could complete our research," he pushed on. "But afterwards, we began to realize just how significant Tobias was."

"Significant how?" I asked, staring out across the huge empty space around me.

He grunted, and I heard a sound like splintering

glass. "Your brother isn't merely a candidate like the rest of us. His life *began* here. He has been immersed in the fallout throughout the entire course of his development. We believe that the last one hundred days have shaped Tobias in ways that are completely unique."

Calvin's footsteps returned to their steady climbing rhythm. He was coming back up.

I paced back and forth in front of the pillar, bouncing Tobias inside the biohazard suit. "So basically, you're saying that any baby who was –"

"No," said Calvin. "Obviously, our understanding of these developments is still limited, but your own experience should tell you that the fallout affects each person differently. When I tell you your brother is *uniquely* qualified to assist us, I am using the full meaning of the word."

Calvin kept climbing, and now I could hear his footsteps outside my suit as well as through the speaker. He made a noise that sounded almost like it could have been laughter. "In hindsight, the projected due date Dr. Montag gave your parents might have given us a clue that Tobias was destined for some greater purpose in all of this. Though of course, Shackleton would dismiss such a thought out of hand even if it did occur to him."

"Not you, though?" I asked.

Calvin's face reappeared. His eyes locked on to me, still streaked with tears. "Jordan, I've just been dragged out of my death of an existence and handed an opportunity to save the world. How could I *not* believe there was something greater at work here?"

Calvin crawled back out of the pillar, a glass cylinder about the size of an energy-drink can held carefully in one hand. It was capped with metal at both ends, with a bit of silver tubing hanging out the bottom where I guessed it had been disconnected from some machine. Sloshing around inside the cylinder was what could almost have been water but was just slightly too thick.

"All right," Calvin sniffed, pulling himself upright. "This is it."

"What is?" I said stupidly, looking him over again, trying to work out what I'd missed. My eyes kept sliding back to the cylinder in Calvin's hand, but my brain refused to take it in. It was so small, so pathetic, so *unworthy* of all the anguish that had brought us here.

But at the same time, from somewhere deeper than reason, I *felt* it. The weight of this moment. The dread like a bruise. And the tiny shards of hope that maybe — *maybe* — we were actually going to undo it all.

"He'll need to come out of there," said Calvin, looking at the baby-shaped bulge in the front of my suit. "Don't worry, that gas should have dissipated by now."

"*Should* have?" I said, focusing on that to avoid focusing on the thing in his hand, fighting to keep pushing back the tide of suspicion that had been rising against me all day, the relentless dread that there was only ever one way this could end.

Calvin reached back to unzip his suit. He took off his helmet and sleeves, gently switching the cylinder from hand to hand as he did so, and let the top half of the suit fall to his waist. He waved an arm out, demonstrating that he was still alive.

I was already unzipping my own suit.

Calvin stepped forward, clutching the cylinder in one hand and the bit of silver tubing in the other, and all of my worst fears were confirmed in a heartbeat. But somehow my hands kept moving, trembling as they went, time slowing to an agonizing crawl.

By the time I'd peeled back the suit from the top half of my body, Calvin was right in front of me, tube pointed at Tobias like he was going to spray him down with it.

"Here," he said. "Put this –"

Something snapped in my head. I couldn't do it. "No! No – y-you're not –"

"Shackleton believes –"

I stumbled backwards, hitting the pillar, survival instinct obliterating everything else. "I don't *care* what

Shackleton –!"

"*Jordan*!" Calvin bore down on me, matching me step for step, face hard again. He stared at me with such intensity that, for a moment, I was paralyzed.

Calvin took a breath, bringing his temper under control. "Jordan, please understand the stakes here."

"*You think I don't get –?*"

"Disconnecting Tabitha from the system has gained us nothing," he said. "We may slow the rate of dispersal, but there is no stopping Tabitha's release. Not without Tobias. Which, abhorrent as it may be, leaves you with a decision to make: either your brother consumes Tabitha –" Calvin lifted his hands, holding the transparent goop up in front of me "– or Tabitha consumes everyone else."

Chapter 32

LUKE

"I know what you're thinking," said Shackleton, gliding towards me, knife in hand. "Blood. It does seem rather a limited medium, doesn't it?"

I squirmed in my chair, eyes flitting around the room. Searching for an exit. Something I'd missed.

"But the more I explore," he went on, "the more I realize just how versatile it is. As you'll see," Shackleton cast a hand at the painting above his desk, "the tonal range one can achieve with just a bit of practice is quite remarkable."

My wrists rubbed painfully against the handcuffs, hands balling into fists. My legs were still free, but I wasn't dragging this chair anywhere in a hurry, and the guards would be on me at the first sign of a struggle.

"And of course, I need hardly mention the richness of the symbolism." Shackleton circled around behind me, gesturing excitedly with his hands. "Beauty wrought from pain. Life giving way to life. The human struggle for survival and significance, all enacted right there on the canvas."

I hunched forward. I was going to throw up. Any second now, I was going to lose control of my stomach and empty it out into my lap.

Maybe he could make a painting out of that too.

Shackleton moved back into view. Circling. Soaking up the moment. Whatever else was going on in his twisted brain, this part was extremely simple.

He had me.

I'd been a stone in his shoe since the day I got here, and now, finally, it was just him and me, and I was going to pay for the frustration I'd caused him.

"You're not a great appreciator of the arts, are you, Mr. Hunter?" Shackleton stopped behind me, leaning in to examine my bound hands. The blade of his knife gleamed in my peripheral vision.

"No matter. My belief is that great art transcends such limitations. The true artist cuts through the intellect and into something deeper. Something *visceral*." Shackleton's spit flecked against my cheek.

"Above all else, I want my work to provoke a *reaction* –"

I jerked my head sideways, smashing it into Shackleton's. He reeled back, grunting, and I sprung up from the chair, still anchored by the handcuffs but maneuverable enough to throw a leg out at his stomach. Shackleton dodged, surprisingly agile for an old man who'd just been smashed in the head. My foot swung wide and I lost my balance, crying out as my wrists jerked against the cuffs.

The office door burst open and two black-sleeved arms dropped into view, dragging me roughly back up into the chair. My eyes blurred with tears. I blinked them away and saw a guard with a shaved head standing over me with a pistol. Shackleton stood behind him, smoothing his hair back into place.

"Thank you, Officer Lee." Shackleton bent down, retrieving his knife from the carpet. "While you're here, would you mind holding our guest still for me? His restlessness is stifling my creative process."

Officer Lee glanced at the blank canvas. A glimmer of recognition passed across his face. He moved to the back of my chair, and I felt the cold muzzle of his pistol press against my temple. His right hand came down on my fist, pinning it to the arm of the chair.

"Please," I whimpered, not daring to turn my head, "don't let him do this."

Shackleton crouched at my hand. I flinched as he reached for me, but Lee mashed his palm down harder, holding my hand in place.

"Lee!" I gasped. "Lee, listen – We can stop him! We can stop *all* of this! Just –"

Lee knocked his pistol against my head. "Quiet."

Shackleton pursed his lips, prying my forefinger out from my clenched fist. "Officer Lee," he said slowly, without looking up, "when we've finished here, would you mind putting in a call to maintenance for me? I suspect –" My knuckle cracked loudly as he pressed my finger down against the wood of the chair. "– that I may need to have the carpets redone."

"No – no, no, no – no, please – *please* –!" I was trembling uncontrollably now, tears rolling down my cheeks.

Shackleton brought the knife gently down against the base of my finger, lining it up. He angled his hand, slowly increasing pressure, and I felt the blade pierce the skin. I gasped, head twisting away, pain spiking up my arm, small and sharp at first, and then –

THUMP. THUMP.

Two sharp impacts as something outside smashed violently against the door. I heard the guard in the corridor thud to the ground, and I realized that *something* had been his face.

315

I winced as Shackleton reared up, taking a little chunk of my finger with him. He glared furiously at the door, and then disappeared behind me.

Officer Lee let me go, rushing to the door. "Sir, permission to –" He cocked his head. "Sir …?"

A burst of compressed air hissed loudly behind me, followed by a mechanical clattering sound. I tried to swivel around to look, but –

THUMP.

My attention jerked to the door again. Officer Lee reeled back, grunting.

THUMP.

A rifle butt came down across his head again and he slumped to the carpet.

A rush of feet stepped over the bodies. I looked up and saw two faces I hadn't run into since before all this blew up last night: Tank and Officer Miller, both in security gear. Reeve and Katie flew in behind them.

Reeve dropped to one knee beside me, firing his pistol at whatever was making that clattering noise.

I turned again, finally catching a glimpse behind me, just in time to see a bookcase slide back into position against the wall. Another compressed air noise, and then silence. Shackleton was gone.

"Trapdoors under the rugs and secret bookcase doors," said Miller, heading over to examine the back wall. "Shackleton's a sucker for the classics, isn't he?"

"Where did he go?" asked Tank.

"Could be anywhere," said Miller. "Or still back there. It could just be a panic room."

"Doubt it," said Reeve, getting up again. "Not really Shackleton's style to pin himself in a corner like that."

"He's probably headed for the bunker," I said. "Safest place for him to be right now."

Reeve glanced down at me like he'd only just taken in that I was here.

"Well, wherever he went, we're not following," said Miller. He pointed at a little silver circle mounted to the wall. "Thumbprint scanner."

"Oi," said Tank, standing over me, clutching a rifle. "Move your hands."

I flinched, still coming down from the terror of almost losing a finger. Then I realized what he was asking. I stretched my arms out, twisting them so the chain of my handcuffs stretched across the arm of the chair. With a grunt, Tank brought the butt of his rifle down against the chain, smashing it apart and freeing my hands.

"Thanks," I said, sliding the cuffs up my wrists to check on the raw skin underneath.

Tank shrugged. He looked so much older in the

uniform. A different person from the big, dumb school kid I'd met on my second day here.

"Here," said Miller, handing me a handkerchief from his pocket to mop up the blood dribbling from the gash in my finger.

"Thanks," I said again, then turned to Reeve. "Where have you guys been?"

"Loyalty room," said Reeve, as Miller moved to guard the door. "They'd upped the number of guards on duty since last time. We – we lost Wilson on the way in." His expression darkened. "Took them about two minutes to disarm the rest of us. We've been twiddling our thumbs with the rest of the prisoners ever since."

"So how did you get out?" I asked.

"Same way we got up here without getting shot," said Reeve, indicating Miller and Tank. "These two."

"We've been hiding out in the building since last night," said Miller. "Keeping a low profile. I couldn't show my face after yesterday, but your mate here's been posing as a new recruit. And so far, with all the chaos going on, no one's called him on it."

"Tank walked right into the loyalty room and convinced the guards to hand Katie and me over," said Reeve. "Told them Shackleton had ordered him to take us in for questioning."

Tank beamed.

"Plan was to go back in and get the others," said Miller, "but I guess that's out the window now that Shackleton's seen us."

"Speaking of which," said Katie, "shouldn't we be getting out of here?"

The question was barely out of her mouth when the sound of footsteps came racing up the hall. Miller leapt out, rifle raised.

"Whoa – hey!" said a frantic voice outside. "Hey, don't shoot!"

Miller stood aside and Mr. and Mrs. Weir came barreling into the room.

"Luke!" Mrs. Weir's mouth fell open at the sight of my cuffed wrists and bleeding hand. She rushed over and put her hands on my shoulders. "Oh, Luke, we thought we heard something going on in here, but we had no idea it was –"

"It's fine," I said. "I'm fine."

Mr. Weir looked around, scanning the faces in the room, then rushed to Shackleton's desk. He pushed down on the top of it with both hands, and a section of the wood levered up like a laptop screen. I ran around the desk, crowding in with everybody else to see what he was doing.

Mr. Weir's fingers were flying across the keyboard at the base of a monitor. "Controls for the automated defenses," he explained, not looking up. "I've been tinkering on my old mate Ben More's computer for the last few hours. Couldn't access any of this from there, but I could see the pathway I needed to …" He trailed off, focusing.

I stared at the screen, barely breathing, not a clue what I was looking at, but still completely transfixed.

And even though, from what Dad had said, the military weren't in any massive hurry to get here, I still couldn't totally push aside the image of all of them swarming in and tipping the balance back in our favor.

Don't, I ordered myself. *Three hours left. You're not saving humanity with wishful thinking.*

"Guys," said Miller, over at the door, "I know this is important, but I really think we need to –"

"Almost there …" said Mr. Weir.

"Can't save the world if we're dead," said Miller.

"Yeah," Mr. Weir bristled. "Which part of 'almost there' didn't you –?"

A little chime sounded from the speaker above the screen. Mr. Weir stepped back from the computer, fists flying into the air in a startlingly Peter-like expression of triumph.

"Only problem is he can still come in here and reactivate it. If you give me a few minutes, I might be able to lock out the interface and –"

Miller pushed forward.

BLAM!

The computer screen exploded in a shower of shattered plastic.

"Or that," said Mr. Weir, as Miller lowered his pistol again. "That'll work."

"Great," said Reeve. "Time to go."

"We need to get down to the bunker," I said. "Find Shackleton and –"

"Yeah," said Miller. "There's just that small matter of us being completely locked out."

Mr. Weir raised his hand. "Actually …"

Every head turned to look at him.

"Like I said, I've been doing some digging on More's computer. And look, obviously there are no guarantees until we get in there and try, *but,*" Mr. Weir's face twisted into a kind of half-smile, the same look he'd had when he got the transceiver working, "I think I might have just bypassed Shackleton's lockdown."

A ripple of noise ran through the group. My heart felt like it couldn't figure out whether to float into my chest or plummet into my stomach.

I looked around the circle. This was it. A handful of people, half of us barely able to hold a weapon the right way up, and no plan left but a blind attack on Shackleton's last stronghold. But we had only a few hours, and I wasn't about to spend them sitting around waiting to die.

I just hoped Jordan was having better luck than we were.

Mr. Weir looked to me, like for some reason he thought the decision was mine to make. He nodded at the resolve on my face. "What do you say we get down there and end this thing?"

Chapter 33

JORDAN

I reached behind me, heart pounding in my head, drawing Calvin's pistol and training it on his chest.

He took a half-step back.

"That's not going to fix this, Jordan. I drop this canister and it's over." He held the thing out to me, liquid oozing around inside like it had a life of its own. "Seven billion dead. You don't want to have that –"

"Don't you dare!" I shouted, moving shakily towards him. "You sick jerk! Don't you *dare* try to put this on me!"

"Jordan –"

"He's a *baby!*"

"A baby who just *happened* to be brought into the world six months ahead of schedule by the very same force that turned me around and brought me here to help you? Can you honestly –?"

"I'm not going to kill him!" I screamed, and felt Tobias start writhing against me again. "I don't care if –"

"You're *not* going to kill him," said Calvin. "The entire basis of Shackleton's concern is your brother's ability to *survive* Tabitha."

"And what if he's *wrong?* What if –?"

But my rant was cut short as Tobias let loose an ear-splitting scream. He squirmed like a fish out of water, face red, mouth stretched like he was being tortured. I hesitated, glancing up at Calvin again, then stuck the pistol in my jeans and pulled Tobias from the sling.

Tobias kept screaming, and it was like he was draining the fight out of me. I held him to my shoulder, bouncing him up and down, making the closest I could come to a soothing noise, somehow knowing none of it was going to work.

"Can't you – can't you just *destroy* it?" I said desperately. "Bury it underground or something?"

"Don't be an idiot," he barked, in a voice that sounded terrifyingly like the old Calvin. "Do you truly believe I need Tobias's assistance to *bury* this weapon?"

Tobias threw himself against my hands, gasping for breath, and screamed again.

Calvin hunched over. "Tabitha will not be

contained," he said. "It is no mere *weapon*. It is alive –
or near enough. We *brought* it to life a hundred days
ago when we activated the countdown. There is no
turning back from that."

"But this whole place –"

"This facility was set up to allow Tabitha to
disperse with maximum efficiency. To minimize the
window of opportunity for a retaliatory strike from the
outside. But Tabitha doesn't *need* this place. When the
countdown expires, Tabitha will either be released from
the containment capsule or it will *burst* out of it. It will
vaporize instantly, self-replicating with exponentially
increasing speed until it completes the task for which
it was designed. Humanity will be extinguished in a
matter of days."

I could barely hear him over Tobias's shrieking in my
ears, and even the bits that did get through just turned
to dust inside my head. It was too much to even begin
to process. An endless sea, surging and swirling in my
mind's eye, millions upon millions of nameless, faceless
people destined to be tortured to death unless I stood
here and fed poison to my terrified, day-old brother.

"Come on, Tobias," I said, crying along with him now.
"Come on, shh-shh-shh-shh. You're okay. You're okay."

But lying to a baby was about as comforting as lying
to myself.

Visions of our family swam up out of the blur, Mum and Dad and Georgia, all trapped in the Shackleton Building, and Luke …

Luke, on the run if he was lucky. Dead as soon as Tabitha got out.

"Jordan …" said Calvin, edging forward again.

Tobias took a shuddering breath, face bright red from the effort, and cried out again. I held on to him, my arms trembling.

I imagined Shackleton in his office, prowling around above it all, rubbing his hands together at his impending genocide, and the rage that had been simmering inside me boiled over again. My stomach churned with an overpowering disgust at that sick, self-righteous old man and his twisted self-made morals and his filthy lie of a town. With all the strength I had left, I hated this place and I hated *him*.

But more than anything else, I hated that it was all completely out of my control. A hundred days of fighting and it came down to this. A leap into the darkness.

No guarantees. No promises that this was going to turn out okay.

Just faith.

Faith that I hadn't been through all this for nothing, that those glimpses of a bigger picture weren't all just in my head, that somehow that picture was big enough to accommodate even *this*.

Calvin stared down at me, his face white. He looked tempted to just snatch Tobias out of my hands and do the thing himself. "Jordan –"

"Give it to me!" I snapped, sitting down with my back against the pillar, my tears almost drowning the words out. I cradled Tobias in my lap, propped up against my knees. He twisted on his back, still wailing uncontrollably, his tiny fists balled up.

Calvin crouched next to me, holding out the little canister again. I held Tobias's head as steady as I could with one hand, and reached out with the other, taking hold of the tube dangling from the Tabitha canister. I could barely keep my fingers on it.

I held tight to the tube, trying to guide it down towards Tobias's mouth, but I couldn't do it. My mind gave the instruction, but my body refused to cooperate. I just sat there, gazing down at him, sobbing and shaking and sucking in ragged half-breaths.

Calvin's hand came down around mine, cold and strong. I stiffened, but didn't pull away. He held my hand steady, slowly guiding the canister towards Tobias's face.

"It's okay," Calvin whispered, as close as I'd ever heard him to gentle. "It's okay. Just a few minutes –"

Tobias's eyes snapped open. He gazed up at the

tube. And immediately, he stopped screaming. He let out a squeaky gasp, lungs fighting for air, eyes locked on to Tabitha with the kind of focus a newborn baby should definitely not have been capable of.

I froze up again. Calvin's hand tensed on mine.

He kept moving, nudging my hand gently forward.

At the last second, I freaked out again. "No, wait! Wait – I don't –"

Too late.

The end of the tube slipped into Tobias's mouth. Instantly, his lips clamped down around it and he started sucking furiously.

A cold shudder wracked my body. I cringed with disgust, expecting Tobias to spit the stuff back out, but he kept drinking like it was milk.

I pictured Mum and Dad standing over me, watching on in horror as I poisoned their only son. Georgia crying, screaming, begging me to stop. Luke, white-faced, shaking his head, all his love for me curling up and dying.

"I'm sorry …" I murmured, reality and unreality blurring into each other. "I'm sorry … I'm sorry …"

Tobias kept drinking, little gurgling and swallowing sounds escaping his throat as he sucked the canister dry.

Calvin tightened his grip, holding me steady, but he might as well not have been there for all the notice I took. I sniffed, nose running, eyes blurring everything together. "I'm s-sorry … I'm sorry …"

And still Tobias kept going, sucking ravenously, dragging the last tiny droplets down the sides of the capsule until finally – *finally* – all of it was gone.

Tobias squirmed against my knees again. He yawned deeply and the tube dropped out of his mouth.

I stopped moaning. Stopped breathing. Silence flooded the release station. Calvin slowly released his hold on me, pulling the canister out of my hand and laying it on the ground.

Tobias opened his eyes. He gazed up at me, face breaking into a smile, and I felt the air flood back into my lungs.

He was okay.

He was *alive*, and that meant –

I glanced at Calvin for confirmation, not daring to believe that it could really have worked, that all of this could really be over. He hovered over me, half-dazed, a smile pulling just slightly at the corners of his open mouth, and relief washed over me like nothing I'd ever felt in my life.

It was over.

We had done it.

I looked at Tobias again and burst out laughing, overwhelmed with a dizzying rush of elation. I got to my feet, hugging my brother to me, tears still pouring down my face.

And then Tobias began to shake.

At first, I thought it was just my own jittering. But then Tobias took a deep, heaving breath and started screaming like he was on fire.

"No …" I breathed, holding him out in front of me, staggering as the weight came slamming back down onto my shoulders again. "No, no, no, no …"

Tobias convulsed in my hands, his eyes wide open and rolling to the back of his head. He screamed again, weaker this time, like his throat was closing over.

"No, no, no …" My voice dissolved into wordless groaning, and I swayed, almost dropping him. Calvin's hands came down around me, cradling me and the baby, keeping us upright.

Tobias kept trembling and writhing like there was something alive inside him, but I could already feel him growing weaker, see his face turning from red to blue. He let out a pitiful cry and tried to fill his lungs again. He couldn't do it. His eyes squeezed shut with the effort, lids closing over vacant white globes.

The visions of my family returned, wailing and screaming, reaching out to tear the baby away from me, but it was too late. Already far too late. A few more desperate, shallow gulps and his breathing gave out altogether, the shaking slowed to a stop and he fell silent, collapsing heavily into me.

I let out a cry of my own, harsh and guttural and spewing up from the depths of me. I searched him frantically for a pulse, a heartbeat, *anything*. But there was nothing there. Nothing but clammy, lifeless flesh.

Just a tiny body.

Adrenaline exploded inside me and I tore out of Calvin's grip, stumbling back from him. "WHAT HAPPENED?"

Calvin didn't even lift his head to look at me. His eyes hovered over the lifeless form of my brother hanging limp in my arms, and a disbelieving gasp escaped his lips. "It didn't work."

Chapter 34

JORDAN

"IT DIDN'T WORK?" I stormed forward, Tobias's body sinking into my chest. So still. So *heavy.*

Calvin backed away from me. "Jordan, I – We knew it was a possibility. With the disappearance of the fallout, we knew there was a chance this might –"

"NO! You said it would work! You said we were *meant –*" I ducked Calvin as he reached out in a deluded attempt to calm me down. "Get away from me!"

His eyes were red, face stretched with pain. "Jordan –"

"Shut up!" I snapped, fumbling behind me for the pistol. "Shut up. Don't even –"

"We need to get back into town," said Calvin cautiously, realizing I might actually be unbalanced enough to pull the trigger this time. "If the disappearance of the fallout has compromised our resistance to Tabitha, our only remaining hope of survival is to return to Phoenix and find Shackleton. He may know some other way to withstand –"

"You think you deserve to *survive* this?" I spat, my weapon trembling in my hand. "The whole human race is about to be wiped out, and you think *you* –?"

"I am not concerned about me!" said Calvin. "I am trying to save *your* life! You have a family back there who –"

"I JUST KILLED MY BROTHER!"

The words rang in my ears, and a suffocating dread swept over me, blotting out all the light in the room. The pistol slipped out of my grip, clattering noisily to the floor, and I clapped a hand to my mouth, overcome by the crushing horror of what I'd just done, like it had taken saying the words out loud for it to become real.

I stared down at Tobias's unmoving body, cradled in my other arm like he was still a person and not just an empty shell, and I was torn between wanting to hug him to me and wanting to throw his body to the ground. I don't remember consciously making the decision, but the next thing I knew, I'd lowered him back into the sling on my shoulder.

Calvin reached out to me again. "You were doing what you thought –"

"It doesn't matter! It doesn't matter what I thought! He's *dead!*"

My brain fired with images of myself trudging up the steps to the Shackleton Building, delivering my baby brother's dead body back into the hands of my parents. I saw the looks on their faces, looks that refused to go away no matter how much I tried to explain myself. Because there *was* no explanation. No way in the world to justify what I'd done.

It didn't matter what happened after this. It was already over.

"You should –" Calvin began, then closed his eyes for a moment. "We should leave Tobias here. When Tabitha – When the countdown expires, we want to be as far away from him as possible."

"Who *cares?*" I said. "Who *cares* what happens to us? In three hours, the whole world is dead! What difference could it possibly –?"

I cut myself short, seized by a sudden suspicion, and ducked to the ground, scrambling to retrieve the pistol.

I sprung up again, thrusting the weapon back on Calvin's chest. "You *knew!*"

Calvin's hands flew out in front of him. "No –"

"You *wanted* this to happen!" I spat, my guilt shifting into a hot fury that coursed through every part of me. "You didn't bring Tobias out here for us!

You brought him out here for you! For Shackleton! You needed Tobias to – to what? *Incubate* Tabitha? To activate it?"

"No!" said Calvin. "Jordan, that isn't – How could Shackleton have built his whole plan around a child he didn't even know the fallout was capable of creating?"

"Someone could have told him! Someone from the complex, from the future – Someone –" My head spun, trying to fit it together.

I was so desperate for this to be his fault, so desperate for it to be something I'd been deceived or coerced or forced into, but I knew deep down that wasn't true.

I'd done this. I'd brought Tobias out here. I'd made the call.

And now he was gone. And Tabitha was still coming.

Calvin edged towards me, hands outstretched for my gun. Even though I was grieved out of my mind, I could see how distraught he looked. "Jordan," he croaked, pressing his hand around the pistol, "I do not deny responsibility for what has happened here, but – but please believe that my only intention was to help you. I brought you out here because I truly believed your brother had the power to put things right. It was –" His eyes drifted to the sling, a tear spilling down his cheek. "It was supposed to work."

I released the gun. Calvin pulled it from my hands

and stowed it away behind him. He laid his hands on my shoulders. "I am truly, truly sorry."

I couldn't breathe. I felt the evaporating warmth of my brother's corpse against my chest and the devastating weight of all that had happened, of all that *would* happen when the clock ran down to zero, and my resistance crumbled to pieces. I collapsed into him, sobbing.

Calvin's hands slipped around my back as my legs gave way again, and for a long moment it didn't matter who he was or what he'd done, only that he was here and real and holding me together as I cried and cried and cried.

Calvin lowered me to the ground, then stepped out of his biohazard suit. I lay on my side, still crying myself blind, my breath coming in wet, choking moans.

He crouched over me again. I hunched, crossing my arms over my chest as his hands hovered past Tobias. "What are you –?"

Calvin slid his arms under me and hoisted me into the air, cradling me like a baby. He threw one last glance at the countdown screen behind us and then began hulking slowly towards the exit.

"There may be no hope left of saving the world," he grunted. "But that doesn't mean I can't save you."

We slipped out of Shackleton's office, over the unconscious bodies of the fallen guards, and squeezed into
the elevator across the hall. Seven of us, all armed with
either a pistol or a rifle or both.

"Okay," said Mr. Weir, hand drifting to the panel
on the wall. "Moment of truth."

He hit the button. With a jolt and a clunk, the
elevator began sliding downwards. Nervous murmurs
filled the tiny compartment. No turning back now.

"Duck for cover as soon as you can find it," Reeve
said. "Whoever's down there, we don't want to make it
easy for them."

He pushed forward, pistol raised at the doors. Miller
and Tank took up positions on either side of him.

The elevator crept down, torturously slow, like
someone was making sure I had time for the last hundred
days to flash before me while we traveled to the bottom.

And you're still here, I told myself. *All that misery and
you're still here. Surely that has to count for something.*

I held tight to the spare pistol Tank had handed
me, finger still throbbing and oozing blood where
Shackleton had gouged it open. Would I do it? Would

I shoot someone if it meant saving Mum or Georgia or one of the others?

The elevator rolled slowly to a stop, and the sound of raised voices on the other side of the doors snapped me back into focus. There was a ripple of movement as everyone tensed and raised their weapons.

Finally, the doors slid open.

"– don't care *what* she did!" said a voice I couldn't place. "If you touch her again –"

"What?" snarled a second voice. "You'll shoot me?" That was van Pelt, the guy from the roof. "What then, Louisa? What do you think happens when Shackleton finds out he's lost *another* member of his ruling council?"

I peered into the enormous bunker, its walls embedded with a circle of heavy doors leading off into the Co-operative's tunnel network. Shelves stacked with food and other supplies stretched out from the wall to our left, partially blocking the view, but I could still see where the argument was coming from.

In the center were a couple of black leather couches with a coffee table between them. Cathryn was sitting at the foot of one of the couches, weeping into her hands, while van Pelt and a gray-haired woman stood over her, looking ready to tear each other apart.

"Idiot," the woman snorted. "Is *that* what he promised you? A place on some fictitious *council*? And I thought Aaron was gullible."

It was Cathryn's mum, Louisa Hawking. Miraculously, in the heat of the argument, neither of them had heard the elevator door open.

Reeve and Miller crept out towards them, Tank right behind. The rest of us spread out, taking up positions behind the storage shelves.

Cathryn let out a loud sob at her mum's feet.

"Quiet!" Hawking barked, then set her sights back on van Pelt. "I think Shackleton might place a *slightly* higher value on a healthy sixteen-year-old candidate than a worn-out businessman, don't you, Arthur?"

Van Pelt shrank back from Hawking, his hand moving to the pistol on his hip. "My contribution to this cause –"

"Was strictly financial," she finished coldly, "and has already been paid in full."

I crouched behind one of the shelves, looking between the stacks of cans and beyond to the row of unmade beds on the other side, wondering if we should just wait here until they finished each other off.

But then, with a nauseous jolt, I saw them. Mum and the others. All still there, and still alive. Bunched up on one of the beds, with three guards standing around them in a circle – Officer Cook and two of his mates from the complex this morning.

Mum was staring anxiously at Cathryn, a purple mark across her face where one of the guards had obviously struck her. Mr. Burke, still handcuffed, one arm crudely bandaged, sat beside Mrs. Burke. Georgia cowered in his lap, the three of them finally back together again after weeks apart. Soren was perched behind them all on the opposite side of the bed, rocking back and forth, still messed up from his interrogation last night.

Reeve spotted them too and took a hasty step back, out of the guards' line of sight. But their attention was flickering between the prisoners on the bed and the argument across the room.

"Get up," Hawking snapped at Cathryn. She nodded at a bookshelf on the far wall. "Find something to read. If I see you anywhere near the other prisoners again —"

"Find something to *read?*" Cathryn shrieked, standing up, finally taking her hands away from her face to reveal the deep gashes Peter had scratched into her cheeks the night before. "Do you *seriously* think —?"

Her mouth fell open at the sight of Reeve and the others. My insides turned to stone.

Hawking and van Pelt whirled around. The guards at the bed followed suit, and in two seconds, everyone who could lay their hand on a weapon was pointing it across the bunker.

I dropped behind my wall of cans, bracing for the roar. But instead of erupting in gunfire, the whole bunker turned deathly silent.

Nobody moved.

One shot would plunge this place into a blood bath, and it looked like no one on Team Shackleton valued the cause more highly than they valued their own life.

Mum still hadn't spotted me. I saw her glance at Mr. Burke, trying to catch his eye.

No! I thought. *Stop! You're going to get yourself –*

"You okay, Cat?" grunted Tank, ending the silence. He stood maybe two meters back from them, his rifle fixed squarely on Hawking.

"Please," Cathryn begged, "don't shoot her."

"Don't want to shoot anyone," said Tank.

"Then how about you all just back away nice and slow," said van Pelt, sounding a lot less cocky than the last time I'd run into him, "and we forget you ever came down here?"

"Where's Shackleton?" said Reeve.

"Not here," said van Pelt. "Now, unless you want –"

"Give us back our people," said Reeve, not missing a beat. "You hand them over and it's done. We're out of your hair without any more –"

There was a shout across the room, and a blur of movement sprang from the bed.

Not Mum. Soren.

He threw himself at one of the guards, knocking him down to the floor and out of sight.

I heard screams from the bed. The other two guards reeled back as –

BLAM!

– either Soren or the guard fired a pistol blindly into the air.

Mrs. Burke dived to the floor, dragging Georgia with her. Mr. Burke sprang up, his hands still cuffed behind his back, and charged the nearest guard.

"STOP!" Hawking demanded, bringing her gun around. "Stop or I'll –!"

Automatic weapons-fire exploded throughout the room and she hit the floor. Cathryn screamed.

Tank threw up his arms, horrified. "It wasn't me! It wasn't me!"

A roar rose up from right beside me, and Mr. and Mrs. Weir suddenly burst out of hiding. Van Pelt panicked, diving behind one of the couches.

More gunfire. Georgia wailed in terror, somewhere out of sight. I looked back at the bed. Soren was on his feet, spinning in a circle like anyone could be a target. Mum was gone. I raced along the row of shelves, eyes sweeping through the gaps in the groceries, but she was nowhere –

Whump.

I slammed straight into someone running past in the opposite direction.

"*Luke!*"

"MUM!"

She threw her arms around me, weeping with relief, then went rigid again as another round of rifle fire cut the air behind us.

Soren let out a gut-wrenching shriek.

"Quick!" said Mum, breaking away. "We need –"

CLUNK.

The noise cut through everything else in the room. A deep, reverberating sound of metal on metal.

CLUNK.

Mum squeezed down on my hand.

I looked up, searching for the source of the noise.

CLUNK.

It was moving. Circling the room.

It seemed to be coming from inside the walls.

CLUNK.

The firing stopped, everyone else as mesmerized as we were.

CLUNK.

"The doors," I breathed, turning to the wall as the sound boomed closer.

"It's like before," said Mum. "Someone's locking us –"

CLUNK.

The nearest door, almost behind us, shuddered like it had just been struck with a battering ram.

Then a new sound. A clattering, groaning noise.

My eyes swept along the wall and froze on the elevator. A steel door, massive and handle-less like the others, had just rolled in front of it.

CLUNK.

The noise echoed and died.

And there, standing beside the door, still dressed in the same blood-spattered shirt, a pistol in one hand and a riot shield in the other, was Noah Shackleton.

"I wouldn't," he warned, as weapons flew up at him. "You would all suffocate long before anyone found a way to free you."

He strode out across the bunker, surveying the scene with absolute calm, like he was completely oblivious to the sounds of anguish in the air all around him.

I was clenching my pistol now, rage and fear burning through me, chewing me up like acid.

"I understand that emotions are running high," said Shackleton, glancing at Cathryn as she wept over her mother. "However, I think it best that we forego any further action until after Tabitha's release this evening. We will have a far greater chance of coming to an understanding once that whole contentious business is behind us. Until then, I have taken the liberty of placing this facility under lockdown."

"It doesn't matter!" I spat, barging out from behind the shelves before I even knew what was happening. "They don't need us! Calvin's still alive! He and Jordan are out there right now with Tobias!"

I was just ranting. I had no idea if any of it was true anymore.

Shackleton lowered his shield, propping it against one of the couches. "You are correct," he smiled, not missing a beat. "It most certainly *doesn't* matter. Whatever grand designs my former security chief may have concocted, your last slender hope of disrupting my work evaporated with the fallout. As of this morning, Tobias is nothing but an ordinary baby. If an attempt is made to use that child to neutralize Tabitha, he will fail, and he will die. Which leaves us –" Shackleton set his pistol on the coffee table and sank contentedly into the couch "– with nothing to do but wait."

Chapter 35

JORDAN

I barely even noticed as the skid rolled to a stop. I just sat there in the back of the cage, staring with unfocused eyes out at the sky.

The sun edged down slowly towards the deserted houses. The fighting was over now, everything quiet and still. Like it was all dead already.

The last two hours were a hazy mess, but I'd somehow pulled myself together enough to walk. I had scattered memories of trudging through wasteland, of Calvin pulling me down behind some rocks as the guards from that other skid came searching for us.

How did we get back inside Phoenix? I racked my brains and dredged up a vision of Calvin dragging his way up the wall on the rope we'd used to get out. He must have pulled me up with him because there was no way I was capable of scaling any walls.

A clank of metal stirred me out of my daze. Calvin was standing over me, pulling open the back of the cage. He rested a hand on my shoulder.

I staggered out of the skid, Tobias's body still heavy against my chest. It was cold now.

Amy climbed out after me. Silent. I don't know how I'd been expecting her to react, but after a cry of shock at the sight of Tobias, she'd gone completely quiet for the rest of the journey back. Either that or I'd just been too out of it to hear her.

We were behind the medical center. You couldn't see the full extent of the destruction in town from here, but there were still plenty of smashed windows and scorched walls, and the stench of smoke hung heavily in the air.

The rain had disappeared, and now sun streamed down cheerfully between the clouds in a mockery of the devastation on the ground.

Calvin pulled some keys from his belt and unlocked the same door to the medical center that we'd broken through a month ago, on our way to free Mum and Georgia and the others. For all the good that had done.

"He'll be down in the bunker," said Calvin, leading us through a little storeroom and out into a spotless white corridor. "If we can get down there ..."

I trailed off. No end to that sentence. No plan.

We kept walking, out towards the front of the medical center. I folded my arms under the sling, staring down at my brother's body again, shocked at how quickly the color had drained out of it.

Not even a person anymore. Just a thing.

I dragged my eyes up towards Amy. She quickly looked away.

It would have been better if she'd just yelled at me. There was nothing left of me to tear down that I hadn't already demolished myself. I shuffled down the shadowy corridor, Mum and Dad and Georgia still condemning me over and over again inside my head.

We reached the front of the medical center, and Calvin grabbed my arm, pulling me quickly across the reception area, past the smashed glass doors looking out on the carnage in the town center. The Shackleton Building stood just across the street. All quiet. There must surely have still been a few people lying low in houses or getting lost out in the bush, but it wouldn't take the Co-operative long to round them up tomorrow.

Assuming there *was* a tomorrow, even for us. And there was a huge part of me that really hoped there wasn't, that Tabitha would just take us *all* out and be done with it. Better no humanity at all than a humanity with Shackleton in charge.

Calvin released my arm. We were back out of sight of the town center now, moving down the corridor that led to the tunnel entrance.

My hand dropped to my pocket. There was a phone there. It took me a minute to figure out where it had come from.

It was Ketterley's. The one I'd lost in the skid crash this morning. Calvin had insisted on stopping to look for it on our way back.

Why? What were we going to do with it? Call Shackleton and ask him nicely to surrender?

I'd tried to phone Luke. I remembered now: the phone was still working despite all the rain, and I'd tried to call Luke, but the phone had just rung and rung, and I'd burst into tears in the back of the skid.

He was dead. Either gone already or he'd be twisted inside out when Tabitha came through in an hour's time. All our struggling to save him from Peter, and we'd only bought him a few more miserable hours.

"I'm sorry," said Amy.

I jumped, the sound of her voice pulling me back out of myself, into the dim light of the medical center.

"I'm sorry I wasn't more cooperative. I'm sorry I told you not to trust him." Her eyes flickered with that faraway look of hers, like she was listening to a voice that no one else could hear. "You were right. You did the right thing. I know – I know it didn't turn out the way we wanted it to, but that doesn't mean …"

Her brow furrowed as she searched for the words.

My feet crunched on broken glass. There was a huge hole in the widow next to us, like a person had been shoved through it.

"Look," said Amy, as we rounded another corner, "just don't give up, okay? Don't stop hoping. I know that sounds like a stupid thing to say –"

"Don't stop *hoping?*" I shouted, something snapping inside me. "Are you *insane?* Hope is what made me kill him! I murdered my brother because I *hoped* he was going to save us all! Because I was stupid enough to believe we were *meant* to stop this!"

"What if we still are?" said Amy.

"LOOK AT HIM!" I rounded on her, out of my mind, backing her up against the wall and ripping open Tobias's sling. "*DOES THIS LOOK LIKE A HAPPY ENDING TO YOU?*"

Amy cringed away, looking appalled.

Calvin's hand came down on my shoulder. "Jordan …"

I twisted out from under him, shivering all over, no idea what I was even doing anymore, then stopped, seeing a gleaming silver door and realizing where we were.

I spun back to Amy, delirious. She was still pressed up against the wall.

I lost my balance and collapsed, pain spiking through my kneecaps as they smashed into the cold floor. I thrust out my hands just in time to catch myself, chest heaving, throat clenching up, and there was a disgusting splatter as I emptied my stomach out onto the hospital floor. Not that there was anything much to empty.

I hung there, all pain and no vision, gagging and drooling and wishing I could just hurry up and black out, fingers clawing the ground as the world spun around me, Tobias suspended grotesquely from my chest, corpse swaying in the sling.

Hands came down on either side of me, keeping me from collapsing any further. When the feelings finally subsided, I was dragged to my feet, rested against the wall. My chest heaved, throat stinging with bile.

Amy's face blurred into my field of vision. "Jordan ..."

I couldn't even dredge up the will to focus my eyes.

"*Jordan,*" she snapped, grabbing my face with both hands. "Listen, I – I don't pretend to understand why this has happened to us. But I know what I've seen. What *we've* seen. I know what the fallout gave me. And maybe I forgot all that for a while when I suddenly lost my powers, but that doesn't make it untrue. This wasn't all an accident. You know that. One way or another, this isn't – I don't think this is the end."

"Tell that to my brother," I said, stumbling towards

the door. Calvin swiped a key card and the door clunked open, into a tiny room with a trapdoor set into the floor. I followed him inside.

Amy trailed after me. "What if that's –? I mean, what if his death meant more than you think it did?"

"Fallout's gone now," I said, bending down to activate the trapdoor. "None of this *means* anything."

"You say that," said Amy, "but you keep moving forward."

A hiss of compressed air cut through the room, and a square of the floor sank down and rolled away. Calvin checked to make sure I was actually coming, then started down the stairs underneath.

"Don't give up," said Amy, as we headed down after him. "I know you want to, but –"

BLAM!

The sound blasted through the tiny room, so loud that for a second I was sure it was me who'd been shot. But then Calvin pitched forward, tumbling to the foot of the stairs.

Amy screamed, backing up. Not even close to fast enough.

BLAM!

She shrieked and fell down on top of Calvin, blood blossoming under her ribcage.

Adrenaline fired through me, blowing away the

cloud over my mind. But instead of trying to escape, something kept me moving down the stairs, even when I saw the woman striding across the room to meet me.

Dr. Galton, white with surprise, draped in a blood-stained lab coat. She raised a gun to my face with perfect precision.

BLAM!

I reeled back, but there was no pain. No blood.

What ...?

Calvin had Galton down on the floor, arms wrapped around her legs. Blood pooled under him. Galton brought her pistol around again, aiming it down at Calvin's head.

"NO!" I cried, leaping down the last of the stairs.

Calvin thrust out his arm, too late to knock the weapon away.

BLAM!

He slumped down on top of her.

An animal roar exploded from my throat. Galton dropped her hands to the ground, dragging herself free, but I was on her before she could get up, one hand at her throat and the other clamping down on her wrist.

Galton's pistol clunked to the floor. She snarled up at me. "You think you can –?"

I spat in her face. "Shut up."

There was a whimpering moan behind me, and I

glanced back to see Amy twisting around to face us. Blood glistened through the front of her sweater, no more fallout to stop the flow. But as her eyes locked on to mine, a smile spread across Amy's face.

Galton shifted under me, hijacking my attention. She shot me a smile of her own as she eyed the sling hanging down between us.

"What are you hoping to achieve here, Jordan?" she asked, nose wrinkling at the spit sliding down her cheek. "If it's Shackleton you're looking for, you won't find him. He's locked himself in the bunker with your family and your boyfriend. He's not coming out."

"Not even for his daughter?" said Amy weakly.

And for the first time ever, I saw fear flash behind Galton's eyes. "Shackleton doesn't *have* –" she began, but she broke off into a grunt as I flipped her over, pinning her down on her face.

She was weak, I realized, reaching for her gun. Without her powers from the fallout, she was nothing. And with that realization, a fierce energy welled up inside me.

Whatever happened tomorrow, whoever was still around to see it, I knew there was no place for me there. Not anymore. But until then, I had work to do. If there was another way to stop Tabitha, or to at least do something to keep my family safe, I couldn't just sit here and let it slip away.

Amy groaned again. I hesitated, but she shook her head as adamantly as she was still able to. "Take her. Somewhere he can't send someone else to get you."

"No, I'm not just –"

"What are you going to do?" gasped Amy. "Drag me upstairs and operate? Go!"

I faltered for just a few seconds longer before finally pulling away.

"Come on," I grunted, yanking Galton to her feet and digging her weapon into her back. "Your dad thinks it's fun to screw with people's families? How about we go find out how much *he* likes it."

Chapter 36

LUKE

"Luke," said Shackleton, waving me over to the couch. "Come and take a look at this."

I glanced up from my seat on the bed and felt Mum's arm tighten around me. We were huddled together in a little group with Reeve, Katie and the Burkes, keeping as far from Shackleton and his goons as we could.

The two guards who'd survived our initial firefight stood watch on either side of Shackleton, rifles raised. The other one lay on the bed at the end of the row with a sheet pulled over his head. Soren and Miller were stretched out on the beds next to him, both drifting in and out of consciousness, their makeshift bandages slowly darkening with blood.

Hawking was still alive. Not happy, but alive. We'd

hoisted her onto the couch opposite Shackleton and done what we could to stop the bleeding. Cathryn hadn't left her side since. Tank was perched next to her, a hand on her shoulder. For the past hour, he'd been moving back and forth between our side and theirs, split between his loyalty to her and his loyalty to Reeve.

And through it all, Shackleton had just sat there on the couch, smiling around at us, like this was all just something mildly interesting he was watching on TV. He'd sent van Pelt across the room a few minutes ago to pull out a laptop, and was now hunched over the coffee table, attention flashing every few seconds to whatever was on the screen.

I kept waiting for something to happen, for some new terror to sweep in and shake everything up again. But I guessed we were past that. The cards had all been dealt now and everyone was just hanging here in this weird limbo, waiting for the end.

I couldn't even find the energy to freak out about it. I mean, obviously I didn't *want* to die, but after everything with Peter this morning, the idea of doing it all again just seemed painful. I was so exhausted already. Too burned out to even process anything. If this really was the end, then I just wanted it to be *done*.

"Come now, Luke," said Shackleton again, his voice a tiny bit harder this time, "there's no need to be childish.

I have good news. I believe I have located your father."

Mum's grip tightened again. "Luke, don't …"

But I was already pulling to my feet, frustrated at being so easily manipulated but unable to pass up what might be my last chance to catch a glimpse of my dad. I guessed I still had energy to spare for *some* things.

"Drop the weapon," snarled Officer Cook, eyeing Tank's pistol, still heavy in my hand.

"Oh, let him keep it." Shackleton waved the threat away like it was nothing. Like I was just a dog who'd gotten into something he wasn't meant to be eating. He gestured at the laptop screen as I approached. "What do you think, Luke? Is it him? How desperately does your father wish to see you again before this is all over?"

Cook stepped aside as I approached. Shackleton patted the cushion next to his. I ignored him, snatching up the computer.

It was some kind of satellite map, with Phoenix in the middle and the wide expanse of wasteland stretching out all around. A little huddle of triangles were edging slowly in from the top of the screen.

Aircraft.

A rescue party.

For one flickering moment, hope sparked inside me. And then it was gone again, snuffed out by another thought. Whoever was out there, they were as dead as the rest of humanity. Mr. Weir may have deactivated the automated defenses, but even if they made it to Phoenix, Tabitha was going to shred them alive before the hour was out.

Unless Shackleton was wrong about Tobias. Or unless he was more of a threat than Shackleton was letting on. But would Shackleton really just be kicking back in his bunker if he thought there was even a *chance* that Jordan might succeed?

"Yes," Shackleton nodded at the resignation on my face. "Too little, too late, I'm afraid. They'll drop out of the sky a good half-hour before they reach us. Still," he shrugged, "you certainly have to admire their —"

He paused, raising an eyebrow as a burst of classical music rang out from his pocket. An even deeper hush seemed to fall over the room as Shackleton drew out his phone. Over his shoulder, I saw the name on the screen.

Aaron Ketterley.

Jordan.

I lunged, heart exploding against my ribcage.

"HEY!" Cook's fist balled up around the scruff of my neck, yanking me backwards, and Shackleton pirouetted to his feet.

"Manners, Luke," he said, holding up an admonishing finger. He answered the call, tapping the speakerphone button. "Hello?"

"JORDAN!" I yelled.

Loud, shaky breathing on the other end of the line.

Mr. Burke jolted to his feet, snatching the rifle from Katie's lap. Reeve and the Weirs jumped up behind him. Cook shoved me aside and swung his rifle around, the other guard following suit. I could see on their faces how little they liked their chances.

Shackleton ignored them all, focus set on the phone in his hands.

"Jordan," he said calmly. "Is there something I can –?"

"I've got your daughter," she growled, finding her voice.

The contented look on Shackleton's face wavered just for a moment before the mask went back up again, but it was enough for me to see that the threat had hit home. Whatever warped mockery of affection Shackleton was actually capable of showing another human being, he was showing it for Galton.

There was someone in this world that he actually cared about. And that made him vulnerable.

Hawking and van Pelt's heads snapped up at Shackleton, wearing matching looks of incredulity. Apparently not even they knew about him and Galton.

Shackleton stared back at them, calculating. "Let me speak to her," he said finally.

"Fine," said Jordan. "Come out of your bunker and –"

"*Now*, Jordan," Shackleton ordered. "I'll remind you, you are not the only one with a hostage."

"We've got him outnumbered!" I shouted at the phone. "If we have to, we can –"

"No, Luke," Shackleton ducked down, snatching up his pistol and stabbing it at me, "you cannot. Kill me, and you kill everyone else in this room."

"Anyone else starting to think maybe that's not such a bad idea?" said Mr. Weir.

"NO!" screamed Jordan, and I heard what sounded like a strangled gasp from Galton on the other end of the line. "Nobody –!"

"Let her go, Jordan," said Shackleton, the veneer beginning to crack again.

"*Let my family out of there!*"

Shackleton turned slowly, bringing his gun around to face Mr. Weir. "I understand your anger, Jordan. Truly, I do. But we both know you're not a murderer. You're not going to –"

"*I just killed my brother!*" Jordan roared, with a fury that startled even Shackleton. "*You don't know what I'll do!*"

A stunned, breathless silence swept out across the bunker. Mr. Burke spun to face Mrs. Burke, still huddled with Georgia on the bed, then back to me, searching for an explanation. And whatever fear I'd been nursing

361

as we'd sat trapped in this place, it had nothing on the mutilating despair that crashed over me now. I stared around the room and saw the same thing mirrored on the faces of the others. Defeat.

"Jordan …" her dad began shakily.

"No!" sobbed Georgia, breaking away from Mrs. Burke, her tiny voice swelling to fill the room. "No, no, no, he's not meant to die! He's meant to *win!* He told me!" She crumpled on the floor. "He *told* me!"

Shackleton glanced down at her, and a new look passed over his face. Again, just a flicker, unreadable, then gone.

"If that's so," he said, lifting the phone closer to his face, "if your brother is dead, then you must already know you have failed. The question you should now –"

"FINE!" shouted Jordan, hysterical now. "Fine! I've failed! Now what about you? You want to see your daughter again or not?"

And in a rush, I felt tears surging up into my eyes. What had Calvin *done* to her out there?

"Let me speak to her," said Shackleton again.

"No! You don't get to –!"

"Either you let me speak to my daughter or this conversation ends here."

A moment's pause, and then Jordan let out a frustrated growl. There was a scuffle of movement and, from slightly further away now, Jordan snapped, "*Talk*."

Shackleton, turned again, like he was trying to find somewhere where no one could see his face. He quickly gave up. "Tori?"

"I'm here."

"Will she do it?" Shackleton asked.

"I –" Galton broke off into a spluttering cough. "I don't know. I think she might."

Shackleton glanced up at me, both of us thrown off-balance by the fear in her voice. I spent a horrible moment wondering what Jordan could possibly have done to Galton to get that kind of reaction before my mind clicked to the other side of the equation: Galton wasn't a superhero anymore. Almost her whole life, she'd been just a thought away from crushing anyone who got in her path. Suddenly, all of that was gone. Of course she was terrified.

"Where are you?" Shackleton asked.

There was another burst of shuffling as Jordan snatched the phone away again.

"Okay," she said, between shallow breaths, "you've talked to her. Now here's what you're going to do. You let my family out of there, and then Luke and my dad are going to bring you to the top floor of the Shackleton Building. You're going to tell us how to stop Tabitha, or your daughter is going to die."

I glanced back at Jordan's mum, my stomach turning at the pain on her face.

"Noah!" Galton shouted. "We're up on the med–"

She broke off with a grunt as Jordan barked, "Quiet!"

"Enough!" said Mr. Weir, pushing past Jordan's dad. "Either you do what she says or –"

"Not your father," said Shackleton into the phone. "He stays. If you wish to meet, it will be just Luke and myself, both of us unarmed."

He knows I'm dead when the time runs out, I thought. *All he needs to do is run down the clock and then he can call for backup.*

No response from Jordan. I could hear her crying into the receiver.

"That is my final offer, Jordan," said Shackleton.

I wiped my eyes, looking to Mr. Burke again. He was a wreck. We all were. Hanging in suspense, transfixed by the tinny speaker in Shackleton's hand as Jordan gasped for breath, steadying herself to speak.

When she finally did, it was low and fierce, more animal than human.

"Get up here."

Chapter 37

LUKE

Shackleton snapped the phone shut. "Back on the beds," he said, gun still fixed on Mr. Weir. "All of you."

"Not happening," Mr. Weir snarled.

"Brian ..." said Mrs. Weir, lowering her weapon to reach for him.

He shrugged off her touch. "You want to let him lock us up again?"

"Boss?" said Tank, standing up, looking to Reeve for instructions.

"Don't think we have much of a choice," said Reeve. "Clock's ticking. If there's a hope left, it's with Jordan, not us."

"I think it would be best if we all relinquished our

weapons," said Shackleton. He set his pistol down on the coffee table, like maybe we needed a demonstration.

I came around and put my gun down with his. Then I grabbed Shackleton by the back of the collar, snatching the phone from his hand.

Reeve shrugged off his rifle, and Tank followed his example. One by one, the others reluctantly laid down their weapons, until only van Pelt, Cook and the other guard were still armed.

"Don't kill anyone unless you have to," Shackleton told them. "I want to hold on to them until tomorrow morning's coronation ceremony."

"Yeah, brilliant, wouldn't want to miss that," Mr. Weir muttered, leading his wife back to the beds. Reeve and Mr. Burke trailed after them, whispering, while Tank pulled a wailing Cathryn to her feet.

Van Pelt nodded at the guards, and they closed in on the beds.

I glanced at Mum, barely able to hold my eyes on her agonized face. Probably only fifteen minutes left now. Chances were this was the last time we would ever –

She sprinted across the bunker towards me. I lost my grip on Shackleton, sure one of the guards were going to pull the trigger on her, but they held their fire. She almost knocked me over as she threw her arms around my neck. "Oh, Luke …" she breathed. "I'm –"

"Mum, stop," I said, pulling back enough to look at her, knowing that if I started really crying now, I'd be in no shape to take Shackleton anywhere. "I know. I love you too. But –"

She dragged me to her again, kissing me on the forehead.

"When you're ready," said Shackleton in an undertone.

Mum spun away from me, arms out at Shackleton like she was going to strangle him, but then she caught sight of van Pelt storming over to break them up and she shrank away, back to her place on the bed.

I looked at them all, one last time, then took Shackleton's shirt in my fists and pulled him across to the giant door he'd rolled over the elevator. "Open it."

He bent slightly, holding down the elevator button and speaking into a tiny hole above it that I'd never noticed before. "*Igne natura renovatur integra.*"

CLUNK.

The giant deadbolt inside the wall hauled itself apart and the barricade rumbled open, groaning under its own massive bulk. More thundering clunks rang out around the room as the lockdown was reset.

I glanced back and saw Reeve leaning in close to Jordan's dad, still whispering.

I cringed. *Please, please, don't do anything stupid.*

Shackleton released the button and the elevator doors sprang open. I pushed him roughly inside, hitting the button to take us upstairs, and the doors closed again.

As soon as the bunker was blocked from view, I heard a shout from the other side of the doors. The shouting turned into screaming, which was overtaken almost immediately by a deafening barrage of rifle fire.

I cried out, abandoning Shackleton and throwing myself at the doors, but it was already too late. The elevator jerked upwards, pulling us away from the noise.

I rested my head and hands against the doors, forcing myself to breathe. Surely the guards hadn't just killed them all. Not after Shackleton specifically ordered them not to.

I straightened up again, turning to catch Shackleton's reaction, but it was like he hadn't even heard the shots. He just stared straight ahead, straight through me, his attention locked on the doors. The mask of unconcern was completely gone now, replaced by a look of absolute focus.

We'd lost. He knew that much.

But we could still keep him from winning.

"You have no idea how much it will please me to watch you writhe in agony," he said tonelessly.

I jerked him backwards. "I think I can imagine."

But as the elevator kept rising, a new voice sounded in the back of my mind, hardly audible over the whirlwind of terror and anger, but still making itself heard. A still, small voice, waking me to the reality of what I was doing, quietly questioning whether this was really how I wanted to go out.

Because whatever the stakes, whatever the extenuating circumstances, I was still dragging an old man into a hostage situation to barter for the life of his daughter – and that felt a little too much like *his* tactics for me to actually be okay with it.

Shackleton was as close as I could imagine to pure, unblemished evil. He was a monster. He *deserved* to pay for what he'd done.

But what about me?

If it really was all over, if humanity was doomed and I was going to be unceremoniously torn apart in only a few minutes …

Was I going to spend that time letting myself get dragged down into Shackleton's twisted new reality, or *fighting* it?

The doors opened, and I led Shackleton out onto the scene of destruction left behind by our earlier firefight. It was eerily quiet, the whole place cast in an orange glow by the setting sun outside. Cold wind blew in through the broken windows, rustling papers and raising the hair on the back of my neck.

I jolted, a sudden vibration shooting up my arm as Shackleton's phone began to ring again. I fumbled, almost dropping it, then jerked it to my ear. "Jordan?"

She didn't speak, but I could hear her breathing, even unsteadier than before.

"Where are you?" I asked, dragging Shackleton across the room. "We're here."

Galton growled something I couldn't make out.

"The window," Jordan choked. "We're outside, but –"

"Coming," I said, a chill snaking through me. "Almost there."

"Luke, *wait*," said Jordan. "Galton –"

She broke off as I reached the broken window, and I felt my heart splinter into a thousand tiny shards.

They were down on the roof of the medical center. Jordan was kneeling on the concrete, muddy and trembling, a wet blanket slung over her shoulder. Galton stood over her, pressing a pistol to her head.

Shackleton peered down, face still fixed with that cold, emotionless focus.

"Well," he said, in barely more than a whisper, "doesn't that change things?"

Chapter 38

JORDAN

I couldn't do it.

For all my screaming fury, when the time came, I just stood there, frozen, unable to channel any of it into action. I'd gotten Galton all the way up to the roof, pinned her down, made the call to Shackleton, and then –

I don't even know what happened next.

But suddenly she was darting out from under me, spinning to attack, and the gun was right there in my hand, ready to shoot her in the leg or something, but I couldn't do it, and that moment's hesitation was all Galton needed. She might not have had her powers anymore, but twenty years of hiding them from her father had turned her into a creature of absolute poise and precision. In a single, fluid motion, she'd kicked my knees out from under me and sent me crashing in a heap to the concrete, still trying in vain to protect my brother's dead body.

And just like that, the whole world went spinning back out of my control.

Galton released the fistful of my hair she was holding and tore the phone away from my ear. She glared up across the street at Luke. "Release him."

Luke stepped away from Shackleton, arms spread wide. But instead of disappearing back into the building, Shackleton stayed right where he was.

He wants to see it, I thought, barely keeping my head up enough to look at him. *He wants to watch us die.*

Shackleton reached out to Luke, who handed over the phone.

"Yes," said Galton above me, clearly shaken. "Yes, I'm fine. What do you want me to do with her?"

I stared at the figure in the window. What would give Shackleton more satisfaction? Seeing Luke's reaction as Galton put a bullet through my head, or forcing me to watch as Luke got torn up by Tabitha?

The moment stretched out, and I wanted to be stoical, to go to my death full of rage and defiance, but my gaze drifted to Luke and all of that disintegrated and I slumped down, shuddering for breath, nose and eyes running streams down my face. We were finished.

Tobias's body hung in the sling, cold as frost against my chest. I stared down at our shadows, stretched out across the roof in the setting sun, the dark bulge of the sling protruding from my stomach in a sick parody of a pregnant woman. I turned away, hugging him against my chest, and a roar rose up from the depths of me.

WHY? WHY DID YOU DO THIS TO ME? WHAT WAS THE POINT? WHAT WAS THE POINT OF ANY OF IT?

"Here," snapped Galton. She shoved the phone against the side of my head and I heard Luke gasp into my ear.

"Jordan!"

"Luke!" I croaked, dragging myself up to look at him, lifting my hand to take the phone. "I'm so, so sorry. I didn't –"

"Don't," he said. "Don't be stupid. You have *nothing* to –"

"I killed him, Luke!"

"I know that's not true."

"Luke, you weren't –"

"It doesn't matter!" he said, voice cracking. "I don't care *what* happened out there. You didn't kill him. They did."

And though I knew he was wrong, hearing him even defend me was like a shot of life back into my veins.

"Listen to me," said Luke. "I know this didn't work out the way we wanted it to, but I want you to –"

His voice fell away. Back up at the window, I saw Shackleton snatch the phone out of Luke's hands.

"Thank you, Jordan," he hissed in my ear. "I believe that will be sufficient. Just enough to ensure that your voice is fresh in his mind as he watches you die."

He spoke in a cold, gray monotone, completely different from his normal voice. This wasn't wide-eyed, gleeful, surface-level Shackleton. This was the real deal.

"Now," he said, the words turning darker still, "hand back the phone."

I couldn't move. I just knelt there, frozen in place.

Shackleton's silhouette leaned towards the window. "VICTORIA!" he shouted, loud enough to be heard at a distance, and Galton clawed the phone from my hands. She paused, listening to Shackleton, the cold muzzle of her weapon digging into the back of my head again.

"Really?" she said, with the hint of a sneer. "Are you sure you wouldn't like to stand here and listen to them chat a bit longer?"

She glanced up at the window, listening again. Then a ragged shout rang out from across the street and she started, smacking me in the head with her gun.

It was Luke. He'd just launched himself at Shackleton, knocking him over, the two of them rolling to the ground, perilously close to the shattered window.

And from nowhere, some secret store of adrenaline charged through me and I whirled around, diving into Galton's legs. She thumped to the ground, losing hold of the phone but not her pistol, right arm already outstretched to –

BANG.

I tumbled to the ground, sure I was dead, rolling over in time to catch a glimpse of the hulking figure exploding through the doorway. He barreled out onto the roof, and I felt relief burn through me like wildfire.

"Dad!"

Galton scrambled to her feet, aiming her weapon again. Fast, but not fast enough. Dad grabbed her arm, tearing the gun away, throwing it to the concrete.

He lifted up a massive hand and pounded her into the ground.

LUKE
THURSDAY, AUGUST 13, 4:51 P.M.
9 MINUTES

"Oof!" Shackleton grunted, coughing old man smell into my face as I slammed him down by the shoulders again.

We were right at the edge now, jagged glass rising

up from the ground on my right and scattered across the floor beneath us. Icy wind lashed at my face, spraying me with rain that had apparently decided *now* was a good time to start coming down again.

I glanced through the haze of wet glass, my heart rocketing as I saw Jordan's dad send Galton sprawling. He pinned her down with one knee, dragging her hands around behind her back.

Shackleton bucked under me with strength too big for his aging body. He lunged with his head, trying to smash it up into mine. I ducked and he used the momentum to roll us over.

I slammed into the low wall of cracked glass rising up from the edge of the carpet and heard a sickening *creak* as it shifted under our weight. I pushed off with my feet, and a huge shard of it snapped away, tumbling out of sight through the rain. But it was enough. I was back on top again, kneeling now, a hand to Shackleton's throat to keep him from struggling.

Across the street, I saw Jordan fumbling to pick something up from the roof. She raced over to her dad, one hand still clutched to the bulge at her chest.

Shackleton snarled up at me. "You're dead, Luke."

I cocked my head at the medical center. "She's not."

Down on the roof, Jordan raised a hand to her ear, and another blast of music rang out from Shackleton's phone. It vibrated across the carpet, just out of reach.

I took a hand off Shackleton and lunged. He pushed up from under me, trying to free himself, but my knees kept him down just long enough to grab the phone and pull it open.

"Hey," I grunted, putting the phone on speaker and dropping it on Shackleton's chest, freeing my hands to pin down his throat again. "You okay?"

"Can you see him, Jordan?" Shackleton gasped, before she had a chance to answer. "How long do we have left now, do you think? Five minutes? Six? Your view might not be quite as good as mine when this pestilential blight finally meets his end, but I hate the thought of you missing –"

"Jordan, listen," I said, squeezing down on his throat to silence him, "you need to get out of here, okay? Take your dad. Get your family out."

"*No,*" she choked. "No – I'm not just going to *leave* –"

"I'm dead, Jordan! A few minutes and I'm gone. But I can at least hold Shackleton long enough for you to –"

"Luke," Mr. Burke cut in, "Reeve told us to wait here. He's gone down to the labs under –"

Shackleton's eyes widened.

With a burst of energy, he wrenched his body, throwing me off balance. I flew to the ground, one hand still clawing at his throat, and the phone somehow wound up underneath me, digging into my back.

Shackleton drove a bony fist into my face, and my vision blacked out for a second. By the time the blur cleared, he was back on his feet. A muffled voice screamed up from the phone. "Luke!"

Pain shot through my ribcage as Shackleton delivered a vicious kick to my side, and I rolled towards the glass again. Rain hammered into my face.

"Jordan, listen to me," said Shackleton in a rush, snatching up the phone. "I am prepared to negotiate a prisoner exchange – Luke's life for my daughter's – but only if –"

"No!" I groaned, spitting blood out of my mouth and scrambling back from the edge. "I'm dead anyway! What's the point of –?"

"I can save him," said Shackleton, still speaking to Jordan instead of me. "There is a way. But you must follow my instructions precisely."

"He's lying!" I shouted, pulling myself upright on the nearest desk, fingers slipping in the wet. But even as I said it, I felt a little spark of doubt.

Could there be another way for me to survive this?

"His parents too," said Jordan, voice still thick with tears. "You have to –"

"His mother," said Shackleton. "I can't save his father."

And even though it wasn't new information, hearing

him write off my dad like that was like a sledgehammer to the gut.

I staggered towards Shackleton, hazy doubt forcing its way to the front of my mind. This was wrong. Why were we even having this conversation? What had happened to Shackleton's ecstasy at watching me die?

"You have thirty seconds to return my daughter's weapon and release her down the stairs behind you," Shackleton pushed on when Jordan didn't respond. "And the phone," he added as an afterthought. "You will surrender Ketterley's phone to her as well."

"Something's wrong," I said leaning in. There was a frenetic energy in Shackleton's expression that I'd never seen before. "He's worried all of a sudden. I don't know why, but –"

Shackleton drove his elbow sharply back into my chest and I heaved back, grunting.

"Twenty seconds," he said. "Release her and I will show you how to save Luke."

Jordan's voice gasped out of the speaker. "How do I know you're even –?"

"*Fail* to do so," said Shackleton, venom in every word, "and I will call down to the bunker and have your family executed."

I grabbed hold of him again. "You think I'm just going to let you –?"

"He can't," said Mr. Burke, sounding less than certain. "The bunker is ours now."

"Is it still?" asked Shackleton. "Fifteen seconds."

I moved back to the window, dragging Shackleton with me. A gust of wind swept through and I almost overbalanced.

Mr. Burke was still perched on top of Galton, her pistol aimed down at her with one hand. He and Jordan stared at each other, neither of them speaking.

"Ten seconds," said Shackleton. His voice was icy as ever, but I could feel him shaking. "Nine. Eight."

Jordan jerked around, looking up at us. Even from here, I could see the agony on her face.

"Seven. Six –"

"Do it!" said Jordan, snapping. "Let her go! Dad, come on, we can't just –!"

"Five –"

"He's bluffing!" I said. "Don't –!"

"Four –"

"*Dad!*" Jordan screamed, pulling at him with both hands.

"Three –"

"Okay!" said Mr. Burke, getting up. He spun to face us, hands in the air, and Galton struggled to her feet.

"The pistol," Shackleton ordered.

"No!" I said. "Guys, this isn't –"

Mr. Burke threw out his hand, sending the pistol skittering across the ground towards the stairwell. Galton snatched the phone from Jordan and hurried over to pick the weapon up.

Jordan raced after her, yelling at the phone. "Shackleton!"

Galton whirled around, pointing the pistol at her, and Jordan fell silent.

Shackleton nodded in approval and my stomach lurched again.

Right into his hand.

But how else had they thought it would go? There was no saving me. Of course there wasn't.

Galton raised the phone to her mouth and started moving backwards towards the stairs, careful to keep Jordan between herself and Mr. Burke. "Noah?"

"Victoria," said Shackleton urgently. "Get downstairs. I need you to find Matthew Reeve and –"

With a feral grunt, I smashed my fist into the back of Shackleton's head, and the phone sailed out of his grip. He fell perilously close to the edge of the window, but his hands clenched on air and the phone went tumbling away through the rain.

Shackleton spun, barely missing a beat, and aimed another fist at my face. I ducked, glancing past him to see Galton disappearing down the stairs. Whatever

Shackleton had been trying to tell her, it seemed like she'd gotten the message.

Mr. Burke bolted past Jordan to give chase. Jordan hovered on the spot, torn between going after them and staying here where she could see Shackleton and me.

"GO!" I shouted down at her, moving in to grab Shackleton again. "Get out of here!"

Shackleton stepped back. Too far. His boot crunched down on the glass sticking up from the edge of the floor and he slipped backwards, spinning his arms in a vain attempt to regain his balance.

Instinctively, I reached out to grab him, like I'd blanked out for a second and forgotten who he was. My hand came down around the front of his shirt before I'd even realized what I was doing.

Shackleton glared into my eyes with a look of absolute disdain. He kept falling, feet teetering on the edge. My arm jerked out, straining under his weight but somehow still not letting go.

The wind and rain drove at us from all sides. My shoes skidded on the glass-strewn carpet and I felt my whole body pulled closer to the edge. But just as the signal finally got through from my brain to let go of him and save myself, Shackleton's hands came clamping down around my arm. His fingers dug into me, clawing up my sleeve like it was a rope.

BLAM! BLAM! BLAM!

Gunshots echoed up from across the street. Jordan screamed, and I felt my guts turn to liquid inside me.

"*What was that?*" I demanded, neck straining to see past him.

"That," said Shackleton, a grim smile stretching across his face, "was the end of you."

He flung himself forward, head-butting me in the face. I screamed, crashing to my knees as he dealt a savage blow to my stomach.

"Luke Hunter," he said between breathless gasps.

I opened my eyes and saw him standing over me, legs planted firmly apart against the wind.

"You will never know how very close you may have just come to –" He broke off, his whole body shuddering, as a roar of machine gun fire rose up from somewhere out of sight.

Something wet splashed across my face.

Shackleton's eyes bulged in surprise. He unclenched his jaw, like he wanted to finish his sentence, but all that came out was a mouthful of blood. His body arched backwards, legs slowly folding, like he was jumping off a high-dive. Then he finally tumbled out of sight, crashing down to earth with the rain.

Chapter 39

JORDAN

The whole world slowed to the pace of a dream as I watched Shackleton fall. His body sank through the air, limbs splayed, headfirst by the time it disappeared from view.

A dull thump floated up through the rain, followed by a high streaking sound, like a hand dragging across glass.

Time quickened again, and I knelt at the ledge, needing to know I hadn't just imagined it. I stared over the side of the building, scanning the war zone below.

The shield grid antenna was still stretched out across the street like a barricade. Shackleton had landed right on top of it, then slipped down the side to the ground. He lay facedown on the cracked concrete, legs still propped up against the antenna, blood pooling out beneath him.

Dead.

I stood up again, trembling, leaving the scene behind. And only then did I wonder where the shooting had come from.

I turned around and saw Officer Reeve stretching slowly to his feet at the top of the stairs, fists tight around his rifle. He looked stunned. As unsure as I'd been that what had just happened was real.

Footsteps hammered up the stairwell behind him. Reeve barely had time to look back before my dad charged past him, running to meet me.

Tobias's weight seemed suddenly to double. I stumbled towards my dad, all the relief I *wanted* to feel drowned out in the dread of what he was going to do when he reached me.

But then his arms came crashing down around me, wrapping me into himself for the first time in weeks and weeks, and I knew that somehow the love was still there, big enough to cover even this. He pulled my head into his shoulder, grunting with the pain of some awful injury, stroking my filthy hair, and I broke down all over again, the cold lump of Tobias's body caught up awkwardly between us.

"I killed him …" I sobbed. "He was supposed to save us, and I –"

"Shh," he breathed, choking back his own tears. "Shh … It's okay. It's all going to be okay."

"Jordan." Reeve put a hand on my shoulder, suddenly right behind me.

Dad loosened his grip and I twisted around. "Where's Galton?"

"Bottom of the stairs," said Reeve. "Unconscious."

He held something up into my field of vision and I flinched, thinking it was another gun. On second glance, I realized it was some kind of injection device, pistol-shaped, but with a syringe in place of the barrel and a vial of orange-ish liquid where the chamber would have been.

Reeve pulled on my shoulder, eyes down on the sling at my chest. "I need you to –"

I reeled back, stumbling away from both him and Dad. "What are you doing? What is that?"

"It's –" Reeve faltered, closing the gap again. "It's me. My healing power. Galton was working on a way to extract it. To make it something you could use on –"

"No!" I said. "No – No more – I'm not putting anything else –"

"Jordan, please," said Reeve, "you saw the state I was in after Shackleton put that Tabitha prototype into me. I was a mess. No way could I have survived without –"

"He's not a *mess!*" I said, hugging the body defensively. "He's *dead!*"

Reeve hesitated, absorbing this, like he thought maybe I'd just been exaggerating before. "Okay. Okay, but –"

He faltered again as Dad took a sudden step towards us. He held up Ketterley's phone to show the time.

4:56 p.m.

Four minutes.

"Do it," said Dad. "Try. It's not going to …"

I filled in the blank on my own. *It's not going to make him any deader.*

I looked away from both of them, gaze drifting back to the other side of the street. Where was Luke when I needed him?

Dad moved closer, arms outstretched to take Tobias.

"No!" I said, backing off again. Then, as calmly as I could: "No. Let me do it."

I'd already killed him. If anyone was going to bear the weight of further mutilating his body, it should be me.

I reached into the sling with shaky hands, the pain in my chest redoubling as my fingers slid down over his cold skin. A miserable gasp escaped from my throat as I slowly lifted him free of the blanket, and Dad couldn't hide his distress as he got his first real look at his baby son.

"I'm sorry," I choked, staring down at the pale, life-less thing in my arms and wondering at the stupidity of anyone who ever described a dead person as looking like they were just sleeping.

Tobias wasn't sleeping. He was gone.

Dad steadied himself enough to put an arm around me, but the warmth of his body only made Tobias feel even colder. I shifted him into one arm, and Reeve slid the injector thing into my free hand, and it was so much like the release station all over again that my legs began to buckle.

BANG.

The door at the top of the stairs burst open again, and Luke came pounding out across the roof. He stopped right in front of me, almost falling, doubled over with exhaustion. "Do it," he said, nodding at the thing in my hand. "He was – Something just had Shackleton really freaked out. I think …"

He trailed off, looking right into my eyes, seeing all the anguish there, and I watched his face fill with a deep sadness that cut straight through the whole ugly mess.

He understood.

He saw it all, and he understood what I was going through. And even in the face of his own death, he still had empathy to spare for me.

I lifted the injector, needle hovering over Tobias's rain-soaked body.

"You just – stick it in his arm and pull the trigger," said Luke, the urgency slipping back into his voice.

I brought the needle to rest against Tobias's skin, fist clenched to fight the shakes. Dad's arm tightened around me.

I glanced up at Luke again. If there was even a chance this could save him …

I pushed.

The skin gave under the pressure, and I guided the needle down into the flesh of his arm. I held my breath, pulled the trigger, and the liquid in the vial drained out into Tobias.

Luke looked on, face stretched with nerves.

Please, I begged inside my own head. *I know it's impossible, but please …*

I eased the needle out again, dropping the injector to the ground.

The rain beat down on us, heavier now, but we just stood there, huddled around Tobias. Waiting.

And nothing.

Nothing.

No change.

"Just – just give it a minute," said Reeve feebly,

glancing at Luke. "Give it a chance to …"

But he couldn't even bring himself to finish the sentence.

Silence fell again. Nothing but the patter of rain.

The seconds ticked past, and I felt what little hope I had left tearing away from me. I started shaking again, almost losing my grip on Tobias. Dad pulled me closer into him, but it did no good.

Finally, the last lingering thread of hope snapped inside of me, and I wrenched myself away from him, shoving Tobias into his arms and staggering out of the circle, a furious scream bursting out from deep inside of me.

"Jordan …" Dad choked, but I barely even heard it.

Luke was by my side in a second, arms around me, fighting my attempt to pull away from him.

"*Jordan*," he said. "Come on. You're *not* to blame for – Jordan, *please*. Please listen to me."

I stopped struggling and looked at him, seeing the bitter disappointment etched across his face. He swallowed hard, pushing it aside, tears welling in his eyes.

"Keep fighting," he said fiercely. "Shackleton's gone now. Most of them are gone. You guys need to take charge. Make sure the world that's left is a world worth –"

"I *can't!*" I wept. "I can't do this without you!"

"Yes, you *can*," he said. "Don't be stupid. Of course

you can. You don't need me."

"It was supposed to work!" I sobbed. "He was supposed to *save* you!" I slumped down, head on his shoulder, clinging to him for as long as I still could.

"I – I know. I know he was, but listen –" He lifted my head again. "*Listen* to me, okay? Whatever happens after this – Don't let today be the end of *your* life. You did everything you could today. You – you were amazing. Don't you dare blame yourself."

I tried to answer him, but the words wouldn't come.

He leaned in to kiss me and I stretched to meet him, still sobbing, raking my fingers through his knotted hair. I closed my eyes, fighting back the sickening visions of him tearing apart in my arms, refusing to let my own mind drive me away from him before Tabitha did.

"I love you," he breathed, breaking away, forehead resting against mine. "You're –"

Luke jolted back, eyes wide, as a noise pierced the air behind me. A tiny croaking sound, almost like …

I whirled around, heart thundering.

Dad was staring down into his arms, his brow furrowed in –

In *what*?

Fear? Confusion?

What had he just seen?

Whatever it was, Reeve had seen it too.

I looked down at Tobias. His lips were parted. Just a fraction, but his mouth had definitely not been open before.

And his face. Surely I wasn't just imagining that. It was darker than it had been, like the color was seeping back into the skin.

"Did –?" I faltered, terrified of the warmth flickering to life inside of me, bracing for reality to crash in and snuff it out. "Did he just –?"

And then Tobias's whole body tensed, and his face screwed up, and he let out a scream so loud that I swear they must have heard it all the way down in the bunker.

It was the most incredible sound I'd ever heard in my life.

We stood there dumbly for a long moment, listening to him scream, too stunned to move or breathe or say anything. Then Dad's face lit up with a joy I hadn't seen since we'd touched down here. He gaped over at me, lifting Tobias up into the air, then held him to his shoulder, gently bouncing him, straight into Dad mode.

The phone tumbled out of his hand and I dived to catch it, that flicker of warmth flaring up into a firestorm. My fingers scrambled on the phone, lighting it up again just as the time ticked over.

5:00 p.m.

The end of the countdown.

My eyes locked on to Luke, breath catching in my throat. I spun the phone around, showing him the time. For a long moment, neither of us moved, still too scared to believe it was all really over.

Luke caved first. He leapt forward, crashing into me, spinning me off my feet. I squeezed him back, and he was real and solid and still alive. Time stretched out and out and out, and my brain slowly began to allow the possibility that he wasn't going to disappear on me.

Dad stepped in, throwing one big arm around the both of us. Tobias had stopped crying by now. He smiled at me, the color flooding back into his face, and I felt tears stinging my eyes again. I lifted him up, holding him against me. He wriggled in my hands, warm despite the rain. Really alive.

"We should get down there," said Reeve, coming up behind us. "Make sure the others are all okay. Let them know it's over."

"Right," I said, handing Tobias back to Dad and clearing the rain out of my face.

Luke took my hand, fingers lacing between mine, and we started towards the stairs.

"So," he said, gazing down into a sunset he'd never expected to see, voice lighter than I'd heard it in months, "what do you guys want to do tomorrow?"

Chapter 40

LUKE

It was chaos when the military arrived.

Not gun chaos – most of the guards laid down their arms as soon as the first choppers landed. People chaos. The giddy blur of a town set free after weeks of imprisonment and terror.

Not all of it was happy. Some people took one look at this *new* group of people with guns and freaked out all over again. Others started smashing windows and benches, looking for a way to vent, or maybe just needing to play some small part in bringing this place down. A little gang of kids ran off to trash the school, and came back disappointed that the fire had beat them to it. More than a few people found places to just sit and weep, mourning lost loved ones or simply overwhelmed by it all.

But none of that could shake the wild, unrestrained joy that coursed through the air all around us. It was like those photos of the end of World War II: people hugging and kissing and shouting from the windows and dancing in the rubble.

Day turned to night without anyone noticing. A couple of guys found some secret wine cellar or something in one of the Co-operative leaders' houses and came trundling into town with a shopping cart full of bottles to rapturous applause.

Jordan didn't leave my side the whole night. We and the others kept to the edges of all the partying, as euphoric as anyone but with less energy to show it. A few kids from school came up to thank us or whatever, but mostly people just left us alone, either oblivious to everything we'd done or too caught up in their own celebrations to even notice we were there.

Sometime after midnight, the military guys made a halfhearted attempt to get everyone back into the Shackleton Building for the night, but that fizzled out pretty quickly, and they settled for keeping us contained to the town center.

I'm pretty sure we were the only ones in town who felt like sleeping.

"Crazy how it all works together," said Reeve, cross-legged on the grass with his son in his lap. "I mean, even the stuff you'd think was completely irredeemable. Like that serum – If I hadn't been captured and half-killed by the Co-operative, it never would've been made. We would've been sunk right there at the finish."

I nodded lazily, soaking up the feeling of the sun on my face, of Jordan's head on my shoulder, of clean, dry clothes against my skin and a full stomach for the first time in weeks, my heart swelling with an overwhelming sense of gratitude for the life that had been given back to me.

"Not saying it didn't cost us plenty," Reeve added quickly, glancing at the Weirs, "but ..." He sighed, shaking his head. "I don't know. I don't pretend to understand it. But I have to believe that somehow it all becomes worth it."

Mr. and Mrs. Weir smiled weakly at him, at least *wanting* to believe it. Jordan and I had spent an exhausting couple of hours this morning, piecing everything together with them. I was sure nothing could make losing your kid feel worth it, but the fact that Peter had died making sure we all knew about Tobias had at least given them something solid to hold on to.

We were sitting together in the park – Jordan and her family, Mr. and Mrs. Weir, the Reeves, my mum and me – one of dozens of little huddles spread out all across the grass. They'd moved us out here when the sun came up. Easier to keep us contained, I guess.

There were still a bunch of people missing from the fighting yesterday, and it would be a while before everyone was accounted for. Once that was done, they were taking us all back to the "facility" where Dad and Kara had been yesterday for what was sure to be a long debrief.

Jordan smiled as Georgia got up from her lunch and started climbing her dad's back, perching herself on his shoulders. She stared around the park, then back down at Mr. Burke, ruffling his hair with both hands. "Okay, come on, it's time to get up and play."

"Soon," said Mr. Burke wearily. "Wait until everyone's finished eating."

Georgia sighed dramatically. "We *have* finished!"

"Your brother hasn't," said Mr. Burke, waving a hand at Mrs. Burke, who was feeding Tobias.

"He's not *eating*," said Georgia impatiently. "He's *drinking*. Anyway, he doesn't even know how to play. He's just a baby." She started kicking her legs, digging her heels into Mr. Burke's chest like she was spurring on a horse. "Come on! Giddy up!"

"Georgia, Dad's very tired today," said Mrs. Burke. "Just give him a few more minutes to rest, okay? I'm sure he'll be ready soon."

Jordan stirred next to me. "It's okay," she yawned. "I'll take her."

Georgia clambered down from her dad and ran over. I got up too, not ready to let Jordan out of my sight.

I bent down to kiss Mum on the cheek. "Back soon."

She smiled. "Love you, sweetheart."

"This is all so weird," said Jordan, as we trekked across the grass. "All these people, just sitting around having a picnic. I mean, I know it's over. I know it in my head, anyway. But it still doesn't *feel* over, you know? Like, I keep expecting some new, awful thing to come crashing in on us."

I nodded. "I think it'll be better when they finally fly us out of here."

"Yeah," Jordan sighed. "Whenever that is."

Georgia dragged on her hand. "Hurry *up*. You're being so *boring*."

I smirked, wishing I could just leave it all behind as easily as she could.

"Sorry, Georgia," said Jordan. "Almost –"

"Hey," called a familiar voice from down on the grass. It was Amy, completely uninjured, finally reunited with her parents. She got to her feet, giving

Jordan a hug. "Thanks again."

"Yeah," she said. "You too."

There'd been more vials of whatever they'd pulled from Reeve in a fridge back down in the medical center. We'd used one of them to bring Amy back from the brink. We'd tried the serum on Calvin too, but nothing had happened. Whatever that stuff was, it could heal the wounded, but it couldn't raise the dead.

So what did that say about Tobias?

The playground stood not far from the big taped-off area the military had marked out as a makeshift landing pad for their helicopters. It was vacant at the moment, but I could already hear another chopper thundering towards us.

As soon as we reached the playground, Georgia broke away from Jordan and sprinted up to a little boy her age who was sitting on one of the swings. "Hi, Max!"

The boy jumped off the swing and gave her a big hug. "Hi, Georgia! Where have you been all this time? I couldn't find you anywhere!"

"That's Hamilton's kid," said Jordan, looking around. "Lauren's brother."

Hamilton was standing at the edge of the playground, with a serious-looking women who I guessed was his wife. Officer Chew was with them.

"Hey," said Jordan, walking over, suddenly concerned. "Where's Lauren?"

Hamilton rolled his eyes and pointed across the park to where Lauren and Jeremy were awkwardly making out behind a tree. If they were trying to be secretive, they were doing a terrible job of it.

"Nice to have you back, Lauren!" Hamilton called. "Love you!"

Jeremy jumped bolt upright. His pale face went bright-red. Lauren shot her dad a filthy look and dragged him back behind the tree.

Chew snorted at Hamilton. "Jerk."

"Are you kidding?" he grinned. "What's the point of having my daughter back if I can't at least torment her a little bit?"

By the time the fighting had ended, Hawking, Galton and van Pelt were the only members of the Shackleton Co-operative still left alive. The military had worked out who they were and quickly whisked them away.

Those three were the easy ones.

For now at least, most of Shackleton's security guys had been released back to their families. But what was going to happen, once they got us all out of here? They couldn't just arrest those three and forget the rest ever happened. It was going to take months to untangle it all.

I glanced back and saw Reeve and Katie coming over to join us, swinging Lachlan between their arms. Behind them, Mum and the others were getting up too.

We'd been doing that all day. Gravitating towards each other. Keeping the group together, almost without thinking.

My eyes darted up between the trees as the chopper I'd heard before came swooping in for a landing. It was different from the others that had been coming in and out today. Less aggressive-looking.

"Transport helicopter," Hamilton commented over the noise of the engine. "Maybe they're finally going to start letting some of us out of here."

It was hard to even get my head around the idea of an *outside* anymore. That stuff was all so distant now, like the whole world beyond the wall was just an endless gray fog, with my dad standing somewhere in the middle. But whatever it was, it was better than here.

The chopper touched down, and I watched the blades spin slower and slower, head full of the last hundred days, ten lifetimes of insanity and terror, crammed into the space of a few short months. And somehow, we'd made it through to the other side.

"Reeve's right," I said, turning back to Jordan. "*You* were right. I don't think we did this on our own. Like, I don't think it's an accident we won. This place didn't just *happen* to spit out a baby who could fight off Tabitha."

Jordan smiled, apparently amused that I was finally switching on to this thing she'd been trying to tell me for weeks and weeks. "So what *did* happen?"

"Don't look at me," I said. "You're the one –"

"Luke!" she gasped, clutching my arm and dragging me back around to face the landing pad.

A door at the back of the helicopter had just opened, and an officer had dropped down to the grass, followed by a man and a woman in civilian clothes.

"DAD!" I shouted, breaking into a sprint, straight under the boundary tape, ignoring the shouts of the military people, both of us in tears before we even made contact.

He grabbed hold of me, crushing me into him, and then Kara practically wrenched us apart.

"Where's Soren?" she demanded.

"I – I don't know," I said. The last I'd seen, he'd been eating alone in a corner of the park, looking as sullen as ever. "But Kara –"

She broke away from me, racing off in the direction of the playground, and I felt a lurch in the pit of my stomach. Those two had a lot of difficult conversations ahead of them. After all Soren had done, I couldn't help thinking that even Mr. and Mrs. Weir had it easier than Kara did.

"How are you holding up?" Dad asked, pulling me close again. "These guys treating you okay?"

"Yeah, fine," I said, wiping my eyes clear, dragging

him to rejoin the others. "How did you get them to bring you here? Everyone I spoke to said they weren't going to let you in."

"That was before I became useful," he said sourly, with a sideways glance at the officer who'd come out of the chopper with them. "You guys are first in line to be brought back to base for questioning, and I managed to convince them you'd be more likely to cooperate if I was part of the welcome party."

"Of course," I said, "because without you, we might've all just decided to stay here."

"Right," said Dad, ducking under the barrier. "See? It was all very tactical."

As soon as he was through, Jordan barreled into him. Reeve came up too, and patted him on the back. "Good to see you, mate."

"You're back!" said Georgia, appearing from the playground to latch on to his leg. "I'm glad you didn't die!"

"Me too!" Dad smiled. He spotted Mum hovering at the edge of the group and went over to meet her, pulling her into what had to be the least-awkward hug they'd had since before they separated. "Hey, Em. Thanks for looking after him."

The guy from the chopper cleared his throat. "Your attention please, ladies and gentlemen. I've got a list here of persons of special interest to the –"

"Yep. Thanks, mate," said Dad, holding up a hand. "This is them."

The guy scowled.

Dad clapped me on the shoulder, turning to the others, stretching a hand back in the direction of the chopper. "Any of you guys feel like getting out of here?"

Twenty minutes later, we were strapped in and ready to go. "Everyone okay?" asked Dad, as the pilot came through for a final check.

Weary nods from around the cabin.

Jordan slipped her hand into mine as the whine of the engine was slowly drowned out by the *whump-whump-whump* of the blades above our heads. The chopper lifted off the ground – no screaming, nobody firing on it – and we gazed out the window, watching the town of Phoenix fall slowly away from us.

We rose up over the park, over the little huddles of people who had almost become the last of humanity, and then banked sideways, drifting above the broken wreck of the town center. Shackleton's nightmare vision of a better world, burned to the ground and staying there.

I closed my eyes, concentrating on the warmth of

Jordan's hand, not knowing where I was going, but knowing who I was going with. Trusting that whatever lay ahead was better than what we were leaving behind.

We'd come this far. We'd survived.

I had a feeling we were going to be okay.

THE END

Acknowledgments

Thanks to Hilary Rogers for taking a chance on an up-start twenty-something's wacky idea for a sci-fi series; to Marisa Pintado for all the incredible work you've put into dragging it out of my head and onto the page; and to Jennifer Kean, publicist extraordinaire, for patiently reminding me what day it is and what city I'm in, and for listening to me tell the same stories about myself more times than anyone else on this planet.

Huge thanks to everyone at Hardie Grant Egmont and my wonderful overseas publishers for getting behind this series and pushing it out there into the world, and to all the awesome librarians and book-sellers who've helped people find it (especially Shearer's Bookshop, my not-so-secret favorite).

Thanks to Rowan McAuley for being an amazing first reader and creative collaborator, and for introducing me to that Zac Power kid. Keep on putting my writing to shame with yours!

Thanks to Ben for all the technical advice about guns and bombs and helicopters.

Thanks to Rev Dave for being such an awesome pastor, mentor and friend (and for accidentally being rude from the pulpit); and to my second family at Abbotsford Presbyterian Church. It is an honor and a privilege to journey with you guys.

Shout-out to the A-Team. You know who you are. (Also Moose and Jr. Moose.)

Thanks to everyone at PLC Sydney. You guys are the greatest. Turns out writing is only the second-best job in the world.

Thanks to Kerryn, Sarah, Claire, Phil, Mute and Weezy, all of whom have suffered living with me through at least one deadline; to the Rusbournes, Hardings, Thurstons, Barnetts and Doiners, who've been stuck with me for pretty much my whole life; and to the many, many other friends who've read, critiqued, encouraged, and told me to get on with it.

Thanks to Katie. Best brother-sister combo ever. (It's in print now, Kerryn! Beat that!)

Mum and Dad: I have no possible way of thanking

you enough for your constant love, encouragement and support – and most of all, for showing me the true story that shapes all the others.

Finally, to all of you who've stuck with me all the way to the end of this book, THANK YOU. I hope I've given you an ending worth hanging on for. (If not, I'm sure I'll hear about it!) Looking forward to doing it all again with something new!

Born in Sydney, Australia, in 1985, Chris Morphew
spent his childhood writing stories about
dinosaurs and time machines. More recently he
has written for the best-selling *Zac Power* series.
The Phoenix Files is his first series for young adults.

Books in *The Phoenix Files* series:
arrival
contact
mutation
underground
fallout
doomsday